MONEY BURNS

MONEY BURNS

A FIDDLER NOVEL

A. E. MAXWELL

VILLARD BOOKS

NEW YORK

1991

Library of Congress Cataloging-in-Publication Data
Maxwell, A. E.
Money burns : a Fiddler novel / by A. E. Maxwell.
p.   cm.
ISBN 0-394-58873-8   90-45003
I. Title.
PS3563.A899M66   1991   813'.54—dc20

Manufactured in the United States of America

9 8 7 6 5 4 3 2

First Edition

Book design by Debby Jay

*To our son
Matthew,
who has just learned about money*

MONEY BURNS

MONEY BURNS

1

IT'S ODD TO FIND a crossroads eleven miles from the nearest pavement, but I sensed Fiora was at one when she said, "I have a project that might interest you."

That got my attention, all right. Normally Fiora avoids the subject of my "projects" because she has a prejudice against things that could shorten my life span.

"You have a project that might interest me," I repeated in a neutral voice, wondering if I had heard right.

"Mm-hmm."

Her hazel-green eyes gave me a wary glance—the kind of look I'm used to from other people. No matter what I'm wearing, I seem more physical than metaphysical. That's all right with me. I'd rather intimidate someone than shoot him. Less paperwork that way.

"It's about a bank," Fiora began.

"Nope. No way. Not a chance. No banks, no money-shuffling talk, no bean counting. You agreed to leave civilization behind for a few hours, and I'm going to hold you to it. It's quail guzzlers or nothing."

I had just parked Benny's van in a little turnout on the Main Divide Truck Trail, one of the braided network of rock-

studded, pot-holed, rutted fire roads that meander up the
shoulder of Modjeska Peak. Roads like Main Divide are usually closed to the public, but we had received special dis-
pensation to perform a minor errand of ecological mercy.
Quail guzzlers, to be precise.

Fiora looked away from me and studied the dusty little
path that dropped off the lip of the dirt road and ran downhill
through the chaparral for a few hundred feet to our objective.
I watched her and waited to see if we were going to spend
our day wrangling or fixing quail guzzlers. Frankly, I would
have put money on either end of the question.

Fiora is no longer my wife, but she's still my lover. She's
also an investment banker and a small, elegant blonde with
a natural taste for luxury. She has the figure and the carriage
for silk underwear and lizard pumps. But she wasn't to the
manor born. Wearing Levi's, one of my old white cotton dress
shirts with its tails hanging out, a pair of brand-new ankle-
high trail shoes, and a wool Dodgers cap, she was quite at
ease on Modjeska's ragged slope. The clothes were no more
able to conceal Fiora's unflinching intelligence and decep-
tively fragile beauty here than when I first met her in Montana long ago.

And every bit of that intelligence was at work right now,
trying to decide whether to push, parry, or ignore my fiat.

"Right. Quail guzzlers it is," Fiora said finally.

She gathered up a shovel, a rake, and a short-handled ax
and headed off down the trail. The first fifty feet of the path
was steeply pitched. She scrambled down it with the offhand
grace that had been the third thing I noticed—after intelligence and beauty—when I met her. She moves as flexibly
as a willow in the wind. She isn't visibly muscular, but she
isn't pudding either. Given the right motivation, she could
walk me into the ground.

Particularly since she can usually talk me into carrying
her pack.

Benny Speidel, the Ice Cream King of Saigon—he spent
five years there as quality control engineer in an ice-cream

plant—leaned on his tripod-tipped crutches beside me and watched Fiora merge with the head-high chaparral. The early morning breeze played with Benny's dark beard and his shoulder-length black hair. He squinted in the warm sunlight and smiled gently, taking as much pleasure in Fiora's grace as I did. The relationship between Benny and Fiora is almost as complex as the one between her and me. Or between me and Benny, for that matter.

"Beautiful," Benny said.

"Persistent, too," I muttered. "I'll bet she slipped that damned pager on under her shirt, even though she promised to take the whole day off. How can she enjoy the great outdoors with that thing ticking like a little bomb on her belt?"

"Give it a rest, boyo. You get cranky about banks because you're jealous. They're the only thing in Fiora's life that competes with you."

I grunted and turned away from the trail to look at Benny. "How do you want to do the next bit?"

Benny uses both crutches and a mach-1 wheelchair, but neither would get the job done very well on a steep dirt trail. He could take the trail the same way he surfed—on his belly—but he would come out looking like a back-country dust mop.

On the other hand, it was his choice. Benny's spinal cord may have been lost to a stray round from an M-16 in Vietnam, but everything else about him was one hundred percent cold-rolled steel.

"If you do the first steep bit for me," Benny said, "I'll do the rest."

Benny's legs may not carry much meat, but thanks to wheelchair racing and other sports he's built like a longshoreman above the waist. He's no lightweight, but then, neither am I. I took him piggyback down the steepest part of the trail, then left him to find his own way at his own pace. We both knew I could have done a few laps up and down the trail with him, but there was no need to prove anything.

When I scrambled back up to the van to collect the rest of the gear, Kwame N'Krumah was waiting for me. The dog sat on his muscular haunches in the open cargo doorway, quivering like an overstrung bow, watching me avidly, waiting for his release. Kwame used to belong to my next-door neighbor, who had decided that what every dentist needs is an attack-trained Rhodesian Ridgeback. To him, Kwame was 130 pounds of security robot. To me, Kwame was—and is— a superbly bred and trained predator. He was also one hell of a tolerant pal.

Kwame felt the same way about me. The question of ownership and, more importantly, of responsibility, had come to a head in the past couple of months, when the dentist and his wife went through the kind of divorce that gives marriage a bad name. The wife ended up with the Mercedes, the baby, the cottage, the gardener, and the blue-point Siamese; the dentist ended up with the practice, the Porsche, an apartment at the Bay Club, the bimbette, and the lawyers' bills.

But nobody had Kwame, near as I could tell.

I kept my nose out of their domestic crisis until I noticed that the dog was looking downright ribby. Then I went over and asked if Kwame had been sick. Turned out nobody had remembered to feed him and he was too well trained to eat the Siamese without permission. I made the dentist an offer he was smart enough not to refuse. Since then, Kwame has been living with Fiora and me. We all like it that way.

I went and stood in front of Kwame, admiring both his restraint and his eagerness. Fiora says I delight in tormenting him. Maybe. And maybe Kwame enjoys the game as much as I do. He stared at me, watching for the slightest signal. He almost broke when I grinned; then he settled back, still waiting.

"Okay," I said as I waved my hand.

Kwame leaped past me on legs like coiled steel springs. He lit fifteen feet away. The next leap took him into the brush. He literally vanished, making his own path as he went, a hunter with a mission. I wondered if the California cougar smells something like the black-maned lion of the African veldt.

I gathered up the rest of the tools, checked to make sure the ice chest was in the shade, and set off down the path again. By the time I reached the quail guzzler, Benny was examining it skeptically. Fiora, with her usual bottom-line instincts, had already figured out how the asphalt and concrete contraption worked.

"Water collects here," she said, pointing to the flat-bottomed catch basin that drained into an underground holding tank, "and comes out there." She glanced at me. "Banks and quail guzzlers aren't all that different. What you collect at one end has a direct ef—"

"Fiora," I interrupted. "Smell the chaparral, listen to the birds, look for mountain lions and wild flowers. No money talk. Take the damn day off, will you?"

"You mean I should stop thinking and become a part of Mother Nature's grand design?" Fiora asked, waving her hand.

All around us, southern California's May sunlight poured down clean and hot and pure, raising a fine sweat beneath my shirt. Fiora must have felt it too. She picked up the trailing tails of my old shirt and tied them in a knot, baring her midriff.

"Yeah," I said, looking at the expanse of smooth, taut skin just above the waistband of her jeans. "Nature's grand design."

Fiora gave me a sideways glance and a fey little smile.

"Just what makes you think banks aren't part of Mother Nature's grand design too?" she asked.

Before I could answer, she laughed and darted away, testing the lug soles of her new trail shoes on the drying silt that had all but filled the concrete catch pan of the guzzler. Benny noticed about the same time I did that the pager wasn't on Fiora's belt, after all. We looked at one another, faintly puzzled.

"Maybe you better let her talk about the bank," Benny said.

"We had all night last night, plus the ride up here, if she wanted to talk about goddamned banks."

He gave me a look out of eyes as black as Apache tears, hitched past me, and found a point where he could study the entire guzzler. I followed him, letting go of the question of Fiora in favor of another one, equally vexing. I was on this mountain of my own free will, but I still had some lingering doubts about the wisdom of kindly ecological interventions such as quail guzzlers. That kind of well-meant tinkering often has too many unanticipated, and unhappy, consequences.

In the long run, I have always suspected that man does better to let Mother Nature work toward her own balance. When water dries up in the mountains, the critter population—ground squirrels, rabbits, mice, and quail—dies out or moves on. The process isn't pretty, but it's a hell of a lot more natural than most of what you find in health-food stores.

For better or for worse, though, man is a born tinkerer. The Izaak Walton League built this decrepit quail guzzler, and forty others like it, a quarter century ago, and the critters had come to depend on their concrete waterhole. But now the flat collection pan was filled with silt, and the winter's rainfall had drained out through a wide crack in the covered concrete cistern. In late May, that was no tragedy. There still was plenty of water around. But come August and September, when the seeps dried up and the hot Santa Anas started to blow, the critters were going to be in trouble. And if the prey was in trouble, the predators would be in worse trouble.

I'm fond of fuzzy little things, but my greatest sympathy is with the furred and feathered hunters. The cougars, coyotes, bobcats, owls, hawks, and falcons that make their living at the fringes of the urbanized desert in Southern

California have to be hard, quick, skillful, and daring. Graceful to watch, they are a necessary reminder that the city and the wilderness are part of a continuum. We tend to forget that fact when we're trapped in concrete canyons or free to roam nothing more challenging than manicured greenbelts.

Predators are a persistent lot. Though California has lost the black bear south of the Tehachapis, I can still show you coyote dens in the Hollywood Hills and cougar tracks in the Santa Ana Mountains. Successful predators adapt to changing conditions. Look at man. If that makes you uncomfortable, look at the white-tailed kites and red-tailed hawks that make their living in the freeway medians, taking prey a few feet from the diamond lanes and rush-hour traffic. These birds are an elegant, unflinching reminder that life eats. That's how you know it's alive.

But the competition between man and beast does make for conflicts. While man can be damned slow compared to a cougar or a falcon, predators are still dumb animals. They have no choice but to follow the rule of the gut and the food chain. If the water holes and the quail guzzlers dry up and the prey population begins to disappear, predators will range out, following the most fundamental imperative in nature—survival.

For the clever predator, Suburbia is Fat City. Any coyote can tell you that the generic house cat or canine purse pet is every bit as nourishing as a ground squirrel and a hell of a lot easier to catch. People, of course, don't view their pets as moveable feasts. Sooner or later, the conflict turns ugly.

One of the saddest news photos I saw last year was of a state game warden drawing a bead on a confused, half-grown male cougar that had wandered down from Modjeska's wild shoulder into a housing tract. Civilization scared him. He hid behind a hot tub in somebody's back yard and wished to hell he was somewhere else. The warden wished he was, too. It was seven-thirty in the morning, the time when toddlers come out to grub around in the sandbox and first-graders head for the bus stop. There was no time for playing hide-and-seek with a frightened cat. The warden had a twelve-gauge and an unpleasant job to do.

I only hope he was a good shot.

Not long after that, when the league requested volunteers to help rebuild the quail guzzlers, I signed up. A few hundred gallons of stored water in a gully might be enough to carry a canyon's critters through the dry season, and one canyon full of prey might prevent one cougar from gliding down the mountain on big cat feet, looking for a meal in some suburban back yard. If nobody ever has to shoot a cougar behind a redwood hot tub again, that will be fine with me.

"Can we save it?" I asked Benny.

Normally Benny doesn't tinker with low-tech construction projects. The big New Zealander is more at home with semiconductor chips and fiber optics and the other accoutrements of electronic listening devices and data communications systems. But he had seen the picture of the doomed cat too. Now he was leaning on his sticks and sneering at the catch basin.

"Bugger all concrete," he muttered through his thick beard. "It hasn't been improved since the Stone Age. Fetch that plastic sheeting and resin from the van, boyo. We'll put this thing right in a minute."

"Environmentalists don't believe in plastic. Call it fiberglass or the Izaac Walton League will put a price on your head."

"Promises, promises. I haven't browned off a tree-hugger in months."

"Are you two handsome types going to spend the morning talking or working?" Fiora asked crisply, dumping a shovelful of dirt between us.

Without a word I turned and headed back toward the van. I have never enjoyed competing for Fiora's attention with her passion for purposeful daily activity, but I've finally learned not to get in her way when she is in work mode.

Pain is a great teacher. I may not understand Fiora's drive, but I damn well know it's real.

I was either blessed or cursed, to have been born without the burning spur of ambition in my soul. Then I inherited Uncle Jake's ill-gotten gains—a steamer trunk full of money. Thus freed of the need to make an honest living, I gave up on regular employment. Fiora looks at work differently. She likes it. She has the kind of mind that can see past the abstract numbers to money's tangible accomplishments: a factory that gives work where none existed, a shopping center that pays enough taxes to build roads and schools, a chunk of cash gambled on one person's vision of a better world.

At least, that's how she sees it. Me, I don't see things that clearly. But that's all right. There's a place for folks like me . . . and today it was on the dumb end of a shovel, scraping silt out of a quail guzzler's catch pan, while Fiora and Benny hauled a quarter century's accumulation of damp dirt and algae out of the tank. Fiora, being the smallest and most agile, took the dirty job, dropping down through the inspection cap and mucking out the cistern with a plastic bucket and a trowel.

By the time we broke for lunch, Fiora's jeans were caked with mud and her white cotton shirt was streaked with what my maiden aunt referred to as "perspiration." I collected the ice chest from the van, passed out the goodies, and watched while Fiora sat on a branch of a red-barked madrone and tied into one of Benny's patented half-pound Italian Gut Bomb sandwiches as though she hadn't eaten for a week.

While she munched, she peeled a slice of tomato from one end of the sandwich and held the tidbit out for Kwame, who had smelled civilized food and reappeared with the speed of light. Kwame opened his lion-trap jaws and let Fiora place the tomato on his tongue. He closed his mouth and swallowed. He likes sirloin, but tomatoes and avocados are his real passions.

I looked past Fiora's slender hand and Kwame's washcloth-sized tongue. There are still days when southern California has a view. From the shoulder of Modjeska, I could see the San Gabriel Mountains to the north and San Diego's Point Loma to the south. The patchwork of housing tracts and chaparral between me and the Pacific was like an Arras tapestry, the colors still vivid from the winter rains and the patterns so sharp you could shave with them.

"To think that people get paid for working outdoors on days like this," Fiora said.

"Before you make a career change, see how stiff you are tomorrow morning," I said, digging into the deli container for another marinated artichoke heart.

"You think I couldn't hack it?"

I plopped the artichoke heart on my picnic plate. "You can do anything you set your mind to, and you've proved it more than once."

Fiora snagged the heart off my plate with her fingers. Oil from the marinade dripped on her jeans as she held the food halfway to her mouth. "Well, right now I'm thinking about selling Pacific Rim Investments," she said calmly.

From the corner of my eye I saw Benny freeze with a Foster's Lager bottle halfway to his lips. He stared at Fiora as though she had just announced she intended to shave her head and pierce her nose with pig bones. I'm sure I was staring in the same way. Pacific Rim Investments was the culmination of Fiora's career in high finance, a monument to her determination, guts, and brains. I would have expected her to sell PRI just about the same time I sold myself into the modern slavery known as civil service.

It was so quiet I could hear Kwame drool. Benny put his beer aside and reached for his sticks.

"I'm going for a stroll," he said. "Sounds like you two have some things to talk about."

"Stay put and finish your beer," Fiora said. "I'm not talking about running off to join Mother Theresa. I'm just tired of going to the office every day, and investment banking isn't the kind of business you can run on a part-time basis. I've been thinking I should get rid of the business before I let it go downhill. Maybe I'll try my hand at something else, something Fiddler and I could operate together."

"If I wanted a job, I'd have one," I said. My nickname is Fiddler, as in violinist, not dilettante.

"I'm not talking about a job. I was thinking more in terms of a rescue operation."

"I'm not sure you're thinking at all," I shot back. "A minute ago you were talking about buying out some poor little bank. Now you're talking about selling the one you already own. Make sense, woman."

Fiora smiled. "Quail guzzlers."

Benny snickered. He knew as well as I did that Fiora had me. I could spend the rest of the day wondering what bomb was ticking away under us, or I could talk about what Fiora had been trying to talk about all day.

Banks.

I grabbed a beer bottle from the ice, held the cap against the cooler's metal handle, and slammed down with the edge of my palm. The cap flipped away, beer foamed, and I drank long and hard, trying to cool my temper. There are times when a quick-minded woman is a pain in the ass.

The bottle was more than half empty when I turned to Fiora, ready to give her as hard a time as she was giving me. But it wasn't triumph I saw in her eyes, it was fear or anticipation or hope or all of them mixed together.

Crossroads time, and not one damn signpost in sight.

2

"BANKS," I SAID.

Fiora isn't the type to gloat. She began with perfect calm, as though she hadn't spent the past four hours maneuvering me into her verbal trap.

"Have I ever introduced you to Marianne Bradford Simms?" she asked.

I grunted, which is my all-purpose answer when I don't give a damn.

"She's chairman of the board of Bank of the Southland."

"Bank of the Southland," Benny said to Kwame. "Sounds like another of those go-go cardboard banks."

Benny is a financial conservative. No Eurodollar options, no creative financing or unsecured lines of credit, no rollover loans for him. His investment program consists of what he calls "auric recycling." He buys 999.0 Credit Suisse gold bars and buries them in his back yard.

"The name is new but the institution has been around for a long time. It used to be called Bradford National," Fiora said. She gestured toward the flat coastal plain beyond Modjeska Peak. "The bank's charter dates back to the time when

all you could see from here was orange groves and barley
fields."

I looked out past of the flank of the mountain to the low-
lands, where the coastal plain was now supporting its climax
crop—residential subdivisions with concrete and asphalt
geometries, cedar-shake roofs, and carefully random streaks
of greenbelts or golf courses. I preferred the subtle shadings
of chaparral and canyon, but I was ranch raised; I had no
illusions about the romance of living off the land.

"One of the towns down there is named after the family,
but they could have named the whole county," Fiora said.
"The Bradfords were true pioneers."

Fiora looked out over the man-made landscape that was
the direct result of one family's vision. There was a kind of
hunger in her glance. She doesn't talk about it much, but
she is cursed with the desire to leave the world a better place
than she found it. In her opinion, the Bradfords had.

"I've known Marianne since the commercial banking business went to hell a few years ago," Fiora said, looking away
from the view, fixing me with intense, green-shaded eyes.
"She's a shrewd, tough, honorable woman. She ran that bank
in a time and place when women weren't expected to run
anything more important than errands. A decade ago her
bank was one of the most solid in Orange County."

"What happened?" I asked, interested in spite of myself.
Fiora can always hook me. It's her crackling intensity. I've
never found another woman like her, and God knows I've
tried from time to time.

"Deregulation happened. Her son, Brad, decided Bradford
National was hopelessly old-fashioned. He talked Marianne
into changing the bank's name, opening up five branches
around southern California, and dabbling in everything from
junk bonds to leveraged buy-outs. She gave him his head
and he went crazy, trying to catch the foaming edge of the
wave of the future."

I shrugged. "I was in downtown Bradford a few years ago.
Half the buildings were boarded over, and the other half were

girlie bars and plain old dives. Things change. Maybe demographics just passed your friend by."

Fiora shook her head fiercely. "Marianne isn't a fool. She knows that the all-white farming town of her childhood has become a heavy-metal melting pot—Latins, Asians, Pacific Islanders. But she wants the bank to survive, and she's worried about her son."

Off to the northwest, fifteen miles away, I could just make out the spot where the Costa Mesa Freeway bends around the old downtown district of Bradford. I could hear the intensity in Fiora's voice, but I couldn't understand it. With or without the bank, the freeway would still bend and people would still drive its concrete curve.

"It was Brad, not Marianne, who didn't understand the change and the opportunity," Fiora continued. "He wanted to shut down the old main branch and abandon the town. Marianne refused. She wanted to help the bank change and grow with the new community, just like her father and grandfather did. But Brad wanted to go down to the Gold Coast and play with the big kids. He insisted on opening branches in Newport Beach and Laguna, the high-ticket places every other bank was trying to crack. B of A and Wells Fargo undercut him at every turn."

"Bloody idiot," muttered Benny. "A banker ought to know that more money beats less money every time."

Fiora didn't disagree. "Marianne took back control of the home bank six months ago. She's retrenching, trying to tie into the bank's real power base—the city of Bradford."

"Is it working?" I asked.

"She closed all the branches except Newport and used the savings to build up the main-branch operations. She's made a lot of small business loans of the type that once built the city and the bank into a real force. She had to learn to pronounce a lot of new names and hire bilingual clerks, and she's irritated some of the town's old guard, the ones who believe they'll wake up tomorrow and the community will be all-white again. She's worked sixteen hours a day, seven days a week."

"Why doesn't she just apply for a bailout like everybody else?" I asked, watching the vivid play of color and darkness in Fiora's eyes, wondering how I fit into her complex fiscal equations.

"She wants to come out of this the same way she went into it—with a family-owned bank."

"Will she?"

Fiora grimaced and flipped a hunk of avocado at Kwame, who inhaled it swiftly. "It's too close to call." She took a deep breath and looked at me. "Marianne's biggest problem is that she doesn't have an entirely free hand in the operation. It's a family bank. She controls forty percent of the voting stock, and there's another forty percent in the hands of some cousins, folks who usually take Marianne's advice. The rest, unfortunately, belongs to Brad."

"And I thought you never met a banker you didn't like," I said. "What's wrong with Brad?"

"Don't ask."

"Okay." I raised the beer to my mouth.

Fiora wasn't going to let me off that easy. She picked up the tale without missing a beat.

"Bradford Simms must be thirty by now, but he is still a spoiled, self-indulgent brat."

I swallowed. "Is that what Marianne thinks?"

"God, no. Her one weakness is her son. He's an only child. She raised him alone after his father died twenty-five years ago. She has always, always, had her heart set on his becoming a banker."

"I suppose she gave him lots of money to play with when he was growing up?"

Fiora nodded. "Until a few years ago, he thought the stuff simply grew in his wallet, like dust bunnies under the bed. Seven years at USC, just for a bachelor's degree. Then Marianne personally groomed him for three years. Finally she decided he had to sink or swim on his own. She gave him the keys to the vault and retired."

"And he's sinking fast," I said.

Fiora didn't bother to answer. I leaned over, flipped up the top of the ice chest, and lifted out a glazed strawberry pie. Its peak thrust up like a miniature crimson Matterhorn. The whipped cream around the edges had taken a bit of a beating but was hanging on.

Kwame immediately abandoned the sandwiches and came to me as though he had been bred to hunt Irvine strawberries rather than African lions. While we three humans worked on individual slabs of pie, Kwame lay down with his nose three inches from the tin and waited. He knows he doesn't get refined sugar, but that doesn't keep him from lusting.

Fiora finished her pie first. Without hesitation she ran her index finger around the edge of the tin, going after the whipped cream that was left, patiently waiting for me to ask the question she had been waiting to hear.

I poured the last fragrant drops of coffee from the stainless steel thermos.

"Okay," I said. "Drop the other shoe."

She took a long drink of coffee.

I gave in. "Why are you telling me about the bank rather than telling one of your fiscal cronies?"

"I'm telling you because Marianne asked me to."

"What?"

"Your reputation preceded you, as they say at corporate meetings." Fiora looked at me and smiled sadly. "Marianne heard from a friend of a friend of a friend that my former husband and present lover is good at pulling people out of holes. She's afraid her son has dug himself a big one."

"What kind of hole? Embezzling? Taking kickbacks on bad loans?"

"She doesn't know. After she gave Brad the reins, she tried not to interfere. It worked, too. At least it seemed to. He did surprisingly well at the branch offices, attracting deposits and making loans. There were setbacks, of course, but Marianne expected that. Mistakes are part of learning."

"Sounds like the boy wonder was a slow learner."

"That's the funny part. He started hot and then got real cold. About nine months ago things started coming unraveled. The cousins banded together and told Marianne to take back control or they would sell out." Fiora shrugged. "Technically Marianne took back control, but she actually left Brad alone to manage the Newport branch. He likes to run with the beach crowd, I guess."

"So what happened?"

"He's gone flaky on her," Fiora said succinctly. "Marianne can't get simple answers when she asks simple questions."

"Why doesn't she just walk in one night and take a look at the books?" Benny asked.

That's Benny for you, the compleat pragmatist.

"You're fantastic with computers," Fiora told him, "but you don't know much about being a parent. If Marianne went behind Brad's back, he would think she doesn't trust him."

"Which she doesn't," Benny pointed out.

"There's another problem," Fiora said. "If Marianne went in and looked at the books and found something serious, she would be under a legal obligation to report it, both to the rest of the board and to the bank regulators. That would put paid to an already shaky mother-son relationship. It would also destroy the bank."

"Why?" I asked. "A lot of banks have been audited."

"The local and regional regulators have already put Bank of the Southland on notice that it's subject to close audit procedures with no advance warning. That's the first formal step in a relatively short process that leads directly to outright seizure by the FDIC."

Fiora took the mug from my hand, drank, and returned the mug to me with the kind of fingers-along-fingers caress that is both casual and intimate.

"On the other hand, the Feds can't be anxious to shut

Southland down or they would have done it by now. From what Marianne hinted, there's cause and then some."

Fiora looked thoughtful, then shrugged.

"Maybe the Feds have more banks on their hands than they want," she continued. "But if they're invited in, they would probably have to take formal action of some sort. Big depositors keep track of such actions. One whiff of trouble and there would be a run on deposits. Marianne doesn't have much cushion at the moment. If her reserves drop too low, she won't be able to keep funding loans. The Feds would be all over her. Then there would be an even bigger run on deposits. She could go under in two weeks."

High above us a hawk was keening and crying. I searched until I caught the russet flash of his tail fan between me and the sun. When I squinted I saw there were two birds close together, wings motionless, bodies turning and spinning, suspended within a column of hot pure light.

"Why me?" I asked, following the flight of the hawks. "I've always left high finances to you. If there were some strong-arm type breathing down Marianne's patrician neck, I might be able to help, but . . ."

I looked at Fiora directly, gauging her reaction. We have always tried to maintain separate lives for ourselves, even when we are living together. Especially then. Two purposeful dogs worrying the same bone can lead to real trouble.

"Leave the number crunching to me," Fiora said, taking the mug from my hand, running her fingers over mine again. "All you have to do is meet Marianne and talk to her."

"About what?"

"She wants to look you over and decide if the friend of a friend of a friend was right. She's running on instinct, and her instinct says Brad is up to his lips in shit."

"What if she's right?"

"She wants him washed off, spanked, and sent to bed."

Benny said something I didn't quite hear. Probably because I was swearing under my breath at the time.

"I didn't promise Marianne anything except that you'd talk to her," Fiora said, touching my hand. "She's a good woman, Fiddler. Maybe not a wise one when it comes to loving, but we can hardly hold that against her, can we? Look at us."

Fiora rarely asks me for anything. It's part of her independence. But she was asking now.

"All right."

Fiora's smile put the sun to shame. It made me feel ridiculously good.

"Marianne will meet you at seven forty-five tomorrow for breakfast in Bradford at the café across the street from the bank," Fiora said. "I have an appointment at ten-thirty with Brad. He thinks I'm a prospective investor. Tomorrow at lunch you and I can compare notes."

I stood up and stretched, trying to pull a kink out of my left shoulder. "I'll come with you to talk to Brad."

She shot me a sideways look, taking in the dirty Levi's, sweaty chambray shirt, and scuffed boots. "You don't look like an investor."

"I'll wear a suit."

Fiora blinked. She knows how I feel about suits and ties. "I'd learn more without you," she said. "You make tight-ass executive types very nervous."

"All right, but if you encounter anything in Brad's bank except a typical financial analysis, you're going to turn right around and march away like a good little money shuffler," I warned her.

Fiora looked up and gave me a smile with teeth in it. "You send me down the hill to scare off the rattlesnakes and then tell me I have to run from a little urban scuffling?"

"Bingo."

Benny shifted irritably. He would listen silently all day if Fiora and I read the Greater Los Angeles telephone book to each other, but thirty seconds of our fighting is his limit.

High overhead, the two hawks soared in the brilliant light,

keening to each other and the wind. Fiora watched their graceful flight for a long moment before she looked back at me.

"Why are you the only one who's free?" she asked.

"Neither one of us is free. Love does that to you. Remember that damned museum where you nearly got killed? It's not going to happen again if I have anything to say about it. And I do."

Fiora continued to watch the hawks. Finally she looked at me again. Her eyes were bleak with anger, not at me but at a world that doesn't allow perfect freedom to coexist with love. One or the other, but not both.

"How about this?" Fiora said. "I won't do anything that I don't tell you about in advance. Is that comforting enough for you?"

It wasn't, but it was all the comfort I was going to get.

3

IT HAD BEEN four years since I last drove the Main Street of Bradford. Then it had been a late-Victorian Anglo downtown that had lost the battle of survival to the outer shopping malls. Half the two- and three-story turn-of-the-century business blocks on Main Street had been abandoned, boarded up, their plate-glass windows filmed with dirt. The ticket window in the Art Deco movie theater had been covered with a sheet of plywood, and the red plastic letters on the marquee announced it was CL-S— F— R—ODEL-NG. The only viable commercial activity in town seemed to involve beer, wine, dope, and women. The only patrons or pedestrians were men.

But four years had brought a lot of change. The melting pot of southern California was at a full rolling boil, even at seven-thirty in the morning. Downtown Bradford teemed with vivid, abrasive, aggressive, jangling-joyous activity. Change was bubbling through the old white-bread business district.

The buildings had been transformed. Half of them were gutted and cut up into small shops, the other half redecorated and restocked with a postmodern mix of material goods that reflected the polyglot community. Sony and RCA had a foothold right between the *panadería* and the *casa de cambio*. *Joyería* gold dealers and herbalists occupied adjacent stalls.

The downtown area was not exclusively Hispanic. One block was lined with shops selling kimchee, cut-rate electronics, and intricate Lao Hmong embroidery. The Vietnamese-French influence in the cordon bleu bakery and bouillabaisse café dated back to the days before Dien Bien Phu.

Not surprisingly, immigrant communities place a premium on free movement of people, goods, and money. Travel agencies and air-freight agencies shouldered for sidewalk space. Every fourth shop seemed to offer international money orders, the working wayfarer's version of traveler's checks. Send your money home even if you can't go yourself because you're too busy working to get more money to send home.

I had ten minutes to kill before my unwanted appointment, so I walked awhile, trying to catch the new rhythms of Bradford, California. Merchants had their doors open and their boom boxes playing loud music in two languages and more national accents than I could count. The stores looked chaotic, which is to say prosperous. Workmen were wiring steel rebar into place for the foundation of what a sign announced would be an eighteen-store mall. The sign said construction financing had been provided by Bank of the Southland. The names of the future occupants were Hispanic and Asian.

Three young women in slacks and silk blouses walked by, headed for work as secretaries or shop girls, chattering in the *caló* mixture of English and Spanish that becomes Mexican-border Spanglish. It took me a moment to realize why I was so surprised to see the women alone and unescorted on the streets.

A decade ago, the immigrant enclaves of southern California were largely male, particularly in the Latin communities. Illegal immigration had skewed the population in favor of young, aggressive, ambitious men. The few women around were carefully guarded or sold to the highest bidder. But that had changed. *Mojados* and *alambristas*, wetbacks and wire jumpers, had become legal residents, thanks to federal amnesty. Their women and children could come north to live freely.

With the women had come civilization. The impact was evident everywhere, from the family clothing stores and ice-cream stands to the video stores featuring Bugs and Daffy. Immigration may be by government regulation, but human migration is a different, more appealing process altogether. Downtown Bradford was on its way to becoming a community once more.

A three-story building dominated the intersection of First and Main. A large neon sign proclaimed it to be Bank of the Southland. The building was undergoing a face-lift, complete with modern thermal glass windows and stainless-steel hardware. But nothing could obliterate the old name—BRAD-FORD NATIONAL BANK, FOUNDED 1899—on the red Arizona sandstone façade. You could still detect an aura of Victorian disapproval in the building. Underneath the new hardware there was a rectitude as unyielding as stone itself.

Across the street was a café with a large neon sign that said: CAFE MICHOACANO. Beneath the neon were the faded letters of the former name: BRADFORD CAFE. As I went through the door, the place looked as if not much but the name had changed since Bradford's heyday. The records on the juke box were still Big Band, judging from the Tommy Dorsey tune that was playing. The grill man was still a mahogany-skinned *norteño* with the relaxed look of someone who had arrived a long time ago. Wearing a brimless white paper cap and a spotless white apron, he cracked eggs with one hand and flipped pancakes, hash browns, chorizo, and corn tortillas with the other.

The woman who wanted to vet me as a potential guardian for her wayward son was waiting for me in a booth against the side wall. From there she could keep her eye on the front door of the bank across the street.

At first glance Marianne Bradford Simms was very much the small-town banker, as dated in her tailored business suit and modest makeup as the sandstone building across the street. Then her clear, ice-blue eyes focused on me. She might have been past her prime and under heavy pressure, but there was intelligence, determination, and power in her. At one time she must have possessed Fiora's kind of pouring energy.

No wonder Brad had a hard time holding his own with his mother. I was fully grown, and I still had a hell of a time with Fiora.

"Welcome to downtown Bradford," Mrs. Simms said, offering me her hand without rising. "I hope you don't mind an informal breakfast."

"I prefer them."

Mrs. Simms's smile was a cool flash of teeth. "My grandfather made his first million-dollar loan in this very booth," she said, rapping her knuckles lightly on the table's worn Formica surface. "I've eaten here every morning since I came back to work. It's a good way of getting in touch with the community again."

I folded myself into the booth across from Mrs. Simms. Immediately a sturdy Mixtec waitress appeared and took my order for *huevos rancheros* and corn tortillas. Her English was thick but serviceable. When she spoke to Marianne Simms it was in quiet Spanish, calling her "Señora" with careful respect and asking if she wished more coffee or some *pan dulce*. The banker answered in the same language, fluid and natural. I was surprised but said nothing.

As soon as the waitress left, Mrs. Simms became the Anglo banker again, a woman on a schedule.

"Fiora told me a bit about what you did to Roger Valenti over that O'Keeffe painting," Mrs. Simms said. "I must say it didn't sound gentlemanly at all."

"I'm not a gentleman." I glanced up as the waitress delivered my coffee. *"Gracias."*

"Neither is Valenti," Mrs. Simms said. "He's one of

Orange County's new breed. I call them the Newport Center crowd. Some of them, like Fiora, are brilliant. They have vision and integrity. Others are like Roger Valenti. For them money isn't a means, it's an end in itself. The more the better, without the slightest concept of purpose or perspective."

I said nothing because Mrs. Simms hadn't told me anything about why I was here when I wanted to be somewhere else.

She looked across the street. "George Bradford built that building nearly a century ago. His capital consisted of forty thousand dollars in gold he dug out of the Klondike with his own two hands. It wasn't the gold he wanted, though. It was what it could buy—a bank and a chance to build something lasting."

I drank coffee. Two of the men in my family had gone to the Klondike, but they had gone for gold, period. Any they found ended up in the pockets of whores, thieves, and cold-deck artists. And a good time was had by all.

"What about you, Fiddler? Why do you get up in the morning?"

"To have breakfast with a woman who doesn't want to come to the point," I said bluntly.

Mrs. Simms looked from her grandfather's memorial back to me and spoke with equal bluntness. "You don't sound like a private investigator looking for work."

"I'm not."

"Then why did you accept this job?"

"I haven't."

"Really? Then why did Fiora have a messenger deliver a letter of agreement for my signature yesterday afternoon? Are you a licensed investigator?"

"No. The California Bureau of Consumer Affairs licenses investigators in this state," I said, answering the only question I knew anything about. "Most of what I do isn't on their list of approved activities. That's why I don't take money for it."

"How odd. The letter I signed clearly states that you and Fiora are retained as consultants to Bank of the Southland, and that you are each to be paid at the rate of two hundred fifty dollars an hour."

My reaction to that bit of news was the kind that gives a kick start to your heart.

"I'll donate my fee to the first open manhole I find," I said. "Fiora can do whatever she wants with hers. She always has."

Mrs. Simms watched me for a few moments, obviously reassessing the situation in light of the anger I didn't bother concealing. "With or without license, do you investigate things for a living?"

"Not for a living. I'm gainfully unemployed and I intend to stay that way."

"But you *do* investigate things."

"Yes."

I looked at my watch. There was still plenty of time to wring Fiora's neck before she went to the Newport bank, as long as Marianne Simms got to the point.

"Am I keeping you from something?" she asked crisply.

"Look, Mrs. Simms, you asked me to come here. I'm here. Is there something in particular you thought my 'partner' and I should know, or was this just a dog-and-pony show to make you feel better?"

There was another silence, but it didn't last long.

"I've hired outside counsel to prevent several of the minority stockholders in Bank of the Southland from putting their stock up for public sale," Mrs. Simms said evenly.

"Why bother? Fiora said you and your son own sixty percent of the stock between you."

"At the moment, Brad is one of the stockholders who most worries me. He has become . . ."—Mrs. Simms hesitated, grimaced, and said flatly—"unpredictable."

Thinking of her son added a fast decade to Marianne Simms's looks. She was unhappy and out of her depth and disliked showing it.

"If unpredictable means Brad doesn't always follow his mother's advice, I can't help you, Mrs. Simms. He's old enough to cut the apron strings."

Her eyes narrowed. "Control of this bank isn't a matter of apron strings. Take a look up and down this street."

"I already have."

"What did you see?"

"The main drag of a small California city that's in transition. I saw change, the kind of change that can't be managed the way your grandfather and his cronies managed the economy of the town eighty years ago."

Abruptly Mrs. Simms's eyes took on the quality of fresh-water ice, reflecting the same kind of cold anger I was feeling at the moment.

"Change?" she repeated. "Maybe, but it's nothing new. It has happened here before. If the town survives, it will happen again."

Short, neatly buffed nails tapped on the worn Formica tabletop while Mrs. Simms looked out the window at the handsome sandstone façade of her grandfather's bank. It seemed to calm her. After a minute she turned back to me and began speaking in a flat, take-it-or-leave-it tone.

"One of my grandmothers was born on a small rancho in Jalisco. I've seen several waves of immigration in my own lifetime—Middlewestern Anglos after the Second World War; Mexican braceros in the fifties; the Vietnamese boat people of the seventies; Thais, Samoans, and overseas Chinese in the eighties. I'm not intimidated by the color of anybody's skin, my own included. When I was a girl I was derided for being part Mexican. As an old woman I'm derided for being a white banker, which is to say callous, greedy, and grasping. But I'm the same person now that I was then."

Mrs. Simms sipped at her cooling coffee, then set cup into saucer with a distinct snapping sound. Despite myself, I began to understand why Fiora admired the old lady. Bullshit wasn't this woman's game.

"Relax," I said. "I live with a banker, remember? And one

of my grandfathers was half Cheyenne and half Scots High-lander."

Mrs. Simms examined my face for a moment, as though seeking signs of Indian blood in my gray eyes, dark mustache, and long-fingered hands.

"Fiora says it only shows when I lift scalps," I said.

Mrs. Simms smiled a very feminine smile, as though she suspected that Fiora's scalp was at the top of my list right now. Then she nodded.

"Under whatever name, that bank has watched a great many changes in the past nine decades," she said quietly. "My grandfather didn't found it and my father didn't carry it through the Depression just to see it sold off as a tidy little 'profit center' within some bank holding company."

Her fingernails sounded another muted drum roll. Before I could speak, she was talking again.

"No matter what color its citizens, I understand this community a great deal better than the big banks ever could," she said. "I feel the same way about Bradford's future as Fiora does about the future of the Pacific Rim. I want to put my money where my beliefs are, with the people of this community—the immigrants."

"Don't the other stockholders agree?"

She made an impatient gesture. "The only other stock-holder who matters is my son. I don't know what he thinks. Or wants."

"Ask him."

"I did. That was three months ago. We haven't spoken since."

"Mrs. Simms, you don't need me. You need a family counselor."

She drew a deep breath and faced me without flinching. "It's not that easy. In the modern euphemism, Brad is in the middle of a personal crisis. I am beginning to suspect that it was brought on by substance abuse."

Nice going, Fiora. Remind me to do you a favor sometime.

"Alcohol or some other drug?" I asked finally, wanting all the bad news at once.

"I don't know. He becomes . . . erratic. He's abusive, both of himself and of others."

"How often?"

"Often enough to panic the other family stockholders, but not quite enough to ruin his ability to function. Usually, in fact, he does quite well. Then he goes crazy for a few hours or a few days, does things that make no sense, screams at people."

Mrs. Simms's eyes closed for an instant and her fingers tightened on the coffee cup. "At first I thought it was just left over from his USC days. You know how college boys drink and carry on. When I gave him the branch operations, I hoped it would drag him into adulthood."

I swore under my breath.

"But it didn't work," she said, telling me what I already knew. "Everything I did made the problem worse, not better. That's why I need you and Fiora. I have to know exactly what's happening, both to the bank and to Brad. Then I'll decide what has to be done."

With a sharp movement she set aside her coffee cup and gathered her small purse with the movements of a woman who was getting ready to leave.

"Mrs. Simms, I'm not a glorified baby-sitter. Get a licensed PI. They're cheaper."

Like Fiora, Mrs. Simms was small and self-contained in the same way that a falcon is small and self-contained. Fierce is another word for it.

"I have used several private investigators on banking matters over the years," she said calmly, opening her purse. "There are only two kinds of men who do investigative work for hire, incompetents who would sell their results to the highest bidder and competents who maintain close ties with local law enforcement. I can't afford to take a chance on either type until I know what's really going on. I have no choice but to hold you to the letter of the agreement your partner signed."

She dropped a ten on the table.

"I have already informed Brad through one of his assistants that Fiora, as a potential purchaser of the Newport operation, is to be allowed to examine the branch's books."

Marianne Bradford Simms turned to leave.

"Mrs. Simms."

The older woman was like Fiora in another way; she could read my voice very accurately. Mrs. Simms stopped and turned back, looking warily at me.

"I'm not a gentleman," I said. "Think about that. Then ask yourself if you really want me rooting around in your personal life."

Her flashing smile contained complete understanding and no humor at all. "My grandfather wasn't a gentleman. Civilization wasn't built by gentlemen. It isn't maintained by gentlemen. It is merely exploited by them.

"I'm glad you aren't a gentleman, Fiddler, for I'm very much afraid my son is."

4

IT WAS a quarter to nine when I drove into the parking lot of the upscale community shopping center that housed Bank of the Southland, Newport Beach branch. The center was as far from the melting-pot atmosphere of Bradford as you can get and still stay in the same county: beachwear boutiques, gourmet cook shops, a Schwab discount brokerage outlet, and a running-shoe store—a vest-pocket shopping center surrounded on one side by golf course and tennis courts and on the others by tracts full of houses that start at $750,000 and go up. Steeply.

The shopping center's parking lot was empty except for a few cars in front of the brokerage house. I tucked in among them, trying to look like I belonged.

I was driving the little BMW, a 1972 2002tii, and I had purposely taken the edge off my appearance with a button-down shirt and a pair of cotton slacks. Stock picker, beach bum, idle househusband, or semiserious jogger, I fit anybody's casting list. I walked across the parking lot and approached the front of the bank, looking like someone who expected it to be open. The double doors were still locked but the lights were on inside.

I saw everything I needed in five seconds.

The Newport Beach branch of Bank of the Southland amounted to little more than four thousand square feet of gray-carpeted floor with a vault at one end, teller counter and loan desks down the middle, and a small suite of executive offices at the other end. The office furniture was mass-produced. So was the art on the walls.

Generic branch bank. No surprises. There are probably five hundred like it along the Gold Coast from Mission Bay to Montecito. At least the old Bradford National building with its sandstone façade and substantial presence looked like a bank. Except for the handsome stainless steel and brass vault door that formed the back wall, the Newport branch looked more like an escrow office or an insurance agency.

Banks don't sell security; they sell an illusion of security. The vault door was impressive, but it was hung on a strongroom wall that was probably no better constructed than the rest of the building. That meant a ten-year-old with a ball peen hammer and five uninterrupted minutes could get inside. But put the sign BANK out front, and people think their money is safe.

There was a croissant and coffee bar across the small parking lot from the bank. I walked over and bought a *New York Times* from a news box outside. Inside I got a big cup of Colombian Excelso, black, from the tanned surf bunny behind the counter, and found a table by the window. Now that there was a customer—me—she retuned the radio from Motley Crue to the rondo from Beethoven's Violin Concerto.

The music riveted me. There was a time when I had played the violin. Beethoven convinced me it was a bad idea. I was nineteen and still hadn't learned that perfection is a bitch goddess. The rondo taught me a bleak truth: I might be good, but I wasn't ever going to be great. My fingers would never create the perfection that was in my mind. So I chucked my violin under the wheels of a passing Corvette and concentrated on other, less civilized things.

For a long time I couldn't even listen to Beethoven, certainly not to the Violin Concerto. I'm past that now. I own a half-dozen versions of the piece. Even so, the version coming over the radio wasn't familiar. The orchestra was firm and heavily disciplined—German, probably. The violin was lyric, intelligent, almost delicate. Not weak, mind you, just subtle. Exquisite. Listening to it added a new dimension to a composition that was almost two centuries old. Was that new dimension a woman's touch?

Perhaps.

Probably.

By the end of the piece, I was certain. When the announcer said, "Anna-Sophie Mutter," I wasn't surprised. I made a mental note to buy the CD.

My watch said it was still two minutes to nine when a senior citizen with a passbook in his hand walked up and tried the front doors. They were still locked, but a potbellied bank guard hurried over and unlocked for the old man. Reagan's deregulation did make the term "banker's hours" obsolete. The senior citizen was outside again by 9:04. He wandered into the morning sun looking a little deflated, as though he had just concluded his most important errand of the day.

After that, there was more action in the *Times* than in the bank, which wasn't exactly high praise for the newspaper. For a high-ticket place like Newport, not much money was changing hands through Brad Simms's toy.

At 9:22 the next depositor arrived, a harried young mother driving a Jeep Cherokee complete with twin toddlers strapped into matching car seats. She parked in the red zone outside the front door, where she could keep an eye on the kids, dashed in, transacted her business, and was out again in two minutes. During that time the twins had managed to crawl out of their seats and into a snarl of lap belts and shoulder restraints.

At 9:34, an Asian man in tennis shorts and a floppy canvas

hat pulled up in a Nissan 300ZX and parked. He went in
and came out again two minutes later, stuffing some bills
into the pocket of his shorts.

At 9:38, a Brink's armored truck pulled up in front of the
bank. The truck sat there for a moment, idling, before the
side door on the box opened and the courier stepped out. He
looked as bored as I was. Carrying white canvas bags of
currency in one hand and a single heavy sack of coin in the
other, he walked crookedly toward the bank. He must have
figured he was in friendly territory, because his pistol was
snapped securely, and uselessly, into the worn holster that
flapped on his hip. The bank guard held the door open and
waved the courier inside.

The Brink's man was inside the bank for seven minutes,
during which time another senior citizen wandered in and
came back out. At 9:45 the courier came out empty-handed.
He unlocked the side door of the truck and climbed in. The
truck's diesel engine rattled into life and the vehicle lum-
bered out of the lot.

I sat there drinking coffee, trying to visualize money in
bulk lots, wondering how much the courier had just delivered to the bank. A thousand dollars, a hundred thousand,
a million? How much does a million bucks weigh? How big
a bag do you need to hold it?

I thought about the steamer trunk I had inherited when
Uncle Jake got killed on a run in Mexico. I had never counted
the money inside the trunk. Fiora had. She never told me
how much there was. I never asked. My young uncle was
dead and I had a bullet hole in me and the world wasn't a
playground anymore.

Jake's money had been in tens, twenties, fifties, and
hundreds, used and nonsequential. New money comes in
bundles matched by denomination and serial number, much
more tidy, much more orderly. An odd commodity, money,
varied in form and format. A million dollars in pennies
weighs a couple of tons; a million dollars in thousand-dollar

bills weighs a few pounds, maybe less. A bullet weighs a fraction of an ounce; life weighs nothing.

A movement at the corner of my eye told me that the beach bunny from behind the counter was coming toward my table, coffee pot in hand.

"You want a refill?"

She wore red shorts under her long white apron, a bemusing combination. Beneath her long, sun-bleached blond hair she had the high breasts and flat flanks of an eighteen-year-old child-woman with good genes. It was still spring, but her skin was already the color of light coffee. At that rate, in a decade she would look like a scuffed attaché case and be asking her dermatologist about Retin-A.

But not today. Today she was young and firm and tan and certain she would never be forty. The world was still her playground.

"This shopping center always so quiet?" I asked, holding out my Styrofoam cup for a refill.

"Totally boring," she agreed.

She made the adjective sound like the name of an amphibian: toadally.

"I don't see how the places around here stay in business," I said. "Especially the bank."

"Me neither." She leaned against my table with the generic friendliness of a golden retriever puppy. "My friend Becky, she used to work over there, said it was awful, you know? She got so sick of counting piles of money over and over and over again that she quit. She's working down at the Rusty Pelican now. It's cocktailing, but she gets to meet real people, you know?"

"Money can be boring."

"Toadally."

At 10:10, the action picked up a bit. A metallic green Mercedes 300E pulled into the parking slot marked SIMMS. The driver was a dark-haired man who appeared to be in his thirties rather than his twenties. Either Brad Simms was older than I'd thought or he had just been through a bad few months. He seemed blurred around the edges, as though he were recovering from an illness or coming down with one. He moved a little tentatively—a man who didn't entirely trust his reflexes.

He was wearing the ambitious banker's uniform: tailored gray two-button wool suit with solid red tie carefully knotted, white broadcloth shirt, polished black wing tips. The Latino in the Bradford heritage showed more clearly in the son than in the mother. His dark hair gleamed like rubbed ebony in the sunlight.

Brad walked through the front door of the bank and turned toward the executive office without so much as a nod to his employees. Maybe he was worried about his meeting with Fiora, which was twenty minutes away.

At 10:15 exactly, a Toyota Cressida pulled in and took a slow turn around the parking lot. The driver was Latin, with dark skin and a thick, brushy mustache. He drove slowly, carefully, examining the other cars. On his second pass, I got a closer look at him. He seemed worried, uneasy, a rabbit ready to run. I got a good look at the car, too. The frame on the license plate said RENT AVIS.

Some people fit and some don't. This man didn't. Not in Newport Beach, not behind the wheel of a $17-a-day, 12¢-a-mile rental car. He was too worried for Newport Beach, and he drove too carefully, as though he wasn't entirely comfortable behind the wheel. When he nosed into a space in front of the bank, he misjudged, and his front tires smacked the concrete bumper.

I dropped the *Times* and a tip on the table and sauntered out the front door.

The man was just getting out of his car. He wore a yellow guayabera with dark green slacks and carried brown paper Alpha Beta shopping bags under each arm. Suddenly the passenger door opened and a boy emerged. He was small and slender and must have been scrunched down in the front seat because I hadn't seen him before. He wore jeans, black high-tops and an amusement-park souvenir T-shirt—Disney World, Florida, even though he was less than ten miles from Disneyland, California. I guessed from his size that he was eight or nine.

Man and boy headed for the bank. The man was still nervous. He glanced around again, and this time he spotted me. He couldn't tell whether I was headed for the bank or for him, but he wasn't taking any chances. He spoke sharply to the boy and picked up the pace, walking crabwise to keep an eye on me.

He should have looked where he was going, instead. He tripped on the low step at the front of the bank. On his way down, he instinctively dropped one of the bags and flung out a hand to break his fall. But it was too late. He fell hard on top of one of the bags, ripping it open.

Parcels the size and shape of large bricks tumbled out onto the steps of the bank. The flash of green was unmistakable, even though I couldn't see the denomination. I lengthened my stride a little more, a good Samaritan on the way to giving aid.

"Are you all right?" I asked.

He lay on the torn bag, stunned from having the wind knocked out of him. The boy stood by, staring round-eyed at his father, not sure whether to laugh or cry. I reached for the man to help him up. He panicked.

"No, no, no!"

His face twisted as he scrambled to his knees and away from me. There was more fear than pain in his expression.

"Hey, amigo," I said. *"Ten cuidado."*

The man was too frightened for advice. He lurched, half fell again, then scrambled around on his knees, trying to gather up the bundles of bills and shove them back into the torn bag. There were half a dozen green bricks four or five inches thick. Three were of twenties and three were fifties. Each was bound with rubber bands at either end, giving them the dense, compact look of miniature green cotton bales.

As a personal matter, I don't care much for money. I've

acquired some immunity over the years, living with Fiora. Even so, the sight of several hundred thousand dollars on the sidewalk was arresting. I blew a little tuneless whistle as I picked up a five-inch bundle of fifties and handed it to the frightened man.

"A good night at the cockfights?" I asked.

He snatched the brick without a word and scrambled after the others.

"Are you okay?" I asked again, noticing a nasty scuff and a sheen of blood on his forearm.

"*Sí*. Okay," he said curtly. "Is okay."

Without looking at me, he finished stuffing the money into the torn bag. He picked up the other bag, then steered the boy toward the front door.

"*Andale*, Jaime."

I followed them into the lobby. The man shot me a hard glance, silently warning me to mind my own business. He pushed Jaime against the wall beside a rubber tree, hissed a command in Spanish, and marched to Brad Simms's closed office door. He pushed through the door without knocking. No ordinary customer, this one.

Two tellers, a loan officer, and the guard in the lobby of the bank had all seen just about what I saw. No one reacted.

One of the tellers was an Asian girl with beautiful eyes, a bright, buck-toothed smile, and no chin. I walked over to her queue, pulled out my wallet, and laid a MasterCard on the counter.

"Can I get a cash advance—say, five hundred—on this, please?"

She glanced at the card.

"It's not from our bank, sir. We can call to verify the account, but there would be an extra charge." Her English was faintly accented and very precise.

"That's okay," I said.

She gave me another smile and took the card over to a desk with a telephone. While she was dialing, I motioned to the second teller, a young blonde with railroad-track braces and nothing to do all day but wait for them to be taken off.

"Is he too old for a lollipop?" I asked, nodding toward Jaime, who was trying to fade into the wall next to the rubber tree plant.

The blonde bent over beneath the counter and came up with a small barrel of suckers.

I chose green, red, yellow, and white. Unwrapping the yellow one, I walked over to Jaime. The closer I got, the older he seemed. His clear black eyes had the look you get from war-zone urchins, the ones who gave up trusting other humans about the time they were weaned.

On the other hand, everybody likes candy. I stuck the yellow lollipop in my mouth and spoke around it as I fanned the rest of the suckers in front of Jaime.

"Have one," I said. "Helps to kill the time."

Jaime said nothing, but I still learned something. There was comprehension as well as suspicion in his face. He understood English. But if he was sensitive on the subject, there was no need to let him know I knew.

"*¿Te gustas verde, roja, o blanco?*" I asked.

His eyes widened but he kept his hands stuffed in the pockets of his pants.

"No, thanks."

So English was preferable to my border Spanglish.

"You got something against candy, Jaime?"

He studied my face carefully. I have a few scars here and there. Jaime inspected each mark and old wound thoughtfully.

"My name is Fiddler. Yours is Jaime."

He thought it over, shrugged, and nodded.

"All right, Jaime. Is there any reason you shouldn't have a sucker?"

He shrugged.

"Go ahead," I said. "It's free. No charge."

He gave me a disgusted look and said disdainfully, "No kidding."

Good idiomatic television English, the kind that comes

from Sesame Street, Saturday morning cartoons, and commercials. Much better than his father's. That didn't mean Jaime lived here, much less was born here. Men who run around with grocery bags full of cash tend to change addresses a lot. They also don't pack kids with them unless there's no other choice, which meant that Jaime's papa was probably alone.

"No kidding," I repeated.

He didn't say anything.

I pulled the lollipop out of my mouth and looked at its bright yellow disk.

"A little sweet, but not bad," I said, as though judging a wine rather than a cheap candy. "You sure you don't want one? Your papa won't mind."

At the mention of papa, Jaime glanced toward Brad's office. We were close enough to the door that I could hear low voices, but not so close that I could make out words.

Finally Jaime gave in. He took the green one, pulled the paper off the candy, and put it in his mouth.

"You and your papa both like green, huh?" I said casually.

Jaime didn't like my reference to money. "You a cop?" he demanded.

"Nope. I'm not a crook, either."

Just then the office door swung open and Papa rushed out like a man with a mission. He carried a white cloth bag under his arm. It was a good deal smaller than the shopping bags had been.

Papa took one look at the candy in my hand and snarled, "Go away from my son!"

I backed away slowly, keeping my hands in plain sight. You didn't have to be a genius to see that Jaime's papa was a man in a corner.

And cornered men fight.

5

IT WAS UNCLE JAKE who introduced me to the realities of the underground economy. Illicit businesses operate in cash. Cash can be a pain in the ass to hide, recycle, and explain away. Uncle Jake had smuggled marijuana, back in the days when it was a political statement, and had stashed his cash in a steamer trunk in an upstairs closet. Hide in plain sight was his philosophy.

Things had changed a lot since then. In Jake's day, a hundred thousand dollars was real money. Today, it's a down payment on a doghouse in Santa Monica. Whether it comes from drugs, sex, or the kind of fiscal rock and roll that topples governments, the amount of illicit money to be hidden has vastly increased.

Where better to hide illicit money than in a bank?

As I turned back to the teller's counter, I had a clear view of Brad's office. The door was still the way Papa had left it, half open. One corner of Brad's polished executive desk supported two equal-sized stacks of currency; each of the stacks was two bricks high and three wide. Brad was engrossed in a telephone conversation, oblivious to the mounds of money.

Apparently people regularly walked into his office with bricks of cash in Alpha Beta shopping bags.

Fiora probably would have a clean bureaucratic name for the process, but even I could figure out that folks who do their banking out of brown paper bags are at best unorthodox and, at worst, crooks.

I went back to the counter where the Asian teller was working over my cash advance. After she counted out three hundred-dollar bills, she fished a new bundle of twenties from her cash drawer, broke the paper wrapper, and began counting.

"How many bills in a bundle of twenties?" I asked casually, just a customer making idle conversation.

"One hundred."

"How about in a bundle of fifties?"

"The same. All currency comes in bundles of one hundred."

"How about bigger shipments? How would someone ship, say, fifty thousand dollars in fifties?"

"Everything comes the same way. A hundred bills to a bundle and ten bundles strapped together into a single package." The teller looked up at me, trying to guess the reason for my interest.

"Money fascinates me," I said amiably. "I'm thinking of starting my own collection."

She gave me the smile that said she had heard all the money jokes before—a hundred times.

As I signed for the cash, I pictured bricks of money in my mind. A hundred bills to a bundle, ten bundles to a brick. I was still trying to do the math while I walked toward the exit.

"Is he a regular?" I asked the guard, nodding toward Jaime's papa, who was just getting into his car.

"Banks don't talk about customers."

Which told me that Jaime's papa was, indeed, a regular. I could appreciate the need for the gag rule, particularly for customers who drop off shopping bags full of cash and don't even request a deposit slip, much less a close count of all the green.

The Cressida was already out of sight by the time I hiked across the parking lot and climbed into the boxy little BMW. For the fifth or sixth time that week, I missed my Cobra. A few hundred extra horsepower makes it a lot easier to catch up with somebody in traffic.

Unfortunately, the handmade metal body of the Cobra had ended up bent around a boulder in the desert outside Palm Springs, a casualty of domestic warfare between Fiora and me. The question of liability was still being debated around our old cottage at Crystal Cove. In fact, we were still having difficulties defining our terms. There is a subtle but real difference between "accident"—Fiora's word—and "incident"—mine.

Whatever the name, the event had pretty much totaled the Cobra. The salvage yard wanted to sell it off for parts, but that seemed to me too much like selling off the Mona Lisa for its canvas. Meanwhile, I was stuck with the 2002. The little BMW is less obtrusive, and its two-liter injected engine is quick enough, but somehow it isn't the same as a fire-breathing side-oiler 427.

As I pulled across the parking lot toward an exit, Fiora's glistening silver 750 made the left turn off San Joaquin Hills Road into the shopping center. She spotted me immediately and flashed the BMW's headlights. I didn't want to spend time on long explanations, but the last time one of us had ignored the other's signals, the Cobra had ended up pranged in the desert.

So I drove up beside the driver's door of the 750 and stopped, my window already down. The glass on Fiora's side window slid down like the port of a silver space ship. Fiora looked at me questioningly from behind the wheel. I looked back, feeling my irritation fade as I enjoyed the view. She was wearing a cream-colored dress that clung to her breasts just enough to be interesting and not enough to be obvious. Aviator glasses almost hid her eyes.

"What are you doing here?" she asked.

"I'm consulting. How much is fifty times a thousand times six plus twenty times a thousand times six?"

She blinked, ran the numbers behind her sunglasses, and said, "Six hundred and twenty thousand, why?"

"Somebody just dumped that much cash on Brad's desk. The guy was in such a hurry he didn't even ask for a count or a deposit slip."

"Shit."

"Looked more like money to me."

"Too much money for a branch bank."

"It wasn't my idea to get involved in this," I pointed out, glancing toward the stoplight at San Joaquin Hills Road. Still red.

"Maybe someone won at Lotto Six Forty-nine," she suggested.

"Does the lottery pay off in used, nonsequential twenties and fifties?"

I watched the light while Fiora ran numbers behind her eyelids. As long as the light stayed red, I could wait here as well as at the intersection, but Papa and Jaime were getting farther and farther away.

"A couple of other things you should know," I added. "Marianne says her son's got a substance abuse problem."

Fiora's mouth flattened, but she showed no surprise.

"You might have mentioned that," I said. "You might also have mentioned the letter of agreement and the two hundred and fifty bucks an hour. Each. *Partner*."

Spots of color showed on Fiora's cheeks. I couldn't tell whether they were from anger or embarrassment. She took off her dark glasses, removing an obstacle to understanding, and gave me a look that was equal parts wariness and determination.

"I know how you feel about anything that restricts your freedom," Fiora said, "but I thought this might be a way of regularizing the relationship."

I glanced at the traffic signal again. The cross traffic was now on the yellow cycle. I tapped the accelerator impatiently. The little BMW snarled.

"I don't like regularized relationships with banks," I said. "They might keep me from doing what I think really needs doing."

"I wasn't talking about the bank. I was talking about us. We didn't make it as husband and wife. Maybe we will as partners."

Beyond the parking lot the signal changed to green. I didn't move.

Partners.

Fiora lifted her toe from the brake. The car slid away slowly, like a great silver space shuttle leaving its orbital dock.

By the time I recovered from the shock wave of Fiora's latest bombshell, the light had already cycled to yellow against me. It was now or never for catching Jaime and his papa. I popped the clutch and took off, skating through as the yellow turned red.

Out on the broad boulevard I let the revs run up in first, second, and third, keeping an eye in the mirrors for cops. The Cressida was nowhere in sight. I made all the lights on San Joaquin and then the ones on MacArthur Boulevard, but I never caught up. I turned around just short of the San Diego Freeway and doubled back, checking intersecting streets, irritated as hell. If I was going to use Papa Greenbacks as a lever against Brad Simms, I needed to know where the sacks of cash came from.

As I made the turn back onto San Joaquin, a Newport Beach PD squad car passed me at eighty miles an hour, red and amber lights flashing and yelper in full cry. I pulled over to let him pass. A second patrol car shot by a moment later. I began to get uneasy. Newport likes to keep its cops quiet and efficient; code-three responses by two cars to the same call suggested major excitement.

I fell in behind at a respectful distance and followed until I came over a little rise and saw the Cressida sitting sideways

in the middle of San Joaquin Hills Road surrounded by unmarked sedans and well-marked police cars. The car looked
as though it had gone out of control while making a high-
speed turn from a side street onto the main thoroughfare.
There were broad skid marks scrawled across the asphalt.
The marks ended abruptly against the median curb.

Papa must have been going like a bat out of hell. The
collision with the curb had snapped the rim cleanly off the
Cressida's rear wheel hub. But Papa himself didn't appear to
have been hurt. He was sitting in the grass in the boulevard
median, his head bowed and his hands cuffed behind his
back. A burly Chicano with a full beard and an Ingram submachine gun stood over him, talking. But Papa wasn't
answering.

Jaime was nowhere in sight. Neither was the white bank
bag.

I pulled to the curb and watched for a few minutes, trying
to reconstruct the scene. Besides the two obvious police cars,
there were three unmarked cars parked at various angles in
the roadway, as though they had been pursuing the Cressida
when it crashed. The two uniformed officers from the patrol
cars were busy directing traffic around the accident. Six more
men in casual clothes milled around, probably still high on
the adrenaline of the chase. All were armed.

So Papa had been run down by an undercover surveillance
squad of some sort. As Jake would have put it, the air stank
of things gone from sugar to shit.

I hadn't seen any of the undercover cars in the parking
lot. That suggested they hadn't picked up their quarry until
after he left the bank. Whatever had gone down had happened
in the few minutes Papa and the Cressida had been out of
my sight.

I opened the door, went around to the trunk, and pulled
out a battered Nikon I keep there for moments just like
these. With the strap around my neck, I faked a few overview
shots before I walked across the street. One of the uniformed
patrolmen watched me with a total lack of interest, but when

the guy with the short-barreled Ingram realized I had a camera, he almost drew down on me.

"Hey, you! No pictures!"

I looked at him as though he were speaking Urdu.

"Sarge! Press is here!" the cop with the Ingram hollered.

One of the other plainclothes agents was already moving toward me, scowling. He didn't look much like a sergeant. He had shoulder-length hair and a Browning Hi-Power in a cross-draw holster on his left hip.

"Hey, man," I said easily. "I got a living to earn, you know?"

"You got a press card?"

"I'm freelance, but last I heard, you don't have to have a press card to take pictures on a public street."

"You can't take pictures of prisoners without their permission," the long-haired sergeant said. He positioned himself between me and Papa. "That's the law. Besides, who the hell cares about a routine traffic arrest?"

I looked at the battered Cressida and the assorted police cars scattered across the road, backing up traffic.

"Routine, huh?" I said.

"Sure. Just some mope trying to avoid a speeding ticket. We chased him around for a bit in that housing tract," he said, jerking his head toward the walled tract beside the thoroughfare, "but a kid on a bike could have outrun him. No big deal."

Good undercover agents routinely stake their lives on their ability to lie well. I gave the sergeant an 8.5 for form and a 9.5 for artistic content, mostly on the strength of his grin. It would have disarmed a polygraph.

"All these cars but just the one suspect, huh?" I asked.

The grin went up a few hundred watts. "You know how it is. Newport is a boring place to be a cop. Somebody jaywalks, the locals go bananas."

Behind him, another scruffy type pulled Papa to his feet.

"Better move your car," said the sergeant. "Tow truck coming."

I looped the strap of the camera over my shoulder and shuffled back to the 2002 like an unhappy but docile civilian. If they didn't know about Jaime, I wasn't going to tell them. I started up and made a left turn into the tract. They ignored me.

California housing developments are laid out like Victorian maze gardens—short blocks, cul-de-sacs, blind turns, and pocket parks. Perfect for hide-and-seek. Papa wouldn't have had to be a Formula One driver to stay ahead of the surveillance team for a while. All I had to do was backtrack the scrawling skidmarks he had left on the pavement.

I drove slowly, watching for a spot where he might have stopped for a few seconds, just long enough to ditch his son. It took three or four minutes to reach the T-intersection at the edge of a pocket park. Jaime was peering out from behind a low hedge where he had gone to ground like a good little rabbit. His body language suggested he was lost, unhappy, and determined not to show either. One small hand was wrapped tightly around the white canvas bank bag.

Driving down the wrong side of the street, I coasted over to the curb and rolled down the window before Jaime realized anyone was around.

"Ola, hijo," I said gently. "¿Como estas?"

I slipped the shifter into neutral and stepped out of the car. Before Jaime could decide whether he would be safer running than hiding, I was already too close for either.

"Where's my papa?" he said.

"The police arrested him."

"Did they shoot him?"

"No. He's not hurt at all."

Jaime looked away and blinked furiously, refusing to cry. I could have reduced him to tears with a gentle word at that moment, but I held my tongue. He was going to need composure more than comfort. He seemed to know it, too.

"You sure you're not a cop?" he asked finally, his eyes still avoiding mine.

"I'm not a cop."

Jaime looked directly at me, scared but game. I guessed his age at about twelve, now. A very streetwise twelve. He turned as if to walk away.

"Hold it." I wrapped my hand around his thin arm to make sure I wouldn't have to run him to ground. "Where are you going?"

"Home."

"Where is home?"

He gave me a blank look, then shook his head.

"You don't know where home is?" I asked.

A glimmer of defiance showed, but he said nothing.

"You do know where home is."

A fraction of a nod.

At least I think he nodded. I don't deal with kids on a daily basis.

"So you know where home is but you don't want to tell me," I said, thinking aloud, watching Jaime.

No nod this time.

"You don't trust me?"

His eyes told me he didn't trust anybody in the world except himself and maybe Papa.

I drew a deep breath. "I don't blame you. But we've got a problem, *hijo*. I can't let you go wandering off until I find out what kind of trouble your papa is in, and who else is included in that trouble."

Jaime ignored that gambit too, so I went back to the kind of communication I'm best at. The direct kind.

"Get in the car."

He didn't move. His eyes were dark, blank marbles staring at me.

I pointed toward the open front door of the car. "Take your pick, Jaime. Me or the cops."

Two seconds later Jaime was in the car and scrambling over the emergency brake to sit on the passenger side. The white bag was clutched in his hands. It wasn't the first time someone had preferred me over the cops, but I hardly felt good about it. I hadn't meant to browbeat him.

"Look," I said as I got in, "we're going to take a ride to see your dad's banker, okay? I'm not going to hurt you. In fact, I'm just trying to see that you *don't* get hurt."

Jaime sat staring straight through the windshield. I reached over for the seat belt and snapped it across his lap. He said nothing then or during the whole time I searched for a back way out of that damned labyrinthine tract.

I didn't hear one word of any kind until I walked into the bank with Jaime in tow. The potbellied guard watched until I headed straight for the door to Brad's office, which was now closed.

"Can I help you."

The guard wasn't really asking a question and he wasn't trying to help me. He was trying to stop me. I kept going.

"Hey, you!" he barked.

He had the lungs of a drill sergeant, but his gut had robbed him of a step or two. Before he could get in my way, I opened Brad's door and pushed Jaime through it ahead of me.

Fiora sat in the prototypical petitioner's chair, low and uncomfortable. Brad sat in a tall-backed executive throne, staring through horn-rimmed glasses over carefully steepled fingers. According to the furniture, he should have been comfortable and in command. He wasn't. His face and shoulders were tense. My rude entrance shattered what was left of his composure. He jumped to his feet, ready to fight or to dive for the protection of the cherry-wood desk.

"Hi, *partner*," I said to Fiora.

She didn't acknowledge me. She was too busy looking at the sullen boy carrying the white bank bag.

"Just somebody caught in the high-finance cross fire," I said. "His name is Jaime." I rested my hand on his shoulder for a moment. Jaime was a bundle of tight-strung wires just beneath the skin. I pointed him toward an empty chair at one end of the desk. "Why don't you go sit down over there while I sort out some things."

I tried to make my voice kind. I doubt if I succeeded. I

was well and truly pissed at whatever fiscal shenanigans had put this kid on the firing line.

The guard filled the doorway, looking at Bradford Simms for his cue. "Do you want this guy thrown out?"

It was the best idea I'd heard all day. I looked at the guard, hoping he would provide a moving target for my anger.

"Hell of an idea," I said, smiling.

Either the guy hadn't been a bank guard his whole life or he'd worked some pretty rough banks. His eyes got suddenly blank and cold, and he produced an old-fashioned leather sap from the back pocket of his uniform pants.

6

"THIS IS FIDDLER," Fiora said quickly. "He's my partner."

I watched the guard. He waited for word from his boss. The room was silent for a four-count before it dawned on Brad that he was supposed to be in charge. But young Master Simms was almost as confused and defensive as Jaime.

"Hello, Brad," I said, without looking away from the sap. "Before you give the green light and we trash your fancy office, take a look at the kid. He's the son of your best customer—the guy who dropped twenty or thirty pounds of cash on your desk this morning."

In the silence it was easy to hear Brad's ragged breath.

"Thank you, Bill," Brad said to the guard. "I'll take care of things from here. Please close the door on your way out."

Bill was well trained. He called off without a snarl, backing out of the office and pulling the door closed behind him. When the door clicked shut, I turned and looked at Brad. His voice had been steady, but his color had gone, leaving him an unappealing yellow beneath his tan. He had his mother's eyes—pale blue ice—but he lacked her electricity.

"What is this all about, Mr. Fiddler?"

"Just Fiddler. I'm not the formal type." I grabbed a spare chair and jerked it to a spot beside Fiora. When I sat down, Brad did the same. I looked at Fiora. "Tell him why we're here, pretty lady."

Fiora's eyes flashed anger. She hates that term of "endearment." So do I. That's why I only use it when I'm mad as hell.

"What's this about?" Brad demanded.

Watching me, deciding whether to fight or comply, Fiora tapped her index finger against her Coach bag. The elegantly lacquered nail flickered like a flame against the black leather. Maybe the Cobra hadn't died in vain—she accepted my signal this time, just as I had accepted hers in the parking lot earlier.

"I'm not an investor," Fiora said, turning to Brad. "I'm a financial consultant. Your mother hired us to do a discreet examination of the bank. I apologize for the ruse. It seemed necessary at the time."

The glance Fiora gave me said she still thought it was necessary.

"Examination?" Brad asked angrily as color ran back into his face. "You were hired to spy on me!"

"If Mrs. Simms were only your mother, it would be spying," I said. "But since she's your boss as well, call it management oversight. Since you're too busy sulking to talk to her, she's doing it the hard way. Your choice, wonder boy, not hers."

Brad's color deepened. Anger had a becoming effect on him, flushing out the pallor of fear.

Fiora gave me a wary look, then tried to soothe Brad. "Your mother is very worried about the bank and about you."

"The bank's fine," he said tightly.

"Bullshit," I said. "The bank is up to here in caca and sinking fast. So are you."

"What kind of a consultant are you?"

"The firm's name is Mean, Nasty, Brutish and Short." I stilled Fiora with a look. "Jaime."

The boy jumped when I called his name.

"Bring the bag to me. Please."

Jaime thought of objecting, then looked at my face and decided not to. He stood up, walked over, and handed me the bag.

In the excitement, Brad must not have recognized the bleached canvas. But when Jaime held out the bag, the BANK OF THE SOUTHLAND logo showed clearly. Brad sucked a surprised gasp between clenched teeth.

"That's the bag your father picked up in this office, right, Jaime?" I asked.

The boy nodded.

"Have I looked in it?"

He shook his head.

"Will you let me look in it now?"

Jaime looked worried. He didn't like the idea one bit.

"It's all right, *hijo*," I said, trying to sound more gentle than I felt. "You've done a hell of a good job cleaning up after your papa, but there are some things a kid shouldn't be asked to do. Keeping track of six thousand two hundred C-notes is one of them."

The math was easier for Fiora this time. "Six hundred and twenty thousand dollars? Are you sure?"

"As sure as I can be without a count. Ask wonder boy. Or didn't you bother to count the new bills, either?"

Brad was too busy swallowing to say anything. His Adam's apple bobbed three times before he managed a word.

"Banking transactions are private matters," he said.

I held out my hand. "Jaime."

"Papa told me—"

"Your papa can't help you now. I can. Maybe I can even help him. But you have to help me first."

Quid pro quo. A street kid learns the concept of cooperation just after he learns when to fight and when to flee. Or when to *appear* to cooperate. Jaime knew there was no point fighting over a secret that had already been revealed. He gave me the bag.

I undid the drawstrings with real curiosity. If I was right about what was inside, I'd look like a hero. If I was wrong, I'd look like chewed gum.

I upended the bag on Brad's desk. Six neatly banded blocks of one thousand fresh, crisp notes thumped solidly onto the polished wood. They were all brand new, their edges perfectly squared, as though they had just come from the Comptroller of the Currency. The wrapper bands were marked with the words FEDERAL RESERVE BANK, LOS ANGELES, and Benjamin Franklin peered up at me as though unused to bright light. The extra two hundred bills were used and out of sequence. They were fastened together with a chrome paper clip.

Jaime glanced at the money, then looked away with an indifference that wasn't feigned. The back of my neck tingled. No boy his age should be so blasé about that much cash.

Fiora leaned forward and riffled two bundles at random with her thumb, making sure all the bills were hundreds. They were. I looked at Brad. He wasn't a happy man.

"I'm pretty slick at guessing what's *not* in things, too," I said. "For instance, I'm willing to bet there's no record of this morning's transaction in your desk. Doesn't USC teach its business grads to file federal currency reports for transactions over ten thousand dollars?"

Brad opened his mouth. Nothing came out.

"Jaime," I said, scooping money back into the bag, "I'll bet the pretty blond teller with the railroad-track smile would be glad to show you what a bank vault looks like."

Money might bore Jaime, but the vault didn't. Despite himself, he looked intrigued. Brad looked unhappy. He closed his eyes, swallowed hard, and adjusted to the new reality, the one in which his secrets were no longer his own. He picked up the phone and summoned the teller. She appeared and took Jaime in tow. As soon as the door shut behind them, Brad was on his feet.

"Going somewhere?" I asked.

"The bathroom," he said, gesturing toward a door to one side of the office.

I got up, opened the door, and took a fast look. No exit. No weapons lying around. Not even a telephone. Nothing but a toilet, a mirror, and a washbasin.

"Don't worry," Brad said from behind me. "I'm not going to run. If I were that type, I'd have done it months ago."

I walked back and sat down beside Fiora. Brad pulled the door closed behind him. The sound of running water came through the hollow core door. I assumed he was using the sound to cover the noise of a snort or two.

"That was very neat," Fiora said quietly, meaning it. "But why did you drag that poor kid into the middle of it? Who is he, anyway?"

"The cops snatched his papa on the street a few minutes ago, just after he left here. Papa ditched the cops long enough to kick the kid out in a park. I found him. I had a choice—leave Jaime there or bring him back. I brought him."

"Cops? Who? Why?"

"I've got some really unpleasant guesses. Old papa ain't much in my book, but he's all Jaime has right now. If wonder boy in there knows anything useful, he's going to tell me or he'll walk funny for a week."

The toilet flushed and the washroom door opened. Brad came out, wiping his hands and face on a clean, white terry-cloth towel. I looked for the telltale signs of a coke rush— the flushed face and reflexive sniffles—but didn't see any. The young banker sat in his high-backed executive's chair and cleaned his glasses with the towel.

"Better my mother than the Drug Enforcement Administration, I guess," he said finally, giving us a forced smile. "Actually, it's almost a relief to have somebody else know. Maybe confession is good for the soul after all, assuming I still have one."

"DEA? Jesus, wonder boy, you're a real prize, aren't you."

Fiora jumped in, talking right over me. "Brad, tell us what's been going on. We can help you." She turned to me.

"That's why Marianne hired us, isn't it, Fiddler? To help?"

She smiled at me, but her green eyes told me that it was her turn to talk. I shrugged and kept my mouth shut. Let her try nice on Brad. But if nice didn't get it done, it would be my turn again.

"Talk to us," Fiora said to Brad. "We can't help unless you tell us the truth."

"I-It's hard to know where to begin," he stammered. "It's not as bad as it looks. I haven't been laundering money, not really. I was just exchanging small bills for hundreds."

"How many times?" Fiora asked, her voice gentle.

I almost laughed out loud at Brad's look of relief. The nice lady didn't judge him; she just listened to him. Like most men, Brad looked at Fiora and saw only a petite, pretty blonde with a good body. That was only half of Fiora's truth. The other half was razor intelligence and the kind of pragmatism that Genghis Khan could appreciate.

"Once or twice a week," Brad said. "Maybe three times."

Fiora smiled encouragingly. "For how long?"

Frowning, Brad put on his glasses. "A little more than five months."

I would have lost the thread of the interrogation right there, swamped in zeros. Fiora did the math with one side of her brain while she formulated the next question with the other.

"Tell me exactly how it works," she said gently. "It will help us to help you."

Brad grimaced, but answered. "Ysidro—Señor Ibañez, the boy's father—brings in a bag full of bills, all counted and bundled, and I give him the same amount in hundreds. That's all there is to it."

"What about records? How is it entered in the books?"

"No record. No need of one."

Brad's inflection was perfect, offhand and calm. But he needed a refresher course in lying; he broke eye contact with Fiora after a second. She glanced sideways at me, making sure I was still following.

"Really," Brad said, his voice less controlled now. "I didn't keep any records because the entire transaction was a wash—dollars in, dollars out. Null, zero, no change in the bottom line."

"That's nice," Fiora said, losing some of her niceness. "Unfortunately, you're supposed to file a currency transaction report, even for a straight exchange. Under the law, consolidating a bag of bills is no different from turning cash into a financial instrument such as a cashier's check."

"Perhaps that's how the IRS looks at it," Brad said. "I'm not sure that interpretation has been tried in a court of law."

Nice wasn't getting it done.

I made a rude sound. "Just how long did you expect your luck to hold? And luck is all it is, wonder boy. You've run ten million—"

"More like fifteen," Fiora said.

"—through your bank. Sooner or later even the Feds are bound to catch on."

"Fifteen?" Brad said. "That much?"

"Yes," Fiora said flatly. "That much."

He looked dazed. "I—that's hard to believe. For a while there, I guess things got a little fuzzy around the edges."

"A little fuzzy?" I asked, not bothering to muffle the sarcasm. "The fuzz is in your brain. The Federal Reserve Board probably has buildings full of computers just looking for bankers like you, and you sit there acting like you've been playing for matchsticks!"

Fiora touched my sleeve. I looked at her, locked my jaw, and waited. She had the half-there look she got when she was running an insight to ground. I sat back and let her have at it.

"Does all this money belong to Jaime's papa?" she asked finally.

"Ysidro? He just brings it. He's a banker, like me." Brad's mouth twisted down. "A glorified gofer. Frankly, I like him. Usually he'll sit and talk with me for a while when he brings the money. Today he just wanted to get done and leave."

"What do you and Ibañez talk about?" Fiora asked.

"Money. He used to be the operations director for a bank somewhere in South America."

"What's he doing in Newport?"

"I don't know, exactly. He works for a man named Faustino D'Aubisson."

Fiora glanced at me, asking if the name meant anything. I didn't blink. Fiora bit her lower lip. "Tell me about Mr. D'Aubisson," she said.

Brad looked helpless for a moment, hard pressed to describe the person he had done fifteen million favors for. Finally he shrugged. "Mr. D'Aubisson is a Uruguayan businessman who has interests all over Central and South America."

I made another rude noise. "I'll bet. I'll also bet he spends a lot of time traveling from the highlands of Peru to Bogotá and Medellín. Is he the one who gave you the nose candy?"

"What?"

"The stuff you sucked up into your sinuses in the bathroom just now."

I'd used up my guessing luck on the bag of money. Brad gave me a look that was triumphant, telling me I was wrong. This time he met my gaze and held it when he spoke.

"I don't take cocaine," he said, "and I don't know what Don Faustino does or doesn't do."

"And you don't want to know," I said, disgusted.

Brad didn't bother to deny it. "But I do know that Ysidro Ibañez is no drug dealer. All he does is count money, bundle it, and take it to the bank."

"Like you."

"Yes," Brad retorted. "Just like me."

"Isn't it lovely how all that dirty money never rubs off on a banker's clean hands?"

Brad looked to Fiora. She wasn't nearly as disgusted as I was, but then, she has always had a higher tolerance for the dark side of money shuffling than I've had. It's one of our biggest areas of impolite disagreement.

"Nobody expects you to be a social crusader," Fiora said coolly to Brad, "but I do hope you've managed to keep a degree of ignorance about the source of Ibañez's shopping bags of cash."

"Of course."

Of course. It's called deniability, and it's a very useful thing in a court of law.

"I've never even asked why he wants hundred-dollar bills," Brad added.

"I'll tell you why," I said. "It's easier to smuggle a brick of C-notes out of the country than it is to smuggle a freight pallet of small bills. I imagine your nice crisp C-notes end up in some international bank in Tijuana or Mexicali, where some other fine, upstanding, clean-handed banker takes the cash and transfers it by wire to accounts in Panama."

"I'll have to take your word for it," Brad retorted. "I have no direct knowledge of such transactions."

"And that, of course, makes it all right."

"No." His eyelids flinched. "It merely makes it defensible in a court of law."

"I can't tell you how much better that makes me feel." I ignored Fiora's hand on my sleeve. "How much did this Faustino pay you?"

"Nothing. I exchanged small bills for larger ones as a professional courtesy to a man who has some very large accounts at this branch."

"Without those accounts," Fiora said, "the branch would have been in trouble, right?"

Brad nodded tightly.

"Any more good news for us?" I asked.

He shook his head.

"How much coke were you using when Faustino recruited you? An ounce a week?"

Brad gave me a bitter look. "You sound like you have experience in that line of work. Recruiting and dealing."

I waited.

"I never used an ounce a month," he said.

"Then they bought you real cheap."

His mouth flattened. "I haven't taken anything from them in the past month."

"Did they cut you off?"

"The coke's been there. The coke's always there, waiting for me." Brad's voice was low and tinged with a combination of bitterness, acceptance, and regret.

"Why haven't you taken any?" Fiora asked.

"I don't use it anymore. I quit."

"You quit? Yeah. Right," I said derisively. "Just like that, you quit. Is this the first time you've quit or the fifteenth?"

Fiora started to reach for my sleeve again but I pulled away. I needed to know what we were up against.

"This isn't the first time," Brad admitted. "But it's the last. As of four weeks ago yesterday. Four weeks, twenty-three hours, and fifteen or twenty minutes."

"What about your little trip to the john a minute ago?"

He looked me straight in the eye. "I'll take any test, piss in any bottle you want. You won't find anything stronger than espresso."

I studied Marianne Simms's son for a good fifteen seconds. He really was a handsome son of a bitch with his light eyes and black hair and unbroken nose. But he didn't have half his mother's brains.

"I'm trying to make a clean break with everything that's gone wrong in the last six months," Brad continued. "In fact, I'm having dinner with Don Faustino and some of his people tonight. I'm going to tell them that today's money is the last I'll exchange. I think I can keep the branch afloat, even if Don Faustino closes his accounts." He looked at Fiora. "Tell Mother it's going to be all right. I just need a little more time."

Fiora looked at me, her green eyes asking my verdict.

"He doesn't need time," I said. "He needs a reality check." I turned on Brad. "Do you know where Ysidro Ibañez lives?"

Brad looked surprised. "No."

"Do you have his telephone number?"

Brad shook his head.

"Did he ever mention a wife?"

"No." Brad looked at me and added quickly. "I always assumed he was alone while he was here. It's not like he really lives in the U.S. He just does business here. I've never even seen Jaime until today."

"Great," I said through my teeth. "Come on, Fiora. We've got some talking to do." I got up and headed for the door, then stopped and looked at Brad. "We'll call you in two hours. Until then, keep your mouth shut about us. Don't go anywhere, do anything, or talk to anyone until you hear from us. Got that?"

Brad's eyes narrowed. He didn't like taking orders, but he did it just the same.

He didn't like it when I took the bank bag full of cash with me, but he didn't do anything about that, either.

7

JAIME FELT a little better when I returned the canvas bag to him. Arms wrapped around more than a half million in cash, he sat in the back seat of Fiora's 750iL and examined the leather and wood.

Fiora was already in the other front seat, staring straight ahead, wearing her not-quite-there look again. I wasn't sure whether she was thinking about something or hiding because she knew I was mad. Both, probably.

"Nice car," Jaime said quietly. "Almost as nice as Cochi Loco's. You a dealer?"

First the kid thought I was a cop. Now he thought I was a drug dealer. Jaime lived in a very narrow world. I turned around in the driver's seat and looked at him.

"Put your seat belt on," I said. "Who's Cochi Loco?"

"Cochi Loco has gold all over his Mercedes," Jaime explained. "He works for Don Faustino."

"The Mercedes trim is anodized. It just looks like gold."

"No, no, Cochi's is real gold, eighteen-carat. Papa told me. It cost a thousand dollars just for the hood ornament."

"Must not have to worry about on-street parking," I muttered, glancing at Fiora. "Cochi Loco translates as Crazy Pig. Crazy pigs are dangerous. This is where you get off."

She blinked, then gave me a sideways look. "I know there are dangerous people in the world. I've been watching them work you over for years, remember? And you're still alive. Battered, but alive."

So much for sweet reason.

I started up the car and backed out of the parking slot. As I changed gears I checked the mirrors, even though we weren't going farther than a few hundred feet.

"It was a real nice idea, this partnership," I said, "but it won't work. Neither will your plan."

Fiora stared straight ahead, shoulders stiff, eyes averted. "How can you be so damn sure? You don't even know what my plan is."

"I don't need to know. I'm not letting you play games with the kind of folks who carry their cash around in shopping bags. End of discussion."

I had ample time to appreciate the quiet running of the 750iL while I scouted a hideout. The best I could find was a four-foot hedge of pyracantha bushes that had been planted to break up the expanses of asphalt. I steered the car in behind the thorny wall and shut off the engine. The hedge screened most of the BMW but was open enough that I could see the front of the bank a hundred yards away.

Fiora let the silence expand until it filled the car to the point of suffocation.

"Do you know what a Colombian necktie is?" I asked finally.

"Tell me. Then maybe we can get down to business."

"Right, pretty lady. All you need for a Colombian necktie is a sharp knife and a snitch. You take the knife and slit the snitch's throat vertically, then pull his tongue down through it like a cravat. Sometimes the *traficantes* don't bother to check if their candidate is a snitch. They just cut a throat and leave the tongue flapping to tell the world they're bad-assed motherfuckers."

Fiora's mouth flattened. She looked at me, then gestured with her eyes toward Jaime. But I had been watching Jaime's eyes in the corner of the rearview mirror. He hadn't shown a flicker of interest in either the topic or the language.

"Don't worry about upsetting Jaime," I said. "He's heard worse in English and Spanish."

At the sound of his name, Jaime flicked a glance in our direction, then went back to staring out the window toward the bank.

"What about Brad?" Fiora asked tightly. "The kind of people you're talking about won't let him just walk away."

"Tough. He dug a hole and he dragged his nice little bank down into it with him. If it will make you feel better, I'll call the local cops and let them baby-sit Marianne's little boy. But after that, wonder boy is on his own and our consulting days are history. *Partner.*"

Fiora turned toward me. There was a passionate flush on her face and pure rage in her eyes. "Did I just hear you suggest that we call in the police?" she asked softly.

"Yes, pretty lady, you sure as hell did."

"Unbelievable. Awhile ago I called in the cops and you threw a goddamn macho fit, got in the wind—no phone calls, no postcards, no nothing. Now you calmly suggest I do it all over again. And men call women illogical!"

My adrenaline wanted to argue, but my mind knew Fiora had me. I sank back in the leather seat. In the rearview mirror Jaime's eyes were big and round, as though he were watching an engrossing but confusing soap opera on television.

"This isn't about our personal lives," Fiora continued. "It's not even about Brad Simms. This is about saving a bank that has been the center of a community for almost a century. Banks aren't just buildings. They're institutions, in the same way that universities and churches and newspapers are institutions. Institutions are how power gets exercised in this society, and exercising power encourages one kind of a future or preempts another."

"Fine, but—"

Fiora kept talking. There's no stopping her when she has the moral high ground.

"Marianne believes in the same kind of future I believe in. It's the future you believe in too, a future where all kinds of people get a shot at the gold ring, not just the folks who are born in the right place at the right time in the right skin."

"Fiora—"

"Not yet," she said, still talking over me. "If Marianne and her bank are ruined, the chance of getting the future we want is diminished. And her bank will be ruined the minute someone calls in the police. As you explained so graphically before you walked out on me the last time, police have different priorities. Not necessarily good or bad, just different. You were right, Fiddler. Some things do have to be fought for one-on-one."

It's hard to argue with someone who says you're right, but I had to try.

"I wasn't fighting for anything intangible like a bank," I pointed out. "Your ass was on the firing line."

"I'm not the primary target this time. Brad is. And if he goes down, so does the bank. That won't happen, not if I can stop it."

It was another old argument, one we'll probably never fully resolve. Unlike Fiora, I've never seen an institution I could get excited over. Maybe that's why I've never been able to bond successfully with organized society the way she has. I believe in individual human beings. Despite all her fierce, impatient intelligence, my ex-wife is much more tolerant of chronic institutional stupidity than I am. Maybe that's because she thinks more quickly than I do. She can outwit institutions. All I can do is bull my way through the morass of their restrictions.

"Fiora—"

Simultaneously Jaime said, "There's Mr. Simms!"

Jaime's papa hadn't raised a dumb one. Without even a

hint, the boy had figured out why we were playing hide-and-seek behind the hedge.

Brad was already at the door of his dark green Mercedes, moving quickly, a man with a mission. Fiora looked at the quartz clock on the dash. It was altogether too early for lunch. She mumbled two half-intelligible words.

I raised my eyebrows. "Is that with or without the hyphen?"

Fiora gave me a look.

"You still want to risk a necktie party for this clown?" I asked.

"You expected this, didn't you? You trapped him."

"I just tested his ability to take orders."

"Maybe he had a previous appointment," Fiora muttered.

"Uh-huh. Got any wooden nickels you want to bet?"

I started up the engine, snapped the shifter into gear, and held the big car in place with the foot brake, waiting.

Brad backed out and drove off at a smart clip. On the street he made a left, which brought him past a break in the hedge. He sailed along, eyes front, oblivious to any part of the world that didn't lie directly beyond his hood ornament.

When he was two blocks ahead, I eased out into traffic.

"We're going to follow him? I thought he was your friend," said Jaime, more curiosity than accusation in his young voice.

Fiora spoke before I could.

"We're trying to help Brad," she said, turning to face Jaime. "Sometimes friends have to do things that aren't nice."

"She may be following Brad because she's his friend," I said. "I'm following him because I don't trust the bastard." Without looking away from traffic I said to Fiora, "Jaime's a hell of a lot less naïve than Marianne's brat. Jaime knows how the world really works as opposed to how it says it works or how it should work. Jaime might hope for the best, but he doesn't think it's his by birthright."

Brad was easy to follow. His car stood out in traffic like a green leaf floating on a dull river. As we swept down from the heights of the San Joaquin Hills toward Newport Center, I let him open a six-block interval. He wasn't likely to get away from the big BMW, even if he tried. The 750iL was well-bred and well-behaved—civilized by the standards of the Cobra—but a lot faster than a vest-pocket Mercedes.

"Just out of curiosity," I said, "what kind of deal did you intend to offer Don Faustino and good old Crazy Pig?"

Fiora gave me a wary, sideways look. "I don't know. I have to find out what they want, what they need."

"The devil's own Maytag, no doubt. Making the money into compact bundles isn't enough. They need it cleaned, too."

"Of course. But there are a hundred ways to launder cash. Which way suits Don Faustino's particular needs? What does he have and what does he lack? I can't cut a deal with somebody until I know what he needs. That's why I have to sit down with Faustino. When I find out what he needs, I'll know what to offer."

"Could you really do business with him?"

"Of course not," she said irritably, "but if I give him a convincing illusion, he might let Brad off the hook."

"Wonderful. Bloody wonderful. You were going to walk into a nest of vipers as naked as Godiva, figuring that somewhere along the way you'd find a stick to protect yourself."

"Actually I thought I'd wear that navy Yves St. Laurent wool dress, if it's not too warm. As for a stick, I have you . . . don't I?"

Check.

"Of course you do," I said.

"Thank you."

"Don't bother," I snarled. "You'd be better off with a tommy gun."

Brad had a green left-turn arrow as he approached MacArthur Boulevard, but I wasn't going to be that lucky. I jumped on the accelerator. The V-12 gave a well-bred roar.

The car shot through the intersection as the yellow turned to red.

Jaime whistled through his teeth and grinned when the tires squeaked on the turn.

Once we were straightened out, I backed off to let Brad open up the gap, although that kind of caution probably wasn't necessary. He was an average, unconscious urban driver. Even today, under the gun, he hadn't glanced in his rearview mirror once since he left the bank.

"What kind of a plan did *you* have in mind?" Fiora asked me, her voice as neutral as her expression.

"I didn't say anything about a plan."

"You didn't have to. You wouldn't really have dropped Brad into the laps of the local cops and walked off. That would have exposed him to criminal money-laundering charges and ruined the bank. I'm assuming you intended to let him testify in return for immunity."

"You've got a nasty, manipulative mind, woman. You've been hanging around with the wrong people too long."

"What kind of deal, Fiddler?"

She was right, but I didn't want to give her the satisfaction of hearing it immediately, so I drove in silence for a while. In truth, Brad was in a good position to cut himself a deal with the cops. Faustino trusted him enough to run fifteen million bucks through his bank, and any cop with half a brain could think of something inventive to do with that kind of access to a crooked operation.

"There's no way of exploiting Brad's knowledge without putting him in danger," I said finally. "Cops can't keep an informant's identity secret anymore. Defense attorneys have too much leverage. Brad and the Bank of the Southland would have to be named in court somewhere along the way. There's no way to leverage him out of his legal problems without destroying the reputation of the bank in the process."

The green Mercedes made a right turn onto Coast High-

way. I ran the red light a hundred yards behind him and kept
my interval. Newport Center's early lunchtime traffic thick-
ened around us like cooling grease.

"You're saying some cop would use Brad's position to set
up Faustino, right?" Fiora asked.

I grunted.

"All right," she said. "We'll do it instead of the cops."

"No. En oh. No."

"Why not? It's the kind of solution that should appeal to
you. I thought you liked to hoist folks on their own petards."

"Listen, I don't know who this guy Faustino is, but I can
guess who he's working for. These people aren't asshole
smugglers like Uncle Jake. Big-time cartels are something
you should appreciate. They're into power—pure, raw eco-
nomic power. They don't do millions, they do bee-boy-
billions."

"Would you cross Faustino if you were the only one involved?" Fiora asked.

"No. He doesn't have anything I want."

"What if he had me?"

"You know the answer."

"Tell me."

"I'd go to war," I said flatly.

"Would you take on a cartel for Benny?"

"Yes."

"How about for somebody who was entirely innocent, who
just happened to be caught up in a bad situation?"

"Brad's too old to be that innocent."

"Yes. But we were all young once, weren't we? And some
of us still are, despite the hard crust on the outside."

I looked in the rearview mirror. Jaime was watching the
expensive houses and the fancy restaurants of the Gold Coast
with big, dark eyes.

"Maybe I'd hang around the fringes and snipe," I admitted.
"But I'd be very goddamn careful about how I did it. Folks
like Faustino have a real advantage. They don't care who
gets killed. I do."

"So do I. But how do you expect me to live with myself if I don't follow through on what I believe is right?" Fiora asked. "How do you expect me to live with you? And would you even want me that way?"

Checkmate.

8

I LET THE SILENCE run with us over Harbor Boulevard's diagonal slice through the great flat heart of Orange County. A few decades ago, Harbor Boulevard was a country highway lined with orange groves and lima bean fields. Today the soil supports strip crops of fast-food franchises and light industrial plants, neighborhood shopping malls and mid-range theme restaurants, low-rise office complexes and no-tell motels with waterbeds and triple-X movies.

Once the strip was white bread only—dust-bowl Okies and dusty Swedish lima bean growers. Now the place is pure postmodern California—tortillarias chockablock with sushi and noodle shops, Winchell's Donuts, and 1950s drive-ins with occasional carhops wearing roller skates. Harbor Boulevard may be the only street in America with three video stores side by side, one Korean, one Arab, and one English, and a Spanish-only competitor across the street.

The area was an odd destination for a wanna-be fiscal high roller like Brad Simms. But ten blocks north on Harbor, he turned into the parking lot of the Royal Hawaiian Motel and Coffee Shop. The place was well past its salad days. I could think of several reasons why a young man might check into a motel before noon. Not one of them had anything to do with high finance.

"I suppose you're going to tell me the Costa Mesa Kiwanis Club meets in the coffee shop," I said.

Fiora didn't bother to answer.

A quick U-turn brought us back by the motel on the other side of the street. There was a six-slot parking lot in front of an Okie beer bar that hadn't opened yet. We could see the motel fairly well through the rolling screen of traffic on Harbor Boulevard.

Brad parked in the motel's deserted lot. He got out and peeled off his jacket and his red silk tie. After putting them neatly on the seat of the Mercedes, he shut the door and headed for the office. His car was the only one on the lot. A dark-haired maid pushed a wheeled cart across the pavement to a laundry room.

When Brad walked into the office, a bald man appeared. He greeted the banker like a regular, shaking hands and handing over a key in the same motion. Brad paid in cash.

"Lord," muttered Fiora. "Being a voyeur was never my thing. Do we have to watch and take notes or can we just assume the obvious and get the hell out of here?"

"Remember Benny's Law of the Obvious," I said. "Assumption is the mother of all fuckups. But there's no reason for both of us to stick around. Take Jaime up the street and order lunch. I'll be along in a while."

Fiora's mouth flattened. She shook her head.

"Think it over," I said. "Watching the boy wonder screw some faceless pro or a horny divorcée he met at the Bay Club last week is nothing. That's just your average keyhole-peeping assignment. Think about how you're going to feel when you get to the real slimy stuff. Ask any cop, any private investigator. You have to do things that will make you want to puke. That's what undercover is all about—eating nine yards of shit just to get your hands on the asshole it came from."

Fiora turned, saw that Jaime hadn't reacted at all, and

frowned. She was beginning to understand what I had guessed the instant I saw Jaime's clear black eyes: the kid hadn't spent his years packed in cotton.

We sat awhile in silence. When I glanced in the rearview mirror again, Jaime's gaze had fallen on the cellular phone on the console between the two front seats. He stared at the black handset with something akin to lust. I made a mental note to make sure Jaime was never alone with a phone. I didn't want him sending up a flare to Faustino or Cochi Loco. The last person I needed on my butt at the moment was a thug who bought solid gold trim for his Mercedes.

Brad came out of the motel office and stood in the parking lot watching traffic on Harbor Boulevard with transparent eagerness. Fiora shifted uneasily on the leather seat every time he looked in our direction.

"He can't recognize us at this distance," I said. "Even if he could, he wouldn't. He's got his mind on his . . . business. But if you're worried, we could always pretend we're noontime lovers ourselves."

She looked at me, puzzled.

"Haven't you ever watched a couple neck in the parking lot of a bar?" I asked.

"Not if I could help it."

"That's just what I mean. Most people are too polite to stare."

"Most couples don't bring their kids along."

I looked at Jaime in the mirror. Jaime looked out the window. I wondered how parents got away from their kids long enough to conceive more of them.

We watched Brad toy with the room key, drop it into his pants pocket, and walk a few steps toward his car, then away, then back again. He unbuttoned his collar and leaned against the shiny green fender, fidgeting and waiting.

"Who do you suppose it's going to be?" Fiora asked finally.

"I'm hoping for a professional. This thing doesn't need any more complications."

"You believe in the Easter Bunny too?" she said.

We watched Brad fidget for a few more minutes before a red Pontiac Firebird pulled out of the traffic on Harbor and made an illegal turn across the solid double line in front of the motel. Brad broke into a grin we could see from across the street. The car parked next to his. The driver, a leggy young woman with a full fall of tousled red curls, bounded out of her car and into Brad's wide-open arms.

Jaime's breath sucked in hard through his teeth. His image vanished from the rearview mirror. I looked over my shoulder. He was pressed against the back seat, seeking the cover of the roof pillar, trembling, as frightened as he had been when I caught up with him in the park a few hours earlier.

"Jaime, what's wrong?" I asked.

He scrunched down farther and didn't answer.

I looked around. Only one new ingredient had been added to our little mess.

"Shit!" I hissed.

"The redhead," Fiora said.

"Do you know her, Jaime?" I asked.

"Mama!" The name came to his lips unbidden, like a talisman. "Don't let that woman see me! She'll tell Don Faustino I'm here, and then he will kill us all, even little Josefina!"

I started to ask Jaime if his mother was in California, but he was too busy whispering his rosary to pay attention to me. I turned back and stared through the windshield, wanting to kill something. First the redhead and now this. I had assumed that Señor Ibañez was the only parent in Jaime's life. Why else would a kid be tagging along on his father's business rounds?

But there was no time to hold postmortems on what I should or should not have assumed. Right now, Jaime's family or lack of it was the least of my problems. If what he'd said was true, the sexy redhead trying to crawl under Brad's shirt was linked to Don Faustino. Closely.

Watching Brad and the redhead, there was no reason to doubt Jaime's assessment. Brad didn't look like he kept any secrets from her. And that meant Faustino would find out about Jaime no matter how well he hid and prayed.

From where I sat the redhead looked harmless, attractive, and as eager for Brad as he was for her. She was one of those pale-skinned Irishwomen with full, firm breasts and hips to match. She moved well, like a dancer, and had gone into Brad's arms in a full-length embrace that quickly turned into a lover's kiss, all lips and teeth and tongue. Brad's hands found the small of her back and tried to stay there, but raw desire kept tugging them lower. For the moment Brad still knew he was in public. But if the kiss went on much longer, he wouldn't care where they were.

The lovers broke off abruptly and stood for a few seconds staring at each other, breathing hard. The redhead looked around the parking lot and the street in a single, sweeping glance, as intent as a vixen scenting hounds. She was nervous, which made her far more alert than Brad had been. We were still fifty yards away and seated behind modestly tinted glass, but I knew in my gut that she'd remember the silver BMW if she saw it again.

She took Brad's hand quickly, eager to flee for cover with her mate, and they walked into the motel without looking away from each other.

"It looked more like romance than commerce," Fiora said after a moment.

I grunted. "Did Marianne mention a girlfriend?"

Fiora shook her head.

"Then he doesn't have anything to hide. I wonder who she's making a fool of."

"What do you mean?"

"They're being very careful not to be seen together," I said. "People don't go to a motel by choice."

I pulled the binoculars from beneath the seat, took a good look at the Firebird's license plate, started the car, and moved back into the Harbor Boulevard traffic. We had gone three blocks before Jaime began to relax.

"Know any good taco places around here?" I asked him, fishing for information about more than food.

He shook his head.

"Then what would you say to a burger and some fries?" I asked.

Jaime smiled wanly.

"I'll throw in a chocolate shake too."

His eyes brightened a little. I didn't have the heart to tell him he would have to sing for his supper.

In deference to Fiora's leather upholstery, we sat outside at a table in the sunlight. I put the white bank bag in the trunk, with Jaime's permission. His father had entrusted the money to his keeping, and he took the responsibility seriously. We both knew I could have taken the bag away by force, but neither of us raised the issue.

While the three of us chewed imported beef from the all-American hamburger stand, Jaime kept glancing over at the pay telephone in the Shell service station next door to the McDonald's. I would have given a lot to know who he wanted to call. From his response to the redhead, I doubted if Jaime was going to call Cochi Loco. On the other hand, I wasn't going to risk Fiora's neck by trusting a streetwise kid whose daddy used grocery bags for wallets.

I mopped my hands with the last napkin and fired it at the trash can. "Jaime, you and I have a couple of problems, don't we?"

He looked at me warily before he ducked his head once in agreement.

"You still don't trust me enough to tell me where you live."

"I can't," he said unhappily.

"Why not?"

He shook his head and studied his fingers.

"Do you live alone with your papa here, or do your mama and Josefina live here too?"

Jaime's eyes widened in shock. "How do you know about them?"

Then memory hit him. He had told me about them himself, when he had been too frightened to guard his tongue. Now he made a dismayed sound and crossed himself.

"Easy, *hijo*. I don't hurt people who can't hurt back," I said. I only manipulate the hell out of them. "Are they waiting for you to come home?"

Jaime refused to look at me.

"How about this?" I asked. "You tell me where you live and I'll take you there."

"No. Papa told me. I am to say nothing to anyone, not to the police if they catch me and not to anyone else. Papa said everything will be all right if we are very careful. Don Faustino may learn that I ran away, but he must not find out I'm here with Papa."

There were a lot of possibilities contained in Jaime's rushed words, but the best one was that Ibañez was getting ready to cut and run with six hundred and twenty thousand bucks that belonged to Don Faustino.

Which left unanswered the why and the when of Jaime running away, and why it mattered that Faustino not find out that Jaime was with his father.

"Did your papa tell you these things before the police took him this morning?" I asked.

Jaime hesitated, looking the question over for hidden traps. He didn't see any, so he nodded.

"What if Mr. Simms tells the redhead about you?" I asked coolly. "Who will protect your father then? And who will protect your mother and Josefina? She's your sister, isn't she?"

For a moment I thought Jaime was going to be sick. So did he. Then he clamped his jaws shut and went back to the one thing he had to hang onto in the adult world—his father's instructions. He looked at me and shook his head.

"Jaime," I said, trying to be patient, "I can't protect you and your family unless you tell me where they are."

I didn't have to look up to know Fiora was glaring at me, angry at me in spite of her knowledge that I was only doing what had to be done. Frankly, I didn't care for browbeating a child myself, but as long as Jaime feared Faustino more than he feared me, I was going to have a hell of a time getting the truth out of him.

"Is the place you live a secret because it's also the place where Faustino keeps his money?" I asked.

Jaime glanced up quickly, surprised by the sudden change of subject. His expression was as revealing as if he had answered the question out loud. When he realized that, he looked stricken, as though he had betrayed his father again.

"It's okay, Jaime," Fiora said, putting her arm around him. "Fiddler just guessed. He knows a lot about smuggling and hiding money."

"It doesn't matter," Jaime said defiantly. "The money isn't where Faustino put it. Papa found a better place."

Pride gleamed from Jaime's eyes, replacing misery. Pride makes a good lever, especially on a kid.

"I don't call a white banker's bag in the hands of a kid 'a better place,' " I said.

"Not that money. That's nothing. Papa has boxes and boxes and boxes of—"

Abruptly Jaime stopped talking. He stopped eating, too. His fingers unraveled the top of the hamburger, but none of the bread crumbs got to his mouth. My appetite took a dive too.

Boxes and boxes and boxes.

That much money makes everything else cheap. Especially life.

9

I SWALLOWED HARD. The hamburger tried to crawl back up my gullet. I swallowed hard again. Papa Ibañez hadn't looked like much, but he must have balls of cold-rolled steel to make off with that much money, considering who he was stealing it from. Cartels are noted for a brutal kind of efficiency when it comes to protecting their assets.

When I looked at Fiora, her eyes were wide, thoughtful, and uneasy. She doesn't understand mayhem in any visceral sense, but she does have a fine appreciation of what losing boxes and boxes and boxes of money could do to otherwise decent human beings, much less to folks like Don Faustino.

"Do you know where the money is?" I asked.

Jaime became very interested in his chocolate shake.

"Listen, Jaime. Your papa is in trouble. We might be able to trade him for those boxes of money, but first we have to know what's going on and where the money is."

I might as well have been talking to the trash can.

"Listen up, kid. I don't give a damn about the cash. I don't want to hurt you or your father. But the two of you are in over your heads. Without help, you'll drown. I can't help you unless you help me. I sure as hell can't help your father, and I've got a feeling he needs help right now. You *do* want to help him, don't you?"

Jaime swallowed hard, gave me a miserable look from eyes bright with tears . . . and shook his head in a silent negative.

"I swore on the blood of the Virgin," he whispered.

I can be a cold son of a bitch, and a few times I've used my fists to separate men from what they knew. But no matter how streetwise Jaime might be, he was still a child.

Feeling almost as helpless as Jaime, I looked at Fiora. She put her hand on the boy's shoulder and turned him toward her.

"Jaime," she said gently, "we don't want you to break your vow. Do you believe me?"

The boy looked at her, then nodded hesitantly.

"We want to help you, your father, and Brad—Mr. Simms. Do you understand that?"

Another pause, another search for hidden traps, another slow nod.

"Would you help us and your father if that didn't mean breaking your vow?"

There was no hesitation this time. Jaime nodded so hard his hair bounced.

Fiora smiled. "Okay, why don't try this? We'll ask you questions. You answer the ones you can without breaking your vow. We won't be mad if you tell us you can't answer. That way you can protect your secrets and still have a chance of helping us help you."

Jaime thought about the offer very carefully. After a long silence he sighed and begin to relax. His hand closed around the hamburger he had been nervously crumbling. He took a big bite. As he chewed, he nodded to Fiora.

Fiora smiled again at Jaime. This time it was her spontaneous, thank-you-you're-wonderful smile, the kind that makes every male over the age of three want to do tricks just to see it again.

"Okay," she said. "We'll start with the easy stuff. Your name is Jaime Ibañez. How old are you?"

"Eleven," he mumbled around a mouthful of meat and bun.

"Where were you born?"

"Salgar."

"Where is that?"

Jaime was busy chewing and swallowing, so I answered, "Colombia. I was there, once."

Jaime smiled approvingly at me. Beneath the table, Fiora's hand touched my knee, silently inviting a question.

"Your English is very good. Did you learn it in a Colombian school?" I asked.

Jaime shook his head in a vigorous negative. He liked being able to answer questions for a change.

"For six years I've lived here most of the time with my papa."

"Six years," Fiora said thoughtfully. "Has your father always worked for Don Faustino?"

Jaime shrugged. "I don't know. Papa was a banker in Colombia. Now he's a banker here."

"What does a banker do?" I asked.

Jaime looked that question over very carefully but decided it wasn't dangerous.

"A banker keeps money for other people." The boy tore off a bite and chewed, talking around the food. "We have a machine. It counts money. Papa lets me work it. It's a very simple thing. A hundred bills to a bundle, ten bundles to a brick, ten bricks to a bale." Jaime swallowed, bit off more and chewed thoughtfully. "The hardest part is getting clean afterward. Money is awfully dirty. It smells bad, too, if you keep too much of it in one place."

"Yeah, I've noticed that about money," I said, giving Fiora a glance.

Jaime sucked on his straw.

"Does your papa yell at you at lot?" I asked.

The boy blinked, showing off eyelashes that would have done credit to a Vegas showgirl.

"Yell at me?"

"Does he love you?" I asked, trying for another angle.

"Of course," Jaime said, licking sauce off his finger.

"And you love him."

"He's my papa."

The tone of Jaime's voice said more than the words. He smiled and for a moment became the guileless child again. Whatever else was wrong with the Ibañez family, there was no lack of affection.

"Then why did you run away from him?" I asked.

"From Papa?" Jaime said, surprised. "I didn't! It was Don Faustino I ran away from. In Colombia."

Fiora looked puzzled. "Wait a minute, I'm lost. You lived here most of the time? Is that right?"

Jaime nodded.

"What were you doing in Colombia?"

"Mama and Josefina had to come here, so I had to go there."

"Why?"

Jaime shrugged. "Part of the family always stays in Colombia."

Bad news, but not surprising. Colombians in certain kinds of business have a rather quaint custom. They hold hostages in the old country to ensure the honesty of workers abroad. But Jaime was so matter-of-fact about it that it took Fiora a few moments to catch on. When she did, she looked at me for confirmation. I nodded.

"What happened?" I asked. "Why did your mama and sister have to come here?"

"Josefina got burned real bad. Papa wanted her to come here to a hospital in Irvine that helps people who have been burned. Mama had to come too, because papa couldn't take care of Josefina and be a banker too. That left only me to stay with Don Faustino."

"So your mama and Josefina came here?"

"Yes. She's getting well again now. She can even bend some of her fingers. But she still has to go to the doctor a lot."

"And you began to think you'd never get to come back to California, right?" I asked.

Jaime nodded uncertainly, a little ashamed because he knew he had violated the terms of the family contract.

"How did you get here?" I asked.

Jaime hesitated.

"Did you promise not to tell?" Fiora asked.

He gave Fiora a smile that was half guilty and half proud. "I didn't have to promise that. Papa wasn't even very angry. He tried to act angry, but I knew he wasn't. He missed me, too."

"It's a long way for a boy alone to come."

He shrugged with the elaborate casualness of a child who is too old to admit to fear and too young to be fully comfortable in the dark.

"There's a little airport at the *finca*," Jaime said. "Learjets and regular planes are coming and going all the time, carrying *cocaína* or money, sometimes just flying back and forth to the United States. I waited until one of the Learjets was going to Miami. I hid in a little cabinet under the washing bowl in the bathroom. It was very dark." He blinked away the memories. "After we landed, I waited until it was quiet and then I snuck off."

"How did you get from Miami to California?" I asked.

"I went all over the Miami airport until I found Eastern Airlines. That's the plane Papa and I always took from Miami to California after we visited Mama and Josefina. There are a lot of South and Central Americans on that flight. I found one who spoke only Spanish and paid him to get my ticket. I paid for his ticket too. He pretended he was my papa."

"Neat trick," I said, meaning it.

Jaime smiled. "Papa thought so too."

"How did you get the money?"

"The barn on the *finca* is full of money. The men let us play hide-and-seek there." Jaime looked at the hamburger. "I only took a little. And I confessed to the priest."

Either he had world-class imagination and acting ability or world-class *huevos*. Considering his old man, I'd vote on the side of balls. Whichever, he was quite a kid.

"So you flew to LA?"

He nodded and eyed the rest of my french fries. I don't know about the soul, but confession sure seemed to be good for the appetite.

"Did your papa know you were coming?" I asked, shoving the french fries over to Jaime.

"He was surprised when I called him from the airport last Sunday. At first he was upset, but it didn't last long."

I tried to put myself in Ibañez's place. He would have been overjoyed when Jaime turned up. Then his guts must have turned to water at the thought of what Faustino would do when he found out.

If Jaime had known—truly *known*—what his escapade could cost his family, he would never have done it. But if he understood he had been a hostage, it was a child's understanding, based on the sweet lie that life is forever and death is only a word.

Papa Ibañez had known the truth.

"What happened when you got here? Did your papa take you right home?" I asked.

"No. He was afraid somebody like Cochi Loco would find out I was here." Jaime frowned. "We stayed in a motel by Disneyland the first night. Then Papa found another place, where he said we all could hide—"

We were too close to home, literally. Jaime's face went blank and he clamped his mouth shut. He didn't want to talk anymore, but he still hadn't told me what I had to know.

"Have you thought about this, *hijo*? Your mama is home

alone with all that money and no husband or son to protect her. What will happen to her and Josefina with her burned hands?"

It had been a guess, but my luck was running again. Tears came to Jaime's dark eyes when I put his fears into words. Hating the game and at the same time knowing it had to be played, I went back to chipping away at Jaime's belief that everything would be all right if he just followed Papa's orders.

"You could help your mother and sister, Jaime. I could protect them if I knew where they were."

"Fiddler," Fiora said, "we promised not to—"

"Pass the ketchup," I said, cutting her off.

The look I gave her said shut up.

The look she gave me back said go to hell. She reached over and put her arm around Jaime's shoulder.

"It's all right, Jaime. We said we wouldn't make you break your vow and we won't." She gave me a hard look. Her eyes were cold green jade.

"Jaime, go over and stand by the car," I said.

He headed for the car like a shot, more than happy just to get away from me. When I was certain he couldn't overhear anything, I turned to Fiora. She spoke before I could.

"If you think I'm going to sit by quietly while you trick a scared child into breaking a vow he believes is sacred, you're crazy."

"I was crazy ever to agree to this farce of a partnership," I said, keeping my voice low for the simple reason that I was too angry to yell. "When Jaime's sacred vow costs his mother's life, do you think a hug and a smile from a pretty lady will make it all better?"

Fiora closed her eyes and turned away. Her carefully painted eyelids flickered, as though she were flinching while she watched my prediction come true. She opened her eyes to banish the vision, then tried to argue.

"If living in the same place with the money were all that

dangerous," she said, "Jaime wouldn't have survived six years of it."

"You're great on money, but you've got a lot to learn about the heavy-lifting end of our so-called partnership. When Mama and Josefina lived in Colombia, they were hostages, living guarantees that Ibañez would shut up and count money like a good little banker."

Fiora became very still.

"As a personnel management technique, taking hostages lacks a certain finesse," I continued, "but it by God *works.* When Josefina got burned, Ibañez swapped his son for his wife and daughter. But suddenly he had his son back too. It was the best chance he was going to get. He grabbed it and ran. Problem is, he grabbed the money too."

Fiora turned toward me, listening as only she can, intensity fairly vibrating in her.

"Now," I continued, "Faustino and the crooks he's laundering money for may not know about the missing hostage yet. If Jaime has been telling the truth, he's been gone only three days. The folks in Colombia probably figure he ran off into the hills and got lost. When they can't find him, they'll want a replacement. They'll go looking for Ibañez, but they won't find him and they won't find the rest of his family. At least not right away."

"Go on."

"These cartel types are very resourceful. Sooner or later they'll track down Jaime or his mother and sister. What will Jaime's sacred vow be worth then?"

Fiora didn't say anything.

I waited.

"We've got to find Jaime's home before the Colombians do," she finally said.

"Hell of an idea, pretty lady. Wonder why I didn't think of asking Jaime where he lives. So simple. Or it would have been, if you hadn't let him off the hook just when I had him swimming toward the net!"

I couldn't tell whether Fiora was more angry at me or at the truth of what I said.

"What about Jaime's father?" she asked tightly.

I shook my head. "The cops have him."

"This is America, not Argentina. You can talk to people in jail. Attorneys do it all the time."

10

"MY GOD. It *is* you, Fiddler. I thought my girl had garbled the name."

"Hello, George. I didn't recognize you without the pony-tail."

"Male-pattern baldness ruins the effect," George Geraghty said regretfully.

He rubbed his palm over his retreating hairline and fine thinning hair. He still wore it cut long on the sides, but the bald spot was beginning to make even that style untenable.

"Besides," he added, "you can't be a hippie and represent this new generation of dope dealers in a court of law. They like Italian fashions and good leather."

"So I've heard."

Geraghty looked up at me and shook his head. "Jesus. I had forgotten how big Jake was. You remind me so much of him it gives me chills. Same almost-black hair. Same light gray eyes. Same mustache and go-to-hell smile. Hard to believe you're his nephew and not his twin."

As I shut Geraghty's office door behind me, he stood up and pulled the chalk-stripe vest of his thousand-dollar suit down over an expanding paunch. Even in the days when he had hung around head shops and hippie health-food bars, Geraghty had loved rich food. Living on a dope lawyer's income apparently had increased the problem. His gut pressed against the wood as he leaned forward and offered me his hand across a dark desk big enough to land a Cessna.

"How the hell are you, Fiddler?" he asked, smiling. As we shook hands, he looked at mine. He whistled softly at the scars I'd picked up when somebody had tried to nail me to a packing crate. "What happened?"

"It was a long time ago."

"Must be hard to play the violin," he said.

"I gave it up not long after Jake died."

Geraghty let the subject slide. He knew lots of people who didn't want to talk about their scars.

"Would you like coffee or something stronger?" he asked.

"Coffee," I said. "Black."

Geraghty fussed over an executive bar, but he looked back a couple of times, as though he still couldn't believe his eyes. It reminded me that he, too, had been fond of Jake.

In Uncle Jake's day, George Geraghty had been everybody's image of a radical lawyer. First as a deputy public defender and then as a private defense attorney, Geraghty had loved messing with people's minds. He had worn Brooks Brothers three-piece suits, hair to the middle of his back, and two-hundred-dollar loafers on his bare feet. A Berkeley graduate with politics to match, he had been a contentious law and motions man and a hell of a courtroom attorney. His position was that the cops, not his clients, were the ones on trial.

As a young man Geraghty had taken to defense work out of idealism. But the years had whacked some of the radical righteousness out of him. Even before Jake was killed in Mexico, Geraghty had begun to wonder if mankind's salvation was really as simple as drugs, sex, and rock and roll.

Jake's death hit the lawyer almost as hard as it hit me. He ended up spending a thousand bucks of his own money—bribes to Mexican cops and hospital workers—just to retrieve Jake's dead body from south of the border. Buying back your best friend's corpse takes some of the gloss off the outlaw life.

He had spent another five thousand retrieving me at the same time, but that had been business.

Geraghty handed me a cup of coffee. As he did, he looked me over very closely, seeing how I carried the years, noting the fit and cost of my clothes and the condition of the body beneath.

"What's up?" he asked, sucking in his gut and standing a little straighter after he glanced at my midsection again. "You finally need a lawyer?"

I shook my head. "Doesn't look like you have to worry about clients. You've done real well for yourself."

I did a quick visual tour of the office. It took up a full corner of one of the bright new stainless-steel high rises at Newport Center. One glass wall is executive VP or CEO level; only dope lawyers and rock-star managers rate two.

But what a view.

I walked over and squinted through an antique brass telescope aimed out at the Pacific. I could read names on the transoms of the yachts parked along Big Boat Row half a mile away. Geraghty slumped in the high-backed leather chair and threw one leg over the corner of the flight-deck desk, watching me a bit unhappily.

"Nice," I said, running my palm over the cold, smooth brass of the telescope, enjoying the elegance and precision of the tool.

Geraghty gave me a world-weary smile. "You don't have to rub it in," he said. "I know Jake would feel out of place here. On the other hand, I don't know that he'd be any happier if he knew you had turned his steamer trunk full of cash into something so mundane as a run-down beachfront cottage and a collector's-edition automobile."

I turned the telescope ninety degrees, aiming it in the direction of Goat Hill and squinting through it.

"The cottage is still on the bluff down at Crystal Cove, but the Cobra is in a wrecking yard somewhere over there."

I pointed toward the tower of Hoag Hospital. "I've got a clean conscience, as far as Jake's money is concerned."

"So do I," Geraghty said, a bit defensively.

"Sorry to hear it. I had hoped for enough guilt to let me milk a favor or two out of you."

Immediately he began to relax, as though he was more comfortable dispensing free legal advice than he was trying to live with my disapproval or Jake's. He opened a flat box on his desk and inspected the contents thoughtfully before looking up at me.

"Want a cigar? There's a Cuban over in Santa Ana who makes these. Honduran tobacco, but they're as good as it'll get until we start trading with Cuba again."

"No, thanks. I've given up all my addictions but one."

"Dope?" He looked accommodating, as though he might have some of that around too, if I really wanted it.

"No, thanks," I said. "Adrenaline always was my drug of choice."

"You and Jake. Jesus."

"Just me and Jake. Jesus went straight a long time ago."

"You guys used to scare the hell out of me."

"Things change. I spend most of my time working with underprivileged kids now."

Geraghty threw me a look out of shrewd blue eyes, then selected a stogie. It was the size of the Mont Blanc pen in his desk holder and almost as black. He snipped the cigar's tip with a gold cutter that hung from the key chain across his vest.

"What kind of favor?"

"I need to find out where the cops have a guy they arrested this morning over on San Joaquin Hills Road."

"Newport Beach cops?"

"I wasn't close enough to read the badges. Plainclothes, probably undercover."

"Feds?"

"Could have been."

"Dope?"

"I didn't hear the charge."

Geraghty stuck the cigar in his mouth and chewed gently, moistening it while he reached for the phone and punched a number from memory.

"Get me men's booking, please."

He ran the cigar in and out of his mouth as he waited.

"Name?" he asked me around the cigar.

"Ysidro Ibañez. I don't know his DOB but he's somewhere in his thirties."

Geraghty raised an eyebrow and started to say something to me when someone picked up the other end of the line.

"This is George Geraghty," he said, with the confidence of a man who knows his name will be recognized. "You have a prospective client of mine over there. Ysidro Ibañez."

He waited.

"Yeah? That right?" he said into the phone. "Listen, who booked him and what's the charge?"

Geraghty laid the cigar in a crystal ashtray and grabbed the Mont Blanc from its holder. In the quiet room the gold nib of the pen scratched across a sheet of cream-colored twenty-pound bond. There was a faint wheeze just behind the sound of the pen. It was Geraghty, breathing. Too many cigars and too much rich food.

I didn't care. I could have kissed the fat, tricky bastard on both cheeks.

"Right," he said. "What's the bail?"

More scratching. He cradled the phone, covered the mouthpiece with three fleshy fingers, and pinned me with eyes that were much harder than his body. "I assume you want to see him?"

I nodded.

Geraghty went back to the phone. "Listen, the poor guy's family may want me to represent him. How about if my investigator comes over in the next half hour or so and interviews him?" He listened, then broke in. "I know, I know, technically we haven't been retained yet. But be a good guy and let my man in."

Geraghty listened again, silently parroting the words he was hearing over the phone as he rolled the cigar between his lips. Finally he spoke again.

"You bet I know. Sure, I'll take care of it. No sweat. Now, is my guy in or not?"

Back to holding my breath.

"Great. See you, Manny."

Geraghty hung up, thrust the pen back in its holder, and carefully folded the sheet of heavy bond. He grabbed his cold cigar from the crystal ashtray and set fire to the fragrant tobacco with a gold desk lighter.

"Immigration hold," he said, around the cigar. "That means no bond. The booking agency was listed as Newport Beach PD, but that could be phony."

I made a noise that said I was listening.

Geraghty was listening too. He waved his hand through the cloud of blue smoke in front of his face and looked at me carefully. Whatever he saw made him smile oddly and say Jake's name under his breath. Then the smile faded.

"An immigration hold is a good way to keep Mr. Ibañez on ice," he said. "Narcs use it when they're trying to twist somebody's pecker off."

Geraghty picked up the folded sheet of paper and hesitated, half offering it to me and half withholding it.

"Thanks, George. I really appreciate your trouble." I reached for the sheet.

He kept the paper just beyond my fingertips. "Is there a defendant in it for me? Not some mope from the Guajira, mind you, but a real live defendant?"

"Could be. You know anything about banking law?"

"I'm a quick study."

"If my partner agrees, the job may be yours."

"Partner?"

"Fiora."

"My God. If you've hung onto her for this long, you're smarter than I thought. She ever forgive Jake for trying to make a smuggler out of you?"

"No."

"She must have forgiven you."

"Sometimes."

Geraghty laughed abruptly and offered the folded paper between index and middle finger. "No strings on this one, Fiddler. It was worth a grand just to see Jake's face again."

I unfolded the paper and read a note authorizing me to interview Ysidro Ibañez in behalf of Geraghty's office.

"This cost you a grand?" I asked.

He shrugged. "The booking sergeant put the arm on me— a full table, ten tickets for the jail commander's retirement dinner."

I reached for my wallet. "I don't want you to go in the hole."

"Get out of here. Don't piss me off." Geraghty relit his cigar and squinted at me again. "I would have been on the hook for ten tickets even if you hadn't come through my door. Now I'll get something besides rubber roast beef out of the deal."

"Thanks," I said, meaning it.

I reached the door, then turned and looked around the office.

"Jake wouldn't have minded," I said, admiring the antique telescope once more. "He never gave a damn about what other people did, so long as they left him alone."

"What about you?"

"I'm working on it."

11

URBAN CHANGE was at work in downtown Santa Ana, same as in downtown Bradford. But the process didn't seem quite as yeasty in Santa Ana. Somebody had started to refurbish a 1920s movie theater but gave up halfway through the job. A vacant lot had been turned into a bandit taxi depot, loading six *Méxicanos* at a time for their ten-dollar rides home to Tijuana. The front window of what had been a Rexall pharmacy was now filled with dusty displays of an Indian *curandero*'s wares.

You could still see a solid Victorian skeleton in the old courthouse and behind the fronts of some of the old business buildings, but the recent Anglo construction had all the grace of a concrete artillery emplacement. The blank-faced, twelve-story county courthouse loomed over equally ugly high-rise offices filled with lawyers and lobbyists and social-welfare bureaucrats who fed off the burgeoning county government. Plenty going on, but none of it had the electric cultural synthesis of Bradford.

Maybe Fiora was right. Maybe institutions like banks can determine what kind of change takes place in a community.

The windowless county jail adjacent to the courthouse

was as impersonal as a stop sign. The attorney's interview room had two doors, a table, two chairs, a floor, and four walls plus a ceiling lined with soundproof tile.

Ysidro Ibañez walked through the door from the cellblock and looked around. An orange jail jumpsuit made his dark skin look waxy and cadaverous. The turnkey slammed the door, leaving Ibañez alone with me. I stood up and offered him my hand across the table.

"My name is Fiddler."

Ibañez was a little slow, maybe still shocky. He took my hand by reflex and shook it weakly, Latino style. Then he recognized me from the bank and drew a sharp breath between clenched teeth. Jaime had made the same sound when he saw the woman with the red hair. Slowly he sat down, staring at me.

"Who are you? Why are you here?"

When he wasn't angry or frightened, his English was clear and precise, educated but heavily accented. His expression suggested I was his worst nightmare come true.

"Relax. I don't work for Don Faustino."

The mention of the name made Ibañez glance warily around the room.

"We can talk safely," I said. "The room isn't bugged. Attorneys interview clients here."

Ibañez wasn't convinced. "Are you an attorney? I have not asked for an attorney."

"I'm not a lawyer, but I'll get one for you if you want."

"What do *you* want?"

"To help Brad Simms out of a jam."

Ibañez's dark, wary gaze didn't soften.

"I had lunch with Jaime," I said.

The reaction was gratifying. For a few instants Ibañez forgot to treat me like an enemy.

"Where is Jaime? Is he all right?"

"He's fine. He's staying with a friend of mine."

Ibañez shrugged slightly, as though his son were of little importance.

I waited, but he asked no more questions.

"I have the bag, too," I said, trying to find another pressure point.

His answer was a shrug.

"You can walk away from your son and you can walk away from six hundred grand?" I asked.

He looked at the wall over my shoulder.

"How about the rest of your family," I said. "Can you walk away from your wife and your daughter?"

For a moment Ibañez looked as though he couldn't breathe. He had been hanging tough, protecting his secrets, but now I seemed to have them all. His black eyes closed for a moment, showing me lashes as long as Jaime's. When Ibañez looked at me again, his eyes were empty of fight.

"Talk to me," I said. "Tell me everything you know about dirty money and bankers to match."

Ibañez reached for a pack of cigarettes in the pocket of his coveralls. It took a few tries, but he managed to get a cigarette out and into his mouth. He fished a book of matches out of the cellophane sheath on the cigarette package, but his hands had started to shake. He sat and stared at the matches as though he had forgotten how to use them.

I took the matches from him, lit one, and held it to the end of the cigarette. For a moment Ibañez simply closed his eyes and smoked, watching the back of his eyelids as they showed the movie of his life coming apart. Finally he opened his eyes and looked at me.

"You have the money in the bag. That should be enough for a man like you. Let my son go."

"Sure. Where should I drop him off? In the waiting room at county jail?"

"Take him to Santa Ana."

"Where in Santa Ana?"

He shrugged. "Anywhere. Jaime knows what to do."

"Drop an eleven-year-old kid in the middle of a city? No way. You'll have to do better than that."

"I have no more money."

It was a lie but I let it pass and told him the truth. "I'm not after money."

"Then why did you kidnap Jaime?"

I laughed, but it wasn't a reassuring sound. "Kidnap him? Hell, hombre, I picked him up off the street where you left him holding a bag full of trouble, the kind of trouble that gets grown-ups killed."

"It is not your problem. Let him go."

"No way, pal. I'm not going to set the boy up for a *traficante* shooting gallery."

"Nothing is wrong. This is all a mistake."

"Christ," I said, disgusted. "Jaime's a hell of a lot safer right now with me than if he was living in the same house with a pile of U.S. currency the size of a Volkswagen and a father with the IQ of a body bag."

"I have betrayed no one. Nothing is wrong." Ibañez's voice was forlorn as he repeated the lies. The location of his home was the last of his secrets, and that made him guard it all the more carefully.

"You took fifteen million from Faustino," I said impatiently. "If he hasn't figured it out yet, he will real soon. You can't go back. He'll have to kill you and your whole family as an object lesson to the rest of his troops."

Ibañez swallowed reflexively, trying to keep his jailhouse lunch in place, but said nothing.

"What made you think you could get away with taking your son back from the cartel?" I asked.

He sucked long and hard on his cigarette and blew out a plume of smoke that was as pale as his face had become.

"Please believe me, señor," he said finally. "I did nothing to help Jaime come to the United States."

"Then you have one bright, gutsy son."

A sad smile flickered across Ibañez's face. "*Sí.*"

He smoked in silence for a time as he looked at me, really looked at me. Then he closed his eyes and thought hard. There was no sound for a minute but the soft exhalation of smoke.

"You are not with Don Faustino," he said.

"No."

"What do you want?" he asked for the third time.

"I'd like to help your family. My partner would like to help a lady whose son is neither bright nor gutsy. He's the dumb-shit banker who helped you turn fifteen million dollars in small dirty bills into neat little bricks of clean C-notes."

"If you know about that, Don Faustino truly is losing control of his own organization. I had hoped such a thing might be true, but I was not sure. His superiors will not be pleased. Even his inferiors." Ibañez smiled.

Faustino losing control of his laundering organization was an interesting possibility, maybe the best news I'd heard since Fiora started talking about a crumbling bank when she should have been talking about crumbling quail guzzlers.

It could also be the worst news I'd heard. Power politics are every bit as much a part of life in the underworld as they are in Washington, D.C. When crooks stage a changing of the guard, it can be real hard on everybody—participants, bystanders, and innocents alike.

"Who else knows about the fifteen million dollars?" I asked.

"The police. I thought they were arresting me because I am here illegally, but it turns out they know about the money too."

"With that much cash on the loose, I'm surprised half the crooks in North America haven't come swarming. How did you ever get your hands on so much money at once?"

Ibañez rubbed the bridge of his nose with his thumb and forefinger, trying to find a solution to the maze of money, thugs, and family.

"We store the money in several places—rented houses. When there is enough, Cochi Loco and I collect it. I package it for shipment on one of the Don's airplanes. You understand?"

"Yeah. You're flying the cash to Miami, then on to the *finca* in one of Faustino's private planes. Then you take a commercial flight home. Eastern Airlines. Jaime told me that's how he knew what plane to take to get here."

Ibañez smiled sourly. "*Sí*. You understand. Too much, I think." He shrugged. "All but the last half million had been exchanged for one-hundred-dollar bills. Then Jaime called me from Los Angeles. *Madre de Dios*. I did not know what to do. We would all die when Don Faustino found out."

With shaking hands, Ibañez fished out another cigarette and lit it from the smoldering butt of the first. I watched and waited.

"Then I started thinking," Ibañez said, stubbing out the first cigarette as he drew hard on the second. "With Jaime free, I was free. Not only that, there was enough money to buy my way to a place where no one could touch my family, a place where doctors could help Josefina. I planned very quickly, packed up all that mattered, and left. Everything was perfect—"

"Until the police arrested you."

"*Sí*." The cigarette burned hotly as Ibañez dragged on it. "Now?" He shrugged. "Now it is in the hands of God."

"God's pretty busy these days. You'd better look for help closer to home."

Ibañez looked at me. "You?"

I nodded.

"How?"

"Tell me where your family is. I'll see that they're safe."

"No."

"Then tell me where the money is. I've got a lawyer who can cut you some kind of deal with the cops. You won't have the money when it's all over, but you'll be free."

And, if I were lucky, Brad would also be free.

"No," Ibañez said. "Without money there is no freedom for us."

"Bullshit, hombre. Nobody gets away with stealing fifteen

million dollars, I don't care who it belongs to. I didn't kidnap Jaime, but I'm sure not eager to give him back to a fool like you."

"I am trying to give my children a safer life!"

"Yeah, and you're trying to provide a better, safer life for the fifteen million bucks at the same time."

"You know nothing of what I am trying to escape. You are a rich gringo!"

"Listen, banker. You can have the money, or you can have your family. Take your pick, because you sure as shit can't have both."

Ibañez closed his eyes again. I had no trouble guessing his thoughts. He was scared, with good reason. Like Brad Simms, Ibañez was basically a gentleman who had given in to major temptation and gotten himself and his family into a major hole, perhaps a grave. Neither man had the requisite meanness to be a thug. Neither man was mean enough to go one-on-one with thugs and survive.

Ibañez opened his eyes, took a last hit on the cigarette, and smashed the butt into the ashtray as he stood up.

"Don Faustino does not know Jaime is with me. The police cannot prove I am anything but a poor immigrant without papers. If I am quiet, all will be well."

Ibañez walked to the cellblock door and knocked on it, summoning the turnkey.

"What about Jaime?" I demanded. "Goddammit! What about your son?"

The door opened. Ibañez stepped through without looking back, leaving me with silence and the stink of a half-dead cigarette smoldering in the dirty ashtray.

12

THE DRIVE BACK to Crystal Cove summed up the day. The emergency valve on a tanker full of sludge from the Moulton-Niguel Water District sewage treatment plant came open on the San Diego Freeway just north of Mac-Arthur. There was a time when the Highway Patrol would have waved traffic through the five-gallon puddle until it stuck to enough tires and the problem was solved.

But not anymore. The Chicken Little syndrome is in full cry. Toxic, nontoxic, or totally ludicrous, it doesn't matter. All spills must be handled with extreme caution—in this case by shutting down half the freeway and calling in a uniformed hazardous-material response team. The ensuing bottleneck added more pollution to the environment than a river of sludge would have.

It was quarter of seven when I turned off Coast Highway past the sign that says WELCOME TO CRYSTAL COVE, PLEASE TURN YOUR CLOCKS BACK TO 1947. Sounded like a good idea to me.

The house—cottage, actually—where I live was built eighty years ago. Outwardly, not much has changed at Crystal Cove since then, which is why I like it. There are two dozen houses, all in varying states of disrepair and so small that nobody important wants to own one. And there is a broad, sandy beach at the base of a fifty-foot bluff. The view is unobstructed, and the hillside in back blocks out the road sounds from Coast Highway. Crystal Cove is what California was like fifty years ago—quiet, remote, gentle, clean.

But time warps don't last forever. Crystal Cove's ramshackle cottages are all on land leased from the Irvine Company, which deeded the cove to the state a few years ago. Crystal Cove State Park is still in the planning stages, so the cottages remain in place. But sooner or later, some D-12 Cats will come creaking down the little dirt road and push over my house and my sway-backed garage and uproot my lemon tree and fill in my koi pond.

Fiora, the realist, says I have no complaint coming. She's right. I knew the ground was leased when I bought the place, and I knew nothing lasts forever. That doesn't mean I have to dance at funerals.

When I walked into the cottage, Fiora came out of the bedroom in the cream silk dressing gown she always wears after a shower. She took one look at my face and headed for the refrigerator. She returned with a bottle of Corona so cold it sweated crystal beads. I drank half of it in a single draught, then followed her to the back of the house.

"Jaime is at Luz's place," Fiora said. "He's not happy about it, but he seems okay. She promised to keep him away from the phone. She said she wouldn't do it for anyone but you. She trusts you."

I grunted.

"Did Jaime's papa have anything useful to say?" Fiora asked.

"He trusts God."

"Must be nice."

I didn't say anything. I just watched Fiora as she sat at a vanity table and assembled the components of her business armor.

"The good news," she said, "is that Brad came through

with our invitation for the soirée Faustino is throwing at the yacht club. The bad news is we leave in forty-five minutes."

I took another hit on the beer bottle and admired the fine, damp tendrils of hair that curled against Fiora's nape. The dressing gown wasn't tightly wrapped. While she worked with the curling iron, I ogled.

"Which yacht club?" I asked.

"West Coast."

The last swallow of beer was cold, foamy, and alive. I dropped the bottle into the wastebasket by the vanity. The glass made a heavy, satisfying thud when it hit. I began unbuttoning, unzipping, and shedding clothes. As I passed the closet I saw my blue blazer, gray slacks, and white shirt hanging on the door. Next to them hung an elegant off-white silk dress. Fiora must have decided the navy blue wool was too hot.

Five minutes later I came out of the bathroom wearing a towel and still in a foul mood. I stood beside and a little bit behind Fiora's left shoulder, looking for an excuse to argue. She had traded her dressing gown for lacy underwear and her curling iron for a mascara brush. Another cold-beaded bottle of Corona had appeared on the vanity in my absence, an offering of some sort.

As I reached past Fiora for the beer, I caught the distracting, spicy scent of freshly bathed, powdered, and perfumed woman. The room got a bit hotter, the bottle a bit cooler in my right hand. The idea of fighting began to lose its appeal. I took a swallow of beer and went back to watching Fiora. Her bra looked far too delicate to do anything useful. For that matter, so did her panties.

"Pretty flimsy armor for money launderers," I said.

"Filmy."

"Hmm?"

"Filmy, not flimsy."

"Actually," I said, running my hand over Fiora's bare shoulder, "silky is probably a better word."

The underwire bra was intended to provide a restrained

touch of cleavage for the dress Fiora had chosen. Without the dress, the effect was striking, particularly when combined with the sight of dark pink nipples pressed against sheer lace.

"We don't have time," she said after a minute of silence.

"For what?"

She glanced at me in the mirror. For a moment our eyes locked. The makeup on her face paled in comparison to the blood that rushed to her cheeks and lips. Her eyes took on a smoky green hue.

"For what's making your towel look like a circus tent," Fiora said, looking me over with a smile before she gave her attention back to her makeup.

Her skin was warm beneath my palm. The silk of the bra strap felt rough by comparison. I hooked my finger underneath the strap and rubbed lightly. She pretended she didn't notice.

"Did you really get to talk to Ibañez?" Fiora asked, trading the mascara brush for an eyelash comb smaller than her little finger.

"Just for a few minutes."

"Where?"

My fingertip traveled beneath the bra strap as far as her collarbone, then traced the slight curve of the bone to the point of her shoulder.

"Ibañez is in Orange County Jail. He confirmed everything that Jaime told us, including the money. Fifteen million. There's a no-bail hold on Papa, but I offered him Jaime and a lawyer to hold the cops at bay. All Ibañez had to do was give us back the hundreds."

My finger traversed the slope of Fiora's shoulder and arrived back at the lacy strap.

"What did he say?"

"No sale."

"Why?"

"He can't tell me where the money is partly because it's the same place he has his wife and daughter."

This time when I hooked my finger beneath the strap, I drew it slowly to the side until it no longer supported the weight of Fiora's breast.

"And the other part?"

Fiora's voice was husky and her eyes were very green. The feeling of gravity doubling hit me.

"Greed, maybe," I said. "Fear, certainly. Ibañez figures that if he trusts me and he's wrong, his whole family dies. If he doesn't trust me, only Jaime is at risk, and he was already at risk with Faustino."

The strap slid off Fiora's shoulder and fell uselessly over her upper arm.

"Are you saying that you offered to trade Jaime for the money?" she demanded.

"Not in so many words."

"You really are a ruthless bastard, aren't you," she muttered, jerking the bra strap back into place as she reached for a deep rose lip pencil.

I switched the cold Corona to my left hand and stalked the other bra strap, beginning at her spine and moving in millimeters toward the strap with my index finger.

"I didn't have anything else to use as leverage," I said. "Not that it did much good. Ibañez made the smart call, the only call he could make, given the circumstances."

She looked at me coolly, unconvinced.

"He had nothing to gain by telling me, and he knew it," I said. "If I'm a ruthless bastard, Jaime's lost no matter what. If I'm a good guy, Jaime's safe even if Ibañez hangs onto the money."

Fiora shivered as I finished retracing her spine with my finger.

"Either way, Ibañez has nothing to gain by turning the money over to me. And I think he must have sensed that I liked Jaime."

A strand of honey-blond hair escaped the clip on top of Fiora's head and fell down her back. The curl brushed against my wrist. I felt the light touch all the way to my knees.

"So we're stuck with Plan A," she said.

"Plan A?"

"Supping with the devil, as your sainted aunt would have said."

I didn't answer. My finger had finally reached the other bra strap and slid it off Fiora's shoulder. When she made no move to set things right, I tugged on the strap, slowly peeling lace away from her breast until the dark pink tip was revealed.

No matter how many times I have seen Fiora's body change at my touch, I am still fascinated by the way her nipple turns from silk to nubby velvet, by the catch in her breath, by the look in her eyes when she wants me. Her lips were slightly parted. They didn't need makeup. They were as full and richly colored as the tip of the breast I was teasing.

Fiora's carefully controlled expression melted away as I removed her bra. She studied the picture we made in the mirror. Her smile was both inviting and expectant, like her body humming beneath my fingers. We had our problems as a couple, but sex had never been one of them. She knew it was going to be good. So did I.

With her right hand, she reached over her shoulder, running her fingertips over the terry-cloth towel and me. She plucked at the edge of the towel, peeling it away as gently as I had peeled away the lacy cup of her bra. I reached for her hand as though to stop her.

"Men really are terrible prudes," she said, laughing up at me as she evaded my hand. "It's fine for me to be naked in front of the mirror, but not you, is that it?"

Her fingers slid beneath the towel. I sucked hard on air.

"I just remembered we're supposed to be meeting Faustino," I said.

It was a lie. All I could think about was how good her hand felt. She turned around and hooked her long, polished nail beneath the towel, slowly beginning to loosen it.

"Don't mind me," Fiora said, pushing the towel away. "You just go on thinking about Faustino."

I would have laughed, but I had to fight just to drag air into my lungs.

We hit the sheets at the same instant, fitting together with the steamy ease that was better than memory and anticipation combined. When I could breathe again and the fine tremors in Fiora's body finally passed, we lay locked together on the bed, wondering whether we would ever be closer, more fulfilled, than at that moment. Lazily I tried to remember when the act of physical love had been so intense.

"Santa Fe," Fiora whispered, kissing my neck, answering my unspoken question.

She tried to shift, to make our position more comfortable for me. I gently pinned her in place with my hips, not wanting the sensation of closeness to end. My movement caused a passionate reflex in her. She made a small sound and strained against me. Her response triggered both of us again, turning us into a single, seamless symbiotic creature, making it impossible to tell where one of us ended and the other began.

When I could tell the difference again, I rolled both of us over onto our sides.

"Yes," I said. "Santa Fe. Only better."

Fiora freed one hand and brushed the hair back out of my eyes, studying me with green-eyed intensity.

"You sound sad," she said. "Why?"

"You remember what was happening around us in Santa Fe? People were lying, people were stealing . . . and there we were in a motel bed, making the love of our lives when we were supposed to be doing something else entirely."

"That's bad?"

"You've always thought so up to now."

"I don't understand."

"Adrenaline is a drug that heightens everything," I said simply. "It's more dangerous than cocaine or heroin. I'd hate to see you become like me, addicted to the rough side of life, unable to get off on anything else."

Fiora's expression became suffused by a warmth and

gentleness I wasn't sure I had ever seen before. She twisted against me gently, moving once, twice, until I groaned, amazed that I could still respond, much less feel anything so intense.

"Does that tell you who and what I get off on?" she whispered, smiling and moving slowly, eyes half closed with pleasure as she measured my reaction. "As for the rest of it, the people dying and lying and stealing and cheating, what better time is there to make love, to remind ourselves that not everything human is ugly?"

I stilled the slow movement of Fiora's hips, wanting her to listen to my words instead of my body. "I've never felt more in love with you than I am at this moment, but I'm scared as hell that hanging around with me full time is going to ruin you for the good things in your life."

"This *is* a good thing in my life. One of the best. It's all of a piece, the rough and the smooth. Making love with you isn't something that's separate from the rest of being alive."

"I want to believe you . . ."

"But?"

There was silence while I tried to put words to my fears, words that Fiora would understand. She waited, watching me, saying nothing.

"There are times when I think the world has gone full circle," I said slowly, "that we're back in the Roman Empire again, that the Huns and the Visigoths are at the front gate, and that some of them have already crept in through an unguarded sally port. There are times I fear they are already among us."

"All the better reason for us smooth-handed types to learn how to knock off some of the rough edges we meet," she said, smiling as she traced the line of my mustache with her fingertip.

"It's not that easy, love."

"The important things never are."

"Fiora . . ."

She waited, watching me with changeable green eyes, focusing on me with all of her considerable intelligence.

"Most people have no real taste for living out beyond the fringes of organized society," I said. "The outlaw-and-adrenaline life is dangerous. It killed Uncle Jake and damn near killed me."

Fiora didn't say she knew that as well as I did. Better, perhaps. Her mind has a way of cutting across time and place. Sometimes that talent is useful, sometimes infuriating, most often merely disconcerting.

"Living beyond the pale is dangerous in more subtle ways too," I said. "You find out that turning the other cheek is a good way to get slapped silly, because too many times violence is the only thing that works. You learn that polite society is sometimes best served by impolite methods. Then you learn that polite society may secretly applaud impolite methods, even if it will never admire them publicly."

"Fiddler—"

"Listen to me," I said, cutting across Fiora's words. "Whether you act on what you've learned beyond the pale or not, the experience ruins you for polite society. It turns you into an outlaw in urban clothing, a barbarian in a Brooks Brothers blazer. You are no longer a gentleman."

"Or a gentle woman? That's what you're afraid of, isn't it? That I'll lose my civilized illusions and with them my softness?"

"That's part of it," I admitted. "Look at you, for Christ's sake. Right now you should be in the high-rise office of your high-flying company, closing some deal that will make you and your clients a few billion dollars and change the course of human development in the process. That's what God created you to do. You sure as hell shouldn't be lying around in bed with me, then heading off to try and fast-talk a bunch of billion-dollar thugs out of killing a spoiled, weak, lying gentleman banker who got cold feet and is trying to crawl back into civilization's warm womb."

"I hate to bring this up, Fiddler, but one of your basic assumptions is wrong."

"Such as?"

"You think men fight one another more than women because men are harder than women. In truth, men are softer. If violence were left to women, there would be fewer incidents of physical bloodshed, yes, because you have to push a woman damned hard to make her fight. But once you *have* pushed a woman into battle, you can forget ritual posturing, codes of honor, diplomacy, rules, medals, uniforms, and all the other codswollop so beloved by men. When women fight it's war to annihilation, no quarter, no prisoners—nothing but one winner, one loser, and the peace of the grave."

Even if my head agreed with Fiora, my gut kept reminding me of how physically small and soft she was. Especially now, lying in my arms, her eyes luminous with emotion.

"I don't want you ruined for polite society," I said. "You spent all your life crawling up out of the bleak rural hole you were born into. You won't admit it, but if you go into partnership with me, you could lose for yourself the very thing you're trying to build and defend for others—a civilized future."

"Stop worrying about what polite society thinks of me," Fiora said, touching my lips with her finger to keep me from talking. "I don't give a damn about that. I never really have. In any case I doubt that the people who hold power are nearly as narrow as you think. If I'm wrong, so be it. I've made my choice."

She replaced her finger with her lips. The kiss was like Fiora—complex, unpredictable, silky, hot, fierce.

"While you were gone," she said finally, "I accepted a verbal offer from Ed Hirshman. It will take a few months to work out the details, but I'm getting out of Pacific Rim Investment's day-to-day business. I don't know exactly what I'll do, but I do know it will amount to consulting. With you, if you want. Without you, if that's the way it has to be."

I drew a deep breath and let it out slowly, emptying my lungs, trying to banish the sinking feeling that, at best, Fiora would live to regret choosing me.

And if I wasn't careful, she wouldn't live long enough to regret her choice at all.

13

THE LIMO was waiting for us outside Benny's place in West Newport. I hate limos. I'm one of those unfortunate people who doesn't trust strangers behind the wheel. But tonight a bridal-veil-white stretch Caddie with a wet bar and a 27-inch Sony seemed the perfect nouveau riche touch for a pair of high-flying bankers like us. Besides, anybody who wanted to background us by running a DMV license-plate check would only get as far as Newport Limo Service before the trail ran out.

The driver's name was Denny. He was razor-cut and blow-dried and a little long in the tooth—a rock musician trying to decide whether to give it up or get a new agent. Denny rolled down the glass partition between the front seat and the passenger compartment and laid out the terms up front. Forty bucks an hour for as long as we wanted him, cash or charge card, whichever. We paid for what we drank from the bar. If we didn't see anything we liked in the bar, he could arrange alternative refreshments—the kind that didn't need refrigeration—but the terms on those goodies were cash only, because nobody could figure out what to call them on an American Express sales voucher.

Fiora handled the whole thing nicely. She pretended not to see Denny or to hear what he said. She just told him where we wanted to be.

"West Coast Club. Please raise the partition."

As the soundproof glass slid into place, I pulled down the jump seat, propped my feet on it, and admired Fiora from the corner of my eye. She rested her hand lightly on my outstretched leg and stroked the fabric of my slacks with a proprietary, satisfied smile on her perfect lips. I knew how she felt. While I still wasn't exactly wild about the business angle of our partnership, particularly since it involved dragging her along into the lion's den, there were some rather spectacular side benefits to our new arrangement.

"Newport Beach must be getting broad-minded," I said after a few minutes. "Guys with names like Faustino used to have to use the service entrance at the West Coast Club."

"It started a couple of years ago," she replied absently. "When the peso went to hell, the Mexican oligarchs converted their holdings to dollars and headed north. The rest of Latin America fell in line. There's more flight capital in local banks than there is in some South American countries. Money like that blurs all kinds of social distinctions."

She leaned back against the limo's crushed velour and slowly drummed her nails on the armrest. I could feel her beginning to rev up for the coming meeting. She looked like a cover shot out of *Town and Country*, except for the two little frown lines between her delicately arched eyebrows. She was thinking—not just chasing thoughts, but *thinking*, the kind of head work that allows her to carry on a conversation, a seduction, and a complex financial coup all at the same time, with enough brain cells left over to run a good-sized country.

"Faustino has reciprocal privileges at the West Coast Club because he's a member of the Bahia Caribe in Panama," she said.

"Don't tell me, let me guess," I said, popping the cap on

a Calistoga water from the bar. "Tony Noriega was his sponsor."

"Mmm."

That sound could have meant anything, but it usually means she's thinking. I settled back and did the same. Not in as organized a fashion as Fiora, no doubt. I just sort of let the thoughts, memories, and questions come.

The West Coast Club is genuine Gold Coast ostentation, the kind of place that gives boating a bad name. I hadn't been inside for years, but the telescope in George Geraghty's office had showed me that there were still twenty gleaming white motor yachts moored along Big Boat Row: 104-foot Ditmar and Donaldsons powerboats, 85-foot motor sailers with acres of teak decking, and 72-foot Italian cruisers with twin Caterpillar diesels and 3,000-mile cruising ranges. The sad thing was that those magnificent machines probably didn't get away from the dock for more than a hundred hours a year.

I'm not sure how it is elsewhere, but in Newport Beach, boats seldom really go to sea. These million-dollar ships function as tax write-offs and floating party pads. Most of them spend their entire existence inside the breakwater. Maybe, just maybe, once a month the owner calls his skipper and orders him to lay in a case of gin and a case of Chablis for a spin around the marina with some customers. The longest voyage on their logs is either the one-hour circuit of the harbor during the Christmas Boat Parade or the once-a-year run down to Lido Shipyard for a new coat of paint and a good brisk bottom scraping.

In other words, the West Coast Club was invented for boat people who hate the sea.

I have nothing against the ships themselves. I love good machinery, and good machinery is invariably expensive. But to buy a superbly designed and crafted oceangoing yacht and then leave it tied to a dock like a hamstrung greyhound . . . well, that's an impulse I've never understood. It's also the major reason I've avoided the West Coast Club. Those people aren't my people, and their gods aren't my gods.

The club was formed by some local real estate hustlers and dilettante yachtsmen who couldn't get into the other yacht clubs on the bay. The West Coast Club is privately owned, which means it's expensive but not exclusive. There are only two requirements for membership: money and enough class not to pour chocolate syrup in your Chablis. If you have enough money, the club will suspend the second requirement.

"Besides reciprocal club privileges, what did you find out about this clown?" I asked.

"Not much. I only had time for a couple of calls."

Fiora's "couple of calls" probably had turned up more juicy tidbits than the average FBI background check. That's the joy of being on the inside of the Establishment. It makes tracking the lines of power ever so much easier.

"Anything we can use?" I asked.

"He's got money, lots of it, an open-ended credit line for personal expenses at one of the Arab banks in LA. He's well connected in Panama."

"Even after Noriega's recent problems?"

She shrugged. "On the surface, Faustino looks respectable. Banks, brokerage concerns, a small chain of newspapers in several South American countries. He also owns one of the biggest gold-mining firms in northern Brazil. All on the up-and-up, so far as I could find out."

"Are you saying he's a crook who hasn't been caught yet?"

"No, I'm saying he appears to have pretty well insulated himself from the dirty businesses you usually associate with people who carry cash in shopping bags. The same might not be said for some of his employees, but I'll bet the Don has never in his life seen a gram of cocaine. He looks like nothing more than an aggressive capitalist who doesn't mind where his capital comes from, as long as he gets his cut."

She took the Calistoga from me and sipped.

"Of course that doesn't explain why he travels with a cadre of armed guards. That has caused quite a bit of a stir, in some of the better spots on our lovely Orange Riviera." She shrugged. "As for the rest of it, Faustino lives on the bluffs in La Jolla, in a villa that costs him thirty thousand a month. He's building a five-million-dollar house up in the hills, but he hasn't been invited to join the La Jolla Beach and Tennis Club."

I grunted.

Fiora tapped her fingers again. "I didn't have time to find out whether the money is Faustino's or somebody else's. If it's his, he's powerful in his own right. If not, he's a world-class gofer. But either way, he goes through a whole lot of cash, which is all the folks around here seem to care about."

"He'll fit right in at the West Coast Club," I said. "Out of curiosity, how many calls did you have to make to dig up all this?"

"Three, but only two were helpful. The third was to a guy I know from Harvard. He didn't tell me a thing. I think he's trying to cut a deal with Don Faustino himself and was afraid I'd take his customer away."

"Nice crowd you run with," I remarked.

"There's an old saying among bankers: Blood always washes off of gold."

"Christ. And you call my line of work corrupting."

"No. You do."

There was silence.

Fiora sighed. "Fiddler, I know what you're saying, but do you have any idea how naïve you sound?"

"Hell, yes, but pragmatism only goes so far. At some point you have to say that dirty money is dirty money is dirty money, and you won't handle it anymore."

"Why do you think I'm trying to get out of investment banking?" she shot back. "You would be appalled at how many new residents of this place got rich from drugs or illegal arms sales or plain old political corruption. Well, maybe you wouldn't be appalled, but I was. If it weren't for the Hong Kong Chinese and the honorable Japanese, I couldn't have closed a clean deal in the past six years."

"I hate to tell you, but most of the heroin from the Golden Triangle comes right through Hong Kong. As for Japan, have you ever heard of the Yakuzas?"

"I know, I know," Fiora said irritably, "the whole world's corrupt, one way or another." She looked over at me, then at the gap in my unbuttoned blazer. "And that damn cannon shows when you wear the shoulder harness."

I carry a Detonics, a full-sized weapon built on the frame of a Model 1911 .45. But I'm usually discreet enough to hide it in the small of my back.

"That's why I wore the shoulder rig," I said, smiling at her.

She gave me a look as cold as my smile.

Tough. There were certain aspects of this partnership that she just wasn't confronting yet. Danger was right up there at the top of the list.

"Don't worry about offending Faustino. Anybody whose chief assistant is named Cochi Loco is used to people who carry guns. He'd be disappointed if I didn't reciprocate."

Fiora grimaced. "You're a throwback to the last century."

"Or a harbinger of the next."

"Frightening thought."

She took the Calistoga bottle from me again and drank. When I took the bottle back I could taste her lipstick on the rim. It reminded me of why we were late, which reminded me of things a lot more interesting than South American money launderers.

The driver made the left turn across two lanes of Coast Highway as though limos turned there every day at that time and the rest of the traffic should damn well know it. He dropped us at the front door of the West Coast Club, then moved over to mingle with the other fifteen stretch limos holding down one corner of the parking lot. I could hear their meters running, each accumulating charges of forty bucks an hour. If the bottom line meant anything, this was going to be a hell of a party.

The lobby signs pointed us toward a medium-sized ball-room adjacent to the club's wine cellar. Fifty people were already sucking up Schramsberg and noshing from silver platters of salted fish eggs, half-naked mollusks, and un-cooked hamburger. Raw and expensive seemed to be the theme.

Brad Simms waved nervously from across the room and started toward us. He wore a charcoal suit with a gray silk tie and a gray silk handkerchief in the breast pocket. In this setting he looked hopelessly stiff and formal.

"You aren't going to become all nasty and prickly if I pursue Don Faustino, are you?" Fiora asked softly, giving me a sideways glance.

I smiled lazily and looked for a moment at the glimpse of cleavage her dress provided. "I'm feeling something less than jealous at the moment. I probably won't get nasty until I recover a bit of my—uh, vigor."

"I'll be watching for the first signs."

She took my arm and gave it a little hug. The soft pressure of her breast against my bicep was intentional and effective—a promise.

"Pretend we're no smarter than we were this morning," I said, shifting my arm just enough to let Fiora know that I reciprocated. "I still don't trust anybody here, and that in-cludes the boy wonder."

Fiora said nothing because Brad was upon us.

"Don Faustino's not here yet," he said.

He gave me a nervous grin, then ran his fingers through his carefully styled hair. I wondered who made him more uneasy, me or Don Faustino.

"Slow down," I said under my breath. "Try not to look like a belly dancer at a Quaker social. We're here to convince these people of our innocent intent, so look innocent, dammit."

Surprisingly, Brad grinned, reminding me oddly of Jaime. "It's hard to look innocent when you're not."

"Why are you nervous? This is just a nice little party in a nice little yacht club with all the nice little members. Relax."

"I can't. Faustino isn't going to be happy when I tell him I won't handle his money anymore."

Fiora smiled at someone she recognized across the room and spoke softly to Brad. "That's why you're not going to tell him."

"Huh?"

She glanced at me one last time, just to make sure I hadn't changed my mind. We were at the point pilots call "decision speed." We could still shut down and back out gracefully— but one more step, one more notch on the throttle, another few seconds, and it would be fly or die.

I gave her a nod so faint I wasn't even sure I had done it myself.

Fiora was sure. She gave Brad the up-from-under look and smile, silently telling him she thought he was twelve feet tall and walked on water.

He believed it.

I tried not to feel sorry for him. Fiora has told me point-blank that she has no scruples about using such tactics in business settings. She thinks any man so dumb that he can't look past her body to her brain deserves whatever he gets. Or, as she put it to me, "You're taller, stronger, and quicker than average, but I don't see you going down on your hands and knees so as not to take advantage."

She's right, but I still get uneasy when I watch her go to work on a poor devil like Brad. It seems disloyal to my sex to let it happen without warning.

"Just remember," Fiora said softly to Brad, "I'm your boss, your immediate supervisor at Bank of the Southland."

"What do you want me to do?"

"Leave any banking talk to me. Let me field the questions and answers. That's what consultants are for."

Brad drew a deep breath and blew it out slowly, trying to center himself.

"Okay," he said, "I guess."

"No guessing," I said. "That's the way it's going to be."

He looked unhappily at me.

I smiled. "Suck it up, wonder boy. It's time to introduce us to your friends."

14

DON FAUSTINO'S guest list was impressive or depressing, depending on how you viewed the collective state of the human soul. I shook hands with the biggest Ferrari dealer in the United States. I nodded at sales consultants for Piper and Lear and Beechcraft. I ate raw ground sirloin on crackers with two world-weary attorneys who got rich defending the indefensible, then invested their profits in an upscale chain of California pasta places.

And I listened while Fiora, two venture capitalists, and a state senator discussed half-billion-dollar malls, world-class resort hotels, and local land use policies. In between, Fiora had her cheek kissed by two environmental design specialists, two nationally known political fund-raisers, a Newport Beach city councilman, and a lonely-looking Italian named Alfredo.

Everybody except the Italian seemed right at home. I'm always curious about the one whose bona fides aren't immediately obvious, often being cast in that role myself. So I hung around Alfredo long enough to find out he was a tailor who made thousand-dollar suits for his friends and expensive suits for his clients.

So I was wrong about Alfredo. He actually fit right in. Most of the people in the room were for hire and on the make, handmaidens eager to service great, newly acquired wealth. I wondered how many of these hustlers took their fees in grocery sacks full of currency. Most of them, probably. Money corrupts. Untraceable money corrupts absolutely.

The underpinnings of another sunshine state, Florida, had already been rotted by illicit cash from the cocaine trade. Cops stealing confiscated currency and judges taking fat envelopes under the table. Now it was California's turn to be debased. Like Florida, we were beginning to integrate billions of dollars in illicit money into the legitimate local economy.

But Fiora was right. It wasn't just narcodollars. The world is awash with hot money, billions and billions of dollars rolling around the international financial system looking for safe haven, the personal fortunes of every high-level crook from Ferdinand Marcos to José Rodriguez Gacha, the proceeds of scams and subterfuges that range from tax avoidance in Argentina to the sale of arms in the Middle East.

For the first time in a long time, I wondered whether I should have destroyed Uncle Jake's steamer trunk. Once, long ago, far away, in another country, I had suggested that to Fiora. She was always more pragmatic about some things than I am. She told me to do whatever I wanted with my half, but she had no such qualms about hers. What was good enough for the Kennedys, the Rockefellers, and the Carnegies was good enough for her.

In the last few days, though, I had gotten the feeling she might be changing her mind.

"Which one's the South American?" The question came from an anxious little man standing beside me in a silk sports coat. He wasn't really talking to me. He was talking either to himself or to everyone else in the crowd, as though we were all in the same game together, with the same goal, working the same mark. He looked familiar, yet out of place. Then I remembered. He was a Hollywood producer named

Rich something-or-other. We had met one night in Century City, at one of those business parties Fiora was trying to leave behind.

With that memory came the rest. Rich was "in film, not television." He had mentioned that repeatedly, as though it should matter to me. He had the face of a whippet—intelligent, intense, and fractured. He ran his nervous eyes over the room like a political advance man counting the crowd.

"Faustino? He's not here yet," I said.

"When's he coming?"

"I don't know."

"Son of a bitch. If I don't connect quick, I'm dead meat. I gotta get back to LA by nine, talk to another money guy. I got a camera crew that's supposed to start principal photography on a feature next week, and Cabot and Forbes just jerked my line of credit. I can't shoot a frame without hard cash for the techs, and now this South American putz pulls a no-show."

Rich's eyes went from me to Fiora, then back, assessing our clothes. He must have recognized Fiora's dress for what it was—an expensive piece of wearable art.

"This film's really hot, a sure thing," he said. "ROI is five hundred percent in three years, guaranteed."

I looked bored, which wasn't hard.

"ROI is return on investment," he explained to Fiora.

She really was on her best behavior. She left his jugular intact.

"We're selling the partnership at ten grand a share," Rich said earnestly. "We'll work out any kind of invoicing arrangement your accountant wants. Double, triple, whatever. We can run as much money as you want through our accounts without . . . any . . ." His voice slowly dried up.

I looked at Rich and realized that he had shifted his focus from Fiora's dress to my sport coat, which had opened enough to reveal the Detonics in its harness under my right arm.

"Any amount within reason, of course," Rich added quickly. "Even movies can soak up only so much cash before people start asking where it's coming from."

Rich glanced uneasily at the butt of the gun again and did what screenwriters call "a fast fade to black." He was pure Hollywood; real blue steel made him nervous.

"Phony invoices," Fiora mused aloud. "That's why features end up costing fifty million bucks. Half of that money never existed in the first place, not until it got run through some shell corporation in Aruba."

A ripple of sound ran through the room. A group of Latinos had entered. Brad's banking reflexes were great: he'd already started snaking through the crowd toward the newcomers.

At first all I could see were the heads of three dark-haired men moving in wedge formation through the crowd. All three of the men were big; one of them was as big as me. His black eyes picked me out of the crowd instantly, paused long enough to memorize my face, then moved on. As his head turned, light gleamed from a small gold earring in his left ear.

The three men watched the crowd with the alert, expressionless faces of Secret Service men flanking a political candidate. Their charge turned out to be a handsome Creole wearing a tropical-weight suit and the benign smile of a parish priest in a holy-day procession.

The bodyguards recognized Brad. They parted, allowing him to move into the inner circle. Faustino greeted him amiably with a touch on the sleeve and a weak handshake. But the Creole's eyes never ceased canvasing the room, marking off the attendance against a mental list. No wonder the handmaidens of plutocracy had gathered so attentively. Faustino looked like a man who never forgot a slight. When he pressed on to greet other guests, Brad fell in half a step behind, a faithful altar boy. All of which was pretty much as expected.

What was surprising was the way Brad studiously avoided noticing the woman at Faustino's side. She was the same redhead who had nearly ravished him on the asphalt in front of the Royal Hawaiian. Now she ignored him. They stood two feet apart and couldn't see each other at all.

Fiora had seen her too. "I guess we know now who they were hiding their affair from. She must belong to Faustino. Ain't love grand."

I studied the party. Fiora's conclusion explained the available facts. But something didn't add up. Brad just didn't seem man enough to steal the boss's girl.

"Stay put right here," I told Fiora. "Don't commit us to a damn thing until I've had a private chat with our client's lying son."

I waited until Faustino was distracted by a blond starlet, then caught Brad's eye and gestured. He came rushing over like the well-trained gofer he was.

"Who's the redhead?" I asked bluntly.

He flushed beneath his saltwater tan. "Jill—Ms. Swann—is a tax consultant. She's been doing some work for Don Faustino."

"I thought she might be the physical fitness instructor from the Royal Hawaiian," I said. "She sure could teach me flat-back aerobics anytime. Tell me, wonder boy, does she charge by the hour?"

Ah, sweet innocence. Brad's flush deepened and he dropped his shoulder, trying to get his fist up and cocked to punch the leering grin off my face. He was game and mad as hell, but a few workouts at the health spa hadn't replaced what had been lost to cocaine. I caught his fist with one hand, turned his wrist, and twisted it behind his back. Everybody else was too busy watching the Don to notice as I levered Brad around and headed toward the terrace doors.

"Take it easy," I said between clenched teeth as I shoved him along. "You don't want to slug me. I'm the guy who's trying to save your ass."

He didn't like it, but his arm slowly began to relax.

"That's better," I said, releasing some of the pressure on his wrist and shoving him into the cool night air.

I gave the room behind me a fast scan. The tall bodyguard with the earring might have seen something, but if he had, he wasn't doing anything about it. I followed Brad out into the night and closed the glass doors behind me. The terrace overlooked Big Boat Row and the bay. It was deserted. Brad walked over to the wrought-iron rail and stared blankly at the small waves nibbling on the handsome, useless, million-dollar hulls.

"Dying for a toot, aren't you?"

He turned and gave me an angry look. "No."

"Good. That's how you know you're getting better. The pains get farther apart. Sort of the reverse of having a baby, although either way you end up with a new life."

"Who the hell are you?"

"Ask me something you don't know. Ask me how I found out you're screwing Faustino's redhead. Then I'll ask you how long you've been screwing her."

"None of your goddamn business!"

"Wrong again. You have a real talent for it."

"We don't need you! We can take care of everything. The bank will be clean. It will all work out. Just give us time to do it our own way!"

"Us?"

"Jill and me."

"Jill and you. Jesus, what a pair to draw to—a crooked banker and a crooked tax lawyer, riding off into the sunset together. What will you do for a living, set up abusive tax shelters?"

"Jill's not a crook. She's a . . . it's just that . . ."

I waited, but Brad didn't have words to describe Swann and he sure as hell hadn't liked mine. For a few unhappy minutes we listened to waves lap against hulls.

"And I suppose you're in love with her," I said finally.

"Yes." Quick, firm, positive.

"Shit." I sighed. "She's the one who drew you into this mess, isn't she?"

"No," he said instantly.

God in heaven. The poor guy didn't even have a clue. He had been trolled up by flashy bait, hooked, netted, gutted, filleted, and thrown on the grill. His skin was curling at the edges from the heat, and he thought he was still swimming around free.

"She worked for Faustino before you did," I said.

Brad nodded.

"Love at first sight, huh."

That stiffened Brad's jaw, but he nodded.

"What, exactly, does she do when she's not with you?"

"She sort of—" He stopped, helpless.

"Spit it out, wonder boy. Tell me what she does. Don't worry. I won't run to your mommy. I want to know, just between us men, what the redhead does outside of the sack that gives her a position on Faustino's right arm."

"You'll take it wrong."

"I'll take it any way I can get it. Talk."

Brad hesitated, then muttered, "She sort of helped Don Faustino set up the deal with me and she wants to set up a way for him to handle some money here without sending it back to Colombia."

Brad said it fast and run together, as though it would change the meaning or make the truth less painful. The pretty lady was a walking laundry, but her heart was pure. Just ask the fool who was in love with her.

"Then why is Ibañez carting around sacks of cash?" I asked. "Hasn't Jill ever heard of wire transfers?"

"She hasn't done any deals with Faustino yet. And damn it, she's not a crook!"

"Yeah. Right. Does she know about Fiora and me?"

Brad didn't like having to answer that one, which told me the answer.

"Christ, wonder boy. You're really something. How much did you tell her?"

"I told her you were consultants Mother had shoved down my throat. I didn't mean to, but I'm not real good at keeping secrets from Jill."

Pillow talk. Gets 'em every time.

"It's all right," Brad insisted. "She'd never tell Don Faustino. She's convinced her whole deal would fall through if he found out we were lovers. That's why we've had to be so careful. She loves me. She's not the kind of woman who would—"

"Save the glowing descriptions," I interrupted. "You'll need them when you take her home to Mother. Now shut up for a minute."

Brad shut up. I ran the new possibilities around in my head, cutting losses and looking for the least dangerous way to get the job done. There wasn't one. I was glad I had followed my gut instinct and worn the Detonics.

"All right," I said, "here's the new agenda. First, you'll introduce us to Faustino. Tell him we know everything you've done. Then leave us with him. Leave the party. Leave the building. Leave the city. Go to your mother's house and don't come out until we tell you to. Don't call your bank. Don't call a lawyer. Don't call anybody. Most especially, *don't call the redhead*. Got it?"

"But—"

"I mean it, wonder boy. You call that redhead and people will start dying. If that happens, I'll do everything I can to make sure she's the first to go."

"Who the hell do you think you—"

"And you'll be the second," I said flatly, talking over him. "It's time you learned that stupidity is a capital crime."

He looked at my eyes, shut his mouth, and headed back into the room, cutting a straight path for Faustino. I detoured long enough to pick up Fiora.

"Listen up," I said in her ear. "He told the redhead that we're financial consultants. Guess what? That's what the redhead does too. She's trying to dream up a way to launder Faustino's money without physically sending it out of the country. Still want to stay in the game, pretty lady?"

"Yes."

"Then you've got about thirty seconds to come up with a better laundry for Faustino's fifteen million."

"Legal?"

"Hell, no. Why should we handcuff ourselves? Nobody else does."

Fiora smiled her honey-blond, tiger-shark smile. "No problem. It's only the legal schemes that take time."

15

"SEÑOR D'AUBISSON," said Brad, "this is Fiddler."

Faustino's smile was as small and cool as a raindrop. He ignored the hand I held out to him.

"Thank you for the last-minute invitation, señor," I said. "We've been watching your transactions with Brad for some time. We're very impressed."

The smile didn't change, but a cold spark flashed in the brown depths of Faustino's eyes. He gave Brad the kind of look a mongoose gives a snake.

"I am disappointed, Brad," Faustino said softly. "What became of your promise that our banking transactions would remain confidential?"

I put my left arm around Brad, just like we were old buddies, and squeezed hard enough to be sure he wouldn't try to say anything. At the same time I continued to offer Faustino my hand.

"You don't think such a junior member of our staff could have handled your business all by himself?" I asked, giving the Latin tycoon a man-to-man smile. "Two senior staff members have been aware of your exchanges for some time. As Director of Security for Bank of the Southland, I'm one. Fiora Fleming is the other. She heads our international operations."

Fiora's last name wasn't Fleming, but she didn't mind. She knew I wasn't director of anyone's security except hers. Although she stepped forward on cue and smiled, she didn't offer the South American her hand.

Faustino's face said he still hadn't heard anything he liked. Cold, bleak eyes continued to measure me. He said a single word.

"Cochi."

The big man turned, telling me that he was Cochi Loco. All three bodyguards shifted unobtrusively to cordon us off from the rest of the party. Cochi Loco was clearly in charge. He had the look of a guy who could drive a Mercedes with gold trim, wear twelve gold earrings or none at all—and get away with it. Cochi Loco translated as Crazy Pig, but he looked more like a lean, tough, feral boar.

Standing beside Faustino, Cochi's eyes never left the right lapel of my coat, the lapel that covered the butt of the Detonics. Up close the man was even more impressive. His size became less memorable than the bleak intelligence of his inspection. If I were Faustino, I'd be torn between anointing the man my heir apparent and shooting him in self-defense.

"Brad has done an excellent job with your transactions," Fiora said, using her cool, reserved business voice. "However, we wanted to make you aware of the variety of services we could provide for an international businessman such as yourself."

"It seems that everyone in the United States has a plan for my money." Faustino's voice was both amused and cold as he looked around the party. "Miss Swann has been offering to provide similar services for some time."

Fiora's eyebrows raised slightly as she looked Swann over

with the cool thoroughness of a madam appraising a potential employee.

"There's an important difference between Ms. Swann and me," Fiora said.

"Of course," Faustino said. "You are blond."

Fiora's smile was leashed.

"Does Ms. Swann have the resources of a full-service financial institution such as Bank of the Southland?" Fiora asked.

Swann had been examining Fiora carefully, as only one beautiful woman can examine another, looking for flaws and weaknesses.

"I maintain relationships with several banks," Swann said.

"That's not the same as controlling one, is it?" Fiora looked at Faustino, dismissing the redhead in the tight red dress. "You are an intelligent, sophisticated man," Fiora continued. "Your business has special needs. I doubt that you intend to entrust your delicate financial problems to a simple laundress—in your own language, *una chingada.*"

The Spanish verb *chingar* is hard to translate and invariably crude. It suggests a kind of rhythmic scrubbing like the motions of a professional washerwoman. The redhead must have known some gutter Spanish. Her eyelids flinched at the deliberately insulting play on words.

Faustino liked the pun, particularly from the lips of a beautiful woman. The corners of his mouth twitched. Cochi Loco reacted, too. For a few seconds his black eyes looked as though they were alive with more than violent calculations.

But talking dirty in two languages wasn't enough. Faustino began to turn away. Fiora threw me a look that told me to do something, so I played the only trump we had.

"Financial problems are Ms. Fleming's specialty. Security is mine. You could use some help in that area too. Urgently. You have internal problems you may not be aware of."

Faustino's glance flicked sideways to Cochi Loco. The Don asked a quick question in Spanish. His accent was so odd I had to concentrate to catch any meaning. The big bodyguard made a curt negative gesture with his head.

"There is nothing amiss," Faustino said, turning back to me with cool disdain.

"Are you sure?" I asked. "You have a courier called Ysidro Ibañez, correct?"

Faustino didn't answer, but he did stop moving and start listening.

"I should say you *used* to have a courier named Ibañez," I continued. "Now somebody else has him."

Cochi Loco made a sound like I'd just pissed in his shoe.

"Such a thing can be easily checked," Faustino said softly.

"Then do it."

He didn't like my tone of voice. He snapped his fingers. One of the smaller bodyguards did an about-face and moved to a telephone on the bar. We all stood around looking nonchalant while the bodyguard punched in a number quickly. He let the number ring a good long time. No one answered. He hung up and punched in the same number or another one. Either way, there was still no answer. He looked back at us for instructions.

This time Faustino let Cochi Loco snap his fingers.

"Where is Ibañez, Mr. Fiddler?" Faustino asked.

"Just Fiddler. We don't stand on ceremony around here."

"Where is Ibañez?"

"I don't know. Two men kidnapped him at gunpoint this morning. Black men."

Fiora listened to my lie with a cool blank expression on her face. Faustino studied me thoughtfully, then grunted a single phrase that I recognized as Spanish but couldn't understand. Cochi Loco lifted his glance from the outline of the Detonics and looked at my eyes for what seemed like ten minutes. I waited it out.

I had long since lowered my hand, but Don Faustino now offered his, breaking the impasse. I took it. His handshake was mild, yet he held on a bit longer than he needed to. It was a strongman's reminder that power wasn't merely physical.

"I'm very pleased to meet you, Fiddler. And you too, Miss Fleming," Faustino added, turning to Fiora. He took the slender hand she offered, bowed over it, and kissed it with practiced courtliness. "It would be my pleasure to have both of you join me for dinner."

Faustino straightened, offered Fiora his arm, and patted her fingertips when she accepted.

"Come to the wine cellar where we can talk frankly," he said, smiling. "Miss Swann, Mr. Simms, this way, please."

"Brad won't be able to join us," I said. "He has other duties to attend to."

Faustino shrugged, agreeing. "Some other time, my friend."

Brad managed a harried smile, a half bow, and an exit. The redhead noticed his departure with about as much interest as she had taken in his presence.

The three bodyguards moved ahead of us, creating a smooth flying wedge through the crowd. Since everybody was being gallant, I offered Jill Swann my arm. She gave me an icy blue stare and walked to the wine cellar unescorted.

The cellar was dark and cool, evoking unpleasant images of dungeons and torture. I told myself it was just nerves. I didn't like being outgunned three to one with Fiora depending on me. Cochi Loco cleared out stray party guests with a broad-shouldered finesse that was surprising. He might have been a gunsel, but somebody had taken off his rough edges.

While the room was being emptied of unwanted guests, I prowled the wine racks. The West Coast Club had paid for some very good wine advice. Their 1978s included not only the Heitz Martha's Vineyard but the Bella Oaks as well. I pulled a bottle of Bella Oaks out of its sleeve.

"Tell me, señor," I said, turning to Faustino, "do you like good wine?"

He looked faintly amused. "Of course."

"Some say this is one of the finest cabernets in the world. It certainly is one of the best in California."

"As you wish," he said, shrugging.

There was a wine steward's table in one corner of the cellar. Clean glasses, corkscrew, everything in its place. The cork made a subdued yet unmistakable sound as I drew it from the bottle. The wine caught and held candlelight beautifully, creating a ruby glow in each glass. A waiter appeared, offering to take over the job, but I ignored him. I offered glasses to the two women, then picked up the other two glasses and handed one to Faustino. I didn't bother offering any to Cochi Loco. He was present, but he had taken on the social invisibility peculiar to carpets and very good bodyguards.

"To clean money," I said, holding the glass in my right hand.

Four glasses lifted. The wine was good enough to command silence. Faustino sipped again, then said something to Cochi Loco, who had stationed himself a step behind and to the side of his boss's right shoulder. Cochi Loco moved to one of the other bodyguards and said something in a low voice. The bodyguard left the room. Cochi Loco returned to his station behind Faustino.

A moment later the short bodyguard reappeared with waiters bearing trays of soft cheeses, four kinds of pâté, and a thin-sliced baguette of crusty bread.

It was all very deft, this establishing of a pecking order. My treat. No, my treat. Let me educate you in the niceties of fine wine. But let *me* show you how easily I can spend money, how civilized and sophisticated I can be.

Faustino was smooth and competent. He had been born to this. He must have been valuable to the uncouth cowboys of the cartel; he was a man who fronted for them, who moved their money around, who got rich at their expense.

The four of us gathered around the food and made appropriate noises as we picked through the goodies. I watched Swann closely out of the corner of my eye. In spite of the circumstances, she seemed at ease. She was also doing a hell of a job of fading into the woodwork, waiting and watching and speaking only when spoken to. Underneath that red hair and flashy dress was a quick, calculating brain.

That was a disappointment; I had been hoping she had the IQ of well-trimmed ivy.

Immediate appetite satisfied, Faustino settled back in a chair, inspected the depth of the wine's color in front of a candle, and said calmly, "Tell me about Ysidro Ibañez. He is a very trusted, very valued employee."

"He came to the Newport Beach branch this morning, by appointment."

Faustino nodded.

I thought fast, choosing among truths, half-truths, and lies more carefully than I had chosen among the pâtés. If I hoped to get to Ibañez before Faustino, I had to send that slick Creole on a wild goose chase.

"He exchanged six hundred and twenty thousand in small bills for new one hundreds," I said. "Then he left. As it happened, I was at the bank, doing an unannounced survey of security. A few minutes after Ibañez left, so did I. About a mile from the bank, I saw his car pulled over to the side of the road. As I arrived, he was being hustled into another car by two men."

"Did you know them?"

"No."

"What did they look like?"

I shrugged. "I wasn't all that close. They were black, probably in their twenties. They wore enough gold jewelry to make bail on your average felony arrest. They were armed."

Generic rather than specific, simple, plausible, and misleading. All the ingredients of a good false trail.

Faustino tried to look through me with his dark, hooded eyes. "Did Ysidro go willingly with these men?"

"He had an Ingram submachine gun pointed at his head. All I had was a pistol." I shrugged again. "I stayed out of it."

"Where did you say this happened?"

"On San Joaquin Hills Road. His car might still be parked there. It wasn't that long ago."

While I spoke, Fiora had been toying with her wineglass, running her elegant index finger around the crystal rim, setting up subtle vibrations in the crystal as she waited and listened to our conversation. Faustino was doing the same, except that he toyed with his mustache, not his wineglass, and he used his middle knuckle rather than his index finger.

"You were the only witness?" he asked.

"It's an expensive residential area. The homes have high walls and the streets don't see much traffic."

"Did you see the license plates of the other car?"

"I ran the plates but it was a rental. Dead end."

"How convenient for the kidnappers. And for you. All I have is your word that things happened as you have said."

Fiora bore down with her index finger on the rim of the wineglass with just enough force to draw forth a haunting crystal cry. The pure, beautiful note broke the mood of Faustino's bleak inquisition. He looked at her.

"The truth is rarely convenient," she said. "We would prefer to tell you that our banking business can continue as usual, but this kind of incident could jeopardize our standing in the financial community. Think of that, señor. We have no reason to lie about what Fiddler saw."

Faustino studied Fiora as though amused that a woman would speak out while men were taking care of business.

"I can think of six hundred and twenty thousand reasons to lie," he said coolly.

"Are you familiar with the story of the goose that laid golden eggs?" she countered.

Faustino's eyes narrowed. He nodded, but he didn't like being referred to as a goose, not even elliptically. His glance flicked over Fiora's face, then moved over her body, finally settling on her modest décolletage with an insult she would have to have been blind to miss.

"If the parallel between yourself and a goose is unpleasant," Fiora continued gently, "ask yourself why we would be here tonight if we were thieves."

Faustino continued to survey Fiora's breasts as though she had offered them both for a price and he was considering a counter offer. Fiora's jade-green glance moved from her host to Swann.

"Have you noticed how easily boys are distracted?" Fiora asked.

Swann smiled coldly. "If you don't like it, you shouldn't wear silk."

"Men control their sexuality," Fiora said. "Boys are controlled by it. I do business with the former and tie the latter into tiny little knots." Fiora glanced back at Faustino. "Which are you, man or boy?"

Jesus Christ, Fiora.

I felt my right hand tingle. The air smelled burned, as if lightning had struck. Cochi of the gold earring and bleak eyes must have felt a similar shot of adrenaline. He too was poised, ready, awaiting the signal.

Faustino smiled, then laughed softly, deeply. It might even have been genuine. He held his wineglass toward Fiora in silent toast, swirled the deep red liquid in its crystal prison, and drank.

Fiora lifted her own glass to Faustino and said, "If there had been any doubt of the answer, I would never have asked the question."

There was no doubt about Faustino's smile and laugh this time.

"But at the same time," Fiora continued, "I'm surprised to find that you are still relying on such unsophisticated methods of handling your international finances as flying actual cash around the world."

The Creole's smile disappeared. "I wasn't aware that you knew much about my international activities. My business with your bank has been limited to a relatively minor series of exchanges."

"Minor but revealing," she said.

"Really? Please explain."

Fiora sipped her wine delicately. "There's only one reason to turn small bills into hundreds, and that's to save space. Mice are easier to smuggle than elephants."

A smile flickered briefly on Faustino's face.

"Given that, the logical assumption is that you are moving currency offshore," Fiora said, shrugging, "either to Mexico or perhaps to Panama, and depositing it there. As a method of transferring money, physical transportation is slow, cumbersome, and invites loss through theft."

Faustino's thin eyebrows rose. "It is a way of maintaining privacy in one's financial transactions. The United States government seems intent on turning bankers into police informants. I am an honest man who has nothing to hide, but that does not mean I wish my competitors to know how much money I have at all times."

"Have you ever heard of exemptions from the currency reporting law?" Fiora asked blandly.

Faustino's expression became more attentive than it had been when he was leering over her breasts. "Exemptions? I thought the rules applied to all transactions of ten thousand dollars or more."

Fiora flicked a sideways glance at Jill Swann, but said only, "I'll have someone send you a copy of the Treasury Department banking rules. There are many loopholes in the reporting requirement."

For the first time, Faustino's smile was wide and genuine. "I am more interested in the loopholes than I am in the rules, Miss Fleming."

"So am I, señor," Fiora replied.

For a moment I was uneasy. I couldn't tell whether she was lying or telling the truth.

"I can see, señorita, that we have much to talk about," Faustino said, shifting in his easy chair to face Fiora more fully. "But first I have another concern." He glanced in my direction. "Tell me, señor, would you recognize those two black men if you saw them again?"

"Their faces?" I shrugged. "I was more interested in their weapons."

A slight movement of Faustino's fingers brought the biggest bodyguard forward.

"Rafael, this is Fiddler. Take him with you on your search. I am sure his memory is excellent."

It was an order, not an invitation. It meant that I had to go down the false trail I had created and have Faustino's big gunsel with me every step of the way. But that wasn't the worst of it. With me gone, Fiora was on her own with the two remaining gunsels and a businessman who left a trail of slime whenever he moved.

Fiora looked at me, silently asking me not to blow the whole deal to hell.

"If you both hurry, you will be back in time for dessert," Faustino continued. He turned to me. "Fiddler, this is my assistant Rafael Cardona Saenz, but you may call him Cochi Loco. I recently recruited him from the organization of one of my clients. I think he has the makings of a fine international banker."

Banker, my ass, unless it was the Bank of Styx.

Cochi didn't offer to shake hands. Neither did I. He was worried about protecting his right hand—his gun hand. I was simply angry at the situation and at myself. If I went with Cochi, I had to leave Fiora alone, a guest in name but a hostage in truth. If I didn't go with Cochi, I would put everything in danger—Brad and his mother, Jaime and his father, the community bank Fiora was so intent on saving, the whole damn lot.

I yanked the phone pager off my belt and held my hand out to Fiora.

"Give me your purse. The pager might go off at the wrong moment."

"It usually does," she said, handing me her small purse.

I opened the gold clasp and dropped the pager inside. At the same time, I made sure the rectangular leather cigarette case was there. It was. Fiora doesn't smoke, but the .25-caliber Beretta inside the case has been known to.

It wasn't much. Small comforts never are.

I turned to Cochi Loco and jerked my thumb toward the door, impatient to get the wild goose chase over with.

16

JAIME HAD BEEN RIGHT. The chrome trim on Cochi Loco's white Mercedes 560SEC had been replaced with gold. There's no luster like it. I had a good chance to inspect the tri-star emblem on the back deck when Cochi raised the trunk lid and removed a hand-held electronics unit in a black box. He ran up a two-foot antenna on the box and walked all the way around the car, probing with the antenna, paying special attention to the wheel wells and the spaces beneath the bumper.

While he was busy, I rubbed the emblem with my sleeve. It buffed up like the queen's salt cellars. Even the pigtail antenna for the cellular phone had been gold plated. This guy was thorough.

"Pardon me, señor."

Cochi Loco's English was accented but quite clear. I moved away from the trunk.

"Do not move, please. A moment, only."

He pointed the antenna of the black box at me and began tracing the outlines of my body, paying special attention to my crotch, armpits, belt, and legs, the usual places where body transmitters are hidden. I let him finish enough of the job so that there wouldn't be a hassle. Then I knocked the antenna aside.

"I don't think I want to hang around with you guys," I said. "Anybody who has to check his car every fifteen minutes for RF transmitters is too hot for me."

Cochi Loco grunted, considered pushing me to submit to another round of inspection, then decided he had covered the major bases. He hefted the bug detector in his broad palm.

"I know my car is clean," he said with a slight smile. "Can you say the same for yours?"

I changed directions. "You're a little late getting to me. If I had been a cop wearing a wire, I'd already have enough of your boss on tape to make a DA drool."

Cochi's smile didn't inspire a warm feeling in my gut.

"Why do you think we meet in the wine cellar, señor?" he asked in a deep voice. "The walls are reinforced. A body transmitter cannot go through fifteen inches of concrete and steel."

With another grunt Cochi collapsed the telescoping antenna and tossed the RF detector into the trunk. Then he unsnapped a Halliburton case and opened the lid, revealing two guns nested within custom-cut protective padding. One gun was a stainless-steel revolver with a heavy, vented four-inch barrel. The other was a blocky-looking semiautomatic pistol.

Cochi cracked the cylinder of the revolver and loaded it from a box of .44 magnum hollow-point rounds. Then he shoved the three-pound pistol into a shoulder holster beneath his coat and went to work on the second gun. The automatic had a thick magazine that looked able to hold half a box of ammunition. The magazine was made of some kind of tough composite material. So were the handle grips and the frame of the gun itself.

The only plastic pistol in the world is the Glock. It slides right through metal detectors, but that's not why it's made. It's exceptionally accurate and it weighs half as much as the

average 9-millimeter. Those are the kind of features only a
pistolero can appreciate.

Cochi shoved the Glock into his waistband on the side
opposite the Magnum, closed up the case, and slammed
down the trunk lid, ready to hunt elephants with one hand
and hold off a reinforced infantry squad with the other.

"You will drive," Cochi said, tossing me a single key. "I
will tell you directions as we go."

I snagged the key and snapped it back at him in the same
motion. "I'm not your chauffeur."

The key smacked against Cochi's palm. His look said that
he didn't like my attitude. That lent a nice symmetry to the
relationship. I didn't like his.

"I have business on the telephone, señor," Cochi said after
a moment. "It will be better, more helpful, if you drive."

Not an order. A request.

"Always glad to be of help." I held out my hand for the
key.

His grin was feral. It revealed his eye teeth. They were
unusually long, like a wild boar's. He dropped the key into
my hand.

Cochi gave clear, concise road directions while I drove out
of the parking structure and turned north on Coast Highway.
As soon as we were in the open, he picked up the cellular
phone. Speaking in idiomatic Spanish that was almost a
dialect, he made three local calls in quick succession, looking for Ysidro Ibañez.

In the pinkish glow of the dashboard lights, Cochi's blunt,
handsome face lost more and more humanity with each
phone call. By the time he directed me off Coast Highway
and onto a residential street behind the Bolsa Chica power
plant, he looked like a savage stone icon carved on a sacri-
ficial altar.

The neighborhood Cochi directed me to was made up of
three- and four-bedroom, two-bath, single-family homes
built in the 1950s and designed to last no longer than the
the thirty-year term of a GI loan. Once Bolsa Chica had been

Orange County white bread. Now the original owners were cashing out and moving to retirement homes in Indio or Desert Hot Springs. The second wave of settlers was southern California ethnic—Pacific Rim, multicultural, multilingual, multiracial.

At Cochi's instructions I parked in front of a ranch-style house that was surrounded by an industrial strength chainlink fence. The fence looked like overkill to me. The house was nothing special and the yard was an unremarkable scattering of succulents. Someone there thought privacy was valuable. The gate was chained shut with a heavy padlock.

The more I saw, the less I liked. I was beginning to get that old familiar feeling. I thought of Uncle Jake's strategy—hide in plain sight. I wondered what was hidden in plain sight here.

Cochi drew a key ring out of his pocket and sorted through five or six similar keys before he found the one that fit this particular lock. The house was dark and silent, but Cochi Loco was more cautious than his nickname implied. He pulled out the Glock and held it against his leg. Cursing silently about wild goose chases and crazy pigs, I stood to one side, my hand on the butt of the holstered Detonics.

Cochi banged on the frame of the aluminum screen, trying to lure somebody to the front door. Nobody took the bait. He hammered on the door again. The house remained dark and silent. He opened the screen, tried the doorknob, and found it locked. He tried one key, then a second, then muttered an impatient curse. With the easy grace of Baryshnikov at the bar, he squared off, lifted his right foot, and slammed an expensive leather loafer into the door just above the knob, about where a dead-bolt latch would be.

The hollow-core door shattered with a dry report and swung open. Just inside the door was a light switch. Cochi found it, flipped it on, and went inside. Before I followed, I took a fast last look around to make sure we hadn't drawn a crowd of back-shooters. We hadn't.

The furniture in the living room had an aura of well-used

impermanence, as though everything had been rented many times by many different tenants. The present tenant had tried to soften the impression of transience with personal touches—religious portraits and a hand-painted shawl on the wall, colorful woven throw pillows on the couch, and framed family pictures on top of the blond oak cabinet that contained the television.

Cochi quickly moved through the living room, checked the kitchen, and strode toward the back of the house. I started to follow, then stopped to get a better look at the photos.

Jaime Ibañez grinned out of one of the picture frames. The other picture was a department store portrait of the rest of the family: Ysidro Ibañez, his round-faced, dark-haired wife, and a girl who looked about six years old. Even in the cheap portrait, burn scars were visible on the little girl's face and neck, as well.

Ibañez must have been in a hell of a rush to leave. He hadn't even stopped to gather the family photos.

There were three bedrooms in the back of the house. The bigger one had a sagging double bed. The smaller one had a mattress on the floor and broken crayons in the corner. The third bedroom was where business was done. There was a machine the size of a postage meter on a table and several cardboard cartons stacked in one corner. The only unusual feature of the room was a new door, solid wood and unpainted, on the small closet.

Impatient or not, Cochi knew he wasn't going to kick his way through that door. He sorted through the ring of keys methodically, looking for the one that fit the doorknob lock and the shiny brass dead-bolt lock that had been inset above.

I inspected the currency counter on the table and the cartons in the corner. The top box was half full of rolls of tape, the kind used by duct workers. The bottom carton held a stack of tissue-thin square plastic sheeting, a box of double-strength rubber bands, and several sheaves of currency wrapper bands.

Cochi finally got both locks undone. He swung the door open, snapped on an interior light, and began growling oaths that relied heavily on beasts and religious figures in unlikely intercourse. When he turned around, I looked past his broad shoulders. The closet was as empty as Cochi Loco's eyes.

"I suppose that's where your trusted employee kept the cash," I said.

The look Cochi gave me was as bestial as his oaths had been. He shouldered past me, out of the bedroom and out of the house. When I caught up with him, he was already climbing into the passenger seat of the Mercedes.

"How much did you lose?"

Ignoring me, Cochi slammed the door hard enough to make the heavy car rock. He stared straight out through the windshield. A mercury-vapor streetlight shed ugly purplish light on the cedar-shake roofs, mowed dichondra lawns, and the bodyguard's harsh features. I slid into the driver's seat and confronted him.

"How much is missing? Are you and Faustino out of business?"

"As much money as your bank exchanged through Ibañez is gone," Cochi said finally. "More than fifteen million dollars. Don Faustino will be angry. So will your blond banker. She will have nothing to pry out of him, nothing to play with." Cochi's bared teeth flashed coldly in the mercury-vapor light as he turned toward me. "How did *los negros* look? Describe them."

One look at Cochi's face told me that I'd better start to remember faces. Fast. Without missing a beat, I described Bill Cosby and Bubba Smith, right down to the gap in Bubba's front teeth.

Cochi thought about it for several minutes. Then he grunted and settled back into his seat.

"Do you know the place called North Long Beach?"

"Yeah."

"Go there."

I didn't think Bill Cosby or Bubba Smith lived there, but

I decided not to argue the toss. While I drove back to Warner
and headed for the San Diego Freeway, Cochi got on the
phone again. He made two calls in English. Both numbers
had a different area code. At each number, he asked for Freeway Ricky. The second time, somebody must have given
him some grief.

"Why? Do not ask why," Cochi said coldly. "I ask. You
answer. Where is he?"

I could just make out a loud voice in the receiver, back
chat from a man with a black ghetto accent.

"I do not care if his mother is dying!" Cochi snarled. "I
will see him and I will see him quick!"

The voice at the other end of the line dropped in volume.

"Direct me," Cochi ordered.

There was silence while Cochi listened.

"Very good, Day-rel," Cochi said, leaning on the separate
syllables of the name in derisive imitation of black English
cadences. "Now, listen to me. If you call him before I get
there, I will come back and cut off your cock and balls and
stuff them through the hole I will make in your throat."

The guy on the other end of the line lost his taste for
argument. Cochi hung up.

"To deal with such men disgusts me," he muttered. "Do
you know how Freeway earned his name? His men shot a
child while driving on the freeway. How do you say it? A
chicken-shit shooting?"

"That's how I'd say it, but newspapers can't use the word.
They call them 'drive-by' shootings."

Cochi shrugged his broad soldiers and lost interest in the
subject. "Do you know a street called Alondra?"

"It's off the Long Beach Freeway."

He grunted. "Alondra and Sedgewick, west of the Number
Seven Freeway and south of Alondra. It is a black barrio,
yes?"

I nodded.

With another grunt Cochi went back to the cellular phone,
this time punching numbers for what seemed like thirty

seconds; international access, country code, the whole works. The conversation was in clear Spanish, one home boy to another.

"Hey, Panesso, screw your mother," Cochi said cheerfully. "What's happening?"

I couldn't hear the answer.

"Listen, has anybody down there heard from that cuckold Ibañez?"

The answer seemed to be negative.

"No calls, eh? Not even to that scrawny bastard son of his?" Cochi pulled out a cigarette, lit it, and blew smoke.

I hit the window button to let in some fresh air.

"Do me a favor, Panesso. Go find that kid and ask him when he last heard from his papa. Then call me back."

Bloody hell.

Don Faustino and friends were about to discover that they had lost their only twist on Ysidro Ibañez—his hostage son. I started refiguring the angles of the lies I had told and the new ones I would have to tell.

I didn't like any of them.

17

COCHI LOCO was silent for perhaps ten minutes, lost in his own thoughts, making his own computations of angles and trajectories. While he thought, he slowly rolled his head on his neck and shrugged, loosening his trapezius muscles. Either he had studied José Canseco or they took the same steroids and built the same thick necks. After a moment he dropped the back of the seat a few inches, leaned against the padded headrest, and closed his eyes.

For a time there was only silence in the car, a quiet that was underlined by the faint, low growl of the perfectly tuned German engine.

"You drive well, señor," Cochi said finally without opening his eyes. "Would you like a job?"

"I've got one."

"Don Faustino pays very well. A man such as you could be a millionaire within six months. All you have to do is drive money from place to place. No contraband, just money. We need an American like you, a man who knows about money, a man who carries a gun without strutting, a man who can keep his mouth shut."

"Thanks but no thanks. There are some—er, side benefits to my present position."

"The blonde?" Cochi shook his head and made a sucking sound through his teeth. "That one is a—how do you say it?—a man-eater. She will take your balls and your cock as well."

"She likes everything better right where it is."

He half smiled, shook his head, and fell silent again, leaving me to my fate at the blonde's indelicate hands.

Traffic was light. The big Mercedes was made for eighty miles an hour. We were approaching the 605 when the cellular phone buzzed at my elbow. Cochi picked it up without opening his eyes. What he heard jolted him like 220 volts of electricity. He sat straight up and fast.

"Gone? Panesso, if you are joking I will kill you!"

Twelve minutes from question to answer. Cochi and Panesso and whoever else was involved had quite an intercontinental organization.

"How long has he been gone? Then guess, cretin! A few hours? A few days? Weeks?"

I could hear Panesso's voice now, high-pitched and frightened, trying to explain how a boy had managed to escape house arrest and not be missed.

"Yes, yes, he is probably lost in the jungle," Cochi said. "But if he is not, you will be lapping the shit out of your own intestines. *Find him.*"

Cochi slammed the receiver into its cradle so hard he chipped the walnut veneer on the Mercedes console.

"Trouble?" I asked.

A grunt was the only reply.

Sedgewick and Alondra was no more remarkable than the neighborhood we had just left: a little older, maybe, and black rather than Latino. North Long Beach becomes Compton somewhere along the line, but life doesn't change much for anybody.

Surprisingly, Cochi's white Mercedes blended right in. There were a half-dozen fancy cars—BMWs and Mercedeses and one Thunderbird Turbocoupe—already parked on the street in front of the two-story frame house. Iron bars covered the windows and doors. The property was surrounded by a battered chain-link fence. The front yard looked like a war had been fought in it.

Jesus, Fiora, what have you gotten us into now?

"That the house?" I asked.

"*Sí.* It is what they call a cookhouse. It is where *los negros* turn our gentle white lady into the screaming demon called crack."

He grunted again, the chesty sound of a pig expecting food. I began to understand how he got the front half of his nickname. Wondering about the back half of his name made me nervous. The last thing I wanted to do was take on a crack house with a crazy asshole at my side. But it was too late now. Decision point was past.

"How are these folks likely to feel about unexpected visitors?" I asked.

"Unhappy. Park here. We go in together."

Fly or die.

I pulled in between a glistening black BMW and a battered 60s Cadillac urban assault vehicle. Cochi got out slowly, stretched, and humped his back, rolling his shoulders, a big man glad to be out of even the Mercedes' luxurious confines. He yawned. He was about to storm the kind of crack house LAPD used urban tanks to subdue, and he was utterly relaxed. I began to understand how he had gotten the second half of his nickname.

The son of a bitch really was crazy.

But not stupid. He understood the tactical value of an innocent appearance. Without fanfare we headed back along the street, a pair of fools on an evening stroll. There was a lookout, a black teenager with a dark rolled-bandanna headband, leaning against one of the cars at the curb, toying with a glass crack pipe. He must have been sampling his own product, for he stared at us without quite comprehending our reality.

By the time he decided we might be trouble, it was too late. Cochi Loco reached out with one powerful hand, grabbed him by the throat, and stretched him up on his tiptoes. Then Cochi used his free hand to stuff the stainless-steel barrel of the Magnum revolver into the kid's ear.

"Not one word," Cochi said softly.

The lookout made choking sounds. Cochi wasn't impressed. He kept his grip on the kid's throat, making him toe-dance on the broken concrete sidewalk all the way to the front door. Cochi moved to one side and nodded toward the door. I pulled the Detonics with my left hand and tried the knob gently with my right. It turned in my hand. I twisted the knob until the latch was fully withdrawn before I gave Cochi a signal and threw the door open.

Cochi's shoulders bunched as he literally threw the frightened lookout through the doorway and into the house. He followed like a hunting cat, crouched, holding the Magnum with two hands, pointing it with his entire body. I cocked the Detonics and went in the same way, cursing the circumstances that had me paired with a nut case who thought he was a one-man SWAT team.

The lookout lay in a stunned, twitching heap on the floor against the far wall of the entryway. In the adjacent living room, two young black men sat on a tattered couch. Their hands were empty. They wore leather jackets with singlets underneath. Wool Lakers caps sat backwards on their heads. They had been watching an ancient, fuzzy black and white television set in the corner, but now they were focused on the muzzle of Cochi's Magnum.

An AK-47 with a banana clip leaned against the wall at one end of the couch. A short-barreled pump shotgun with a chopped stock lay on a coffee table. Both weapons were just out of reach of the two men on the couch.

The house stank of chemicals and human filth. Sounds came from behind the closed door in what was probably the kitchen: two men arguing so loudly they hadn't heard the lookout hit the wall. Wordlessly, Cochi looked at me and

jerked his thumb toward the door. The motion looked sus-
piciously like another direct order, but this was no time to
show a divided front. I moved quietly toward the voices.

The house had been built a long time ago, back when a
swinging door between kitchen and dining room was standard equipment. I listened at the door for an instant, then
eased it open a crack and looked inside.

The room was littered with torn plastic wrappers and
institutional-size boxes of Arm & Hammer baking soda. Two
young bloods were at work. One had a carefully trimmed
Afro flattop with wide, shaved sidewalls over his prominent
ears. He wore a big gold hoop in his left ear, a flashy watch,
and enough gold rings and necklaces to open a jewelry store.
The other man was six-three or more, beefy but soft, like
an interior lineman gone to seed. He wore a couple of kilos
of gold too. Beneath all the metal, the men were stripped
down to sweaty singlets and loose cotton sweatpants. At the
moment both men were hovering around a gas stove, carefully placing capped baby bottles full of milky white liquid
in large flat-bottomed pans of boiling water.

"Flash one of them others, cuz," the one with the flat-top
said. "See if they's cooked."

His voice was thick, soft, gentle. The voice of a preacher,
a pimp, or a candy man.

The second man gingerly picked up a bottle from the other
pan on the stove. He shook the bottle very gently.

"Yeah, we's ready," he said, examining the thin, milky
liquid. He shoved the hot Pyrex bottle into a pan of ice water
on a cluttered table and cackled. "Sucker *did* rock up!"

He showed his buddy the pure cocaine that was crystal-
lizing inside the cooling bottle.

"Ice them," said Flattop.

The Detonics preceded me into the hot, stinking kitchen.
The two bloods were both so busy admiring the bottle they
didn't even notice me.

"Put it down, slowly," I said.

They stared at me for a long moment. Then they exchanged a single questioning glance.

"Don't," I said flatly. "I'm not a cop. I don't need probable cause to kill you."

The bigger of the two men slowly raised his hands and said to his partner, "Put it down, cuz."

"Ricky," complained the other, "we don't ice these muthas, we lose the whole batch."

"Plenty more where that came from, right?" Freeway Ricky said, giving me a big grin.

I stepped to the side of the doorway and motioned them out of the kitchen. Freeway moved through the door with the muscular, crow-footed shuffle of a weight lifter. When he saw Cochi Loco, Freeway broke into a grin and started to lower his hands. "Cochi! Your man here 'bout scared me half to death! Why you here?"

The bloods worked well as a team. When Cochi turned to look at Freeway, one of the two men on the couch shifted, inching closer to the shotgun on the coffee table. Cochi had covered Freeway and the other cook with his revolver, so I pointed the Detonics in the direction of the two on the couch and shook my head. It was the only warning they would get and they knew it. They went back to sitting very still.

Freeway nodded at me in my Brooks Brothers blazer. "Who he? The Man?"

The voice was strident now, and far too loud.

"Be calm," Cochi said. "This will all be over very quickly and then you will have your answers."

"I ain't doing nothing till I find out what you think you doing! You got no call busting in here with guns, rousting us! We good customers!"

Freeway was yelling full out now. It could have been anger or fear or both together. Cochi laid the stainless steel barrel of his revolver along the naked skull above Freeway's ear.

"Shut up," Cochi said quietly.

Freeway finally got the message. Cochi glanced at me

questioningly. I moved back into the living room as though to get a better look at the men. On the way I wiped the shotgun off the table and kicked it into a corner, a little farther out of reach. The Kalashnikov followed with a clatter. A small lamp burned on the table. I tilted the shade until the light was aimed directly into the room.

Freeway started up again. "Don't do that shit!" he objected, his voice rising to a yell despite the gun barrel against his ear. "What you doing with those guns, man? You gonna kill us or what?"

Cochi flicked the barrel of the gun. It wasn't a hard rap, just enough to get Freeway's attention. He shut up and stood very still. Trying to make it look good, I walked until I was in front of the other cook.

"Smile," I said.

He stared blankly at me.

"Show me your teeth."

It wasn't a smile, but it got the job done. He had a gap between his two front teeth. Other than that, he didn't much resemble my description of Ysidro's kidnappers. I wondered how many crack houses Cochi would break into until somebody got killed or we found a black man who looked more like Bill Cosby.

I stared at each of the other four men in turn, including the lookout, who still was slumped against the wall. I was about to break the bad news to Cochi that these weren't Ibañez's kidnappers when I caught a flicker of movement in the shadows at the top of the stairs.

Suddenly I knew why Freeway Ricky had been making so much noise.

"Freeze!"

It was the only thing I had time to say, but it was too late to pull punches and I knew it. Even as I spoke, I was bringing the Detonics up and the muzzle of an Uzi was swinging toward me. Before the shooter could bring the gun to bear, I triggered five rapid shots, aiming for the spaces between the close-set posts of the stair railing.

Two of the shots shattered wooden posts. The other three found a softer target. The gunman slammed against the opposite wall and the Uzi made a terrible racket as it clattered down the stairs. The gunman's body followed, face down. He made a lot less noise.

I kept the Detonics muzzle on the staircase shadows, but no one else appeared. My ears rang from the sound of the five shots. I was disoriented, floating on pure sound. Automatically I shifted position until I could watch the stairway and the living room at the same time.

Cochi Loco had his back to me. He was holding Freeway by the shirt and covering the others with the Magnum. I don't think the bodyguard had even turned around to see why I fired.

"All clear," I said.

My voice sounded flat, inhuman. Cochi turned and glanced at the stairway and then at me. His eyes had the color and warmth of obsidian.

"Well?" he said. "Are these the men?"

I shook my head.

Cochi motioned with his head toward the front door. As I pushed it open, Freeway Ricky found his tongue again.

"You gonna pay for this, assholes! Nobody messes with Freeway! Nobody!"

"Don't worry about your reputation," I said. "Worry about the guy face down on the stairs."

I pulled the front door closed behind me and jogged to the car. The Mercedes started on the first try. Cochi must have been waiting for the sound of the engine. A moment later he backed through the front door with the shotgun and the AK under one arm and the Magnum in the other hand. When he got to the bottom of the stairs, he tossed the two long guns into the bushes.

Watching the front door, he backed across the lawn. Halfway to the curb he began firing at the house, pumping bullet after bullet through the flimsy walls and the door, driving the men inside to cover. The reports from the heavy revolver rolled through the quiet streets like thunder through a canyon.

By the time Cochi's revolver was empty, I had the car turned around and headed back the way we had come. Cochi holstered the Magnum, drew the Glock from his waistband, and opened up again, spacing his shots, firing as calmly as a man at a range. He went through half the clip, walked quickly around the front of the car, then turned and fired some more. Three through the open front door and three more between the bars on the front window.

Either he was lucky or a hell of a shot. Not one of the bullets howled off the wrought-iron security bars on the windows. On the whole, I would have bet he wasn't lucky.

I opened the passenger door. Cochi fired once more over the roof of the car before he slid in and slammed the door. I got us the hell out of there while he pulled a box of ammunition from his suit-coat pocket and started reloading.

"If you want to put more holes in that house, you can do your own damned driving," I said.

My voice was still too flat, too hard. Cochi didn't mind. His answering chuckle sounded like the Poland China boar my grandmother had loved too much to turn into bacon.

I shook my head. The ringing in my ears didn't stop. Five closely spaced shots. No warning. No time. Fly or die, and I was still alive.

We were back on the Long Beach Freeway in thirty seconds. Neither of us spoke again until we were south of the Los Angeles County line.

"Why do they call you Fiddler?"

"I used to be good with the violin."

"You are better with a gun," Cochi said softly. "You would be wasted as a driver. I will make you a better offer. You are very quick, very—how do you say it—*un cirujano?*"

"Surgeons don't use guns."

"*Sí,* but they are very precise when they cut, and their hands do not tremble afterward. You have a valuable talent, señor. A man such as you could make a great deal of money in my business."

"Doing what? Killing other guys like me? No, thanks. I'll stick to banking. The hours are better."

Cochi Loco smiled slightly. "But the work is the same. For men like you and me, señor, the work is always the same."

I shut Cochi out, preferring the ringing in my ears.

18

FIORA SAT in a wide armchair in front of a gas-log fire, a crystal balloon snifter in her hands, her feet daintily crossed on a velvet-covered footstool. She was trying to appear relaxed, but from across the room I could hear her tightly drawn nerves singing like telephone wires in the wind. Don Faustino sat at an angle to Fiora, his thin silk tie slightly loosened and his face a little flushed. He watched her with intense interest and obvious respect.

A cynical friend of mine says that in every important conversation, somebody's buying and somebody's selling. The relationship here was clear.

Jill Swann must have gotten the message already. She had disappeared. So had most of the guests in the dining room. The only people in the wine cellar with Fiora and Faustino were his two bodyguards and a waiter clearing supper plates. I glanced at the table. There were two bottles on it, a Heitz Martha's Vineyard 1969 next to the Bella Oaks 1978. The Bella Oaks is expensive but the Martha's '69 is history, a collector's item, more valuable in the bottle than in the glass. I wondered whether Fiora had nicked the South American bastard for a thousand-dollar bottle of cabernet by accident or out of spite.

Fiora looked up at me over the rim of the snifter. Her jade-green eyes said the cabernet had been no accident and she still wasn't done nicking Faustino. She can be a predator too, in her own intelligent, bloodless fashion.

Her glance went over me like hands, checking for damage. She didn't find any visible wounds, yet she knew just the same. I can withhold much from the world, almost nothing from her. Her eyes said she loved me no matter what, but at the moment I was too cold to be loved. Later I would think about what had happened, what I had done. Later, but not now. Right now that kind of thinking was a luxury I couldn't afford.

Cochi bent down and murmured his report into Don Faustino's ear. I walked over and took the snifter from Fiora. The brandy was warm from her hands, fragrant from her stolen body heat. I knocked back a mouthful as though it were tap water. It wasn't. It was Armagnac, smooth and heady. It burned a hole through the cold in my gut.

"You look like hell," she said quietly.

I didn't doubt it. I went to the sideboard and poured another generous shot from the banjo-shaped Armagnac bottle. This time I gave the liquor half the attention it deserved. Then I looked at Fiora, saw the green shadows in her eyes. She flinched at whatever she saw in my eyes and reached for the balloon glass in my hand.

"We had a little trouble in Long Beach," I said flatly. "How about you?"

"El Patrón and I have been discussing the state of the financial world," she said, inhaling the aroma from the glass without drinking any of the potent liquid. "We also discussed the myopia of governments and the dynamic nature of money. He has some very interesting ideas. Some interesting problems, too. Too much money here, not enough there."

"He's about fifteen million problems short at the moment. I'll tell you about it later."

Fiora's smile curved coldly. At this distance I could see that her pupils were dilated, twin black centers of darkness within the hazel-green beauty of her eyes. That, and the husky quality of her voice, was all that showed she had been drinking. When she wants to, Fiora can focus her will like a laser, burning through the relaxing effects of alcohol. But that kind of focus is tiring. When she lets go, she drops like a stone.

"Time to go," I said, taking back the snifter.

The Creole came to his feet and walked around the table to me.

"Cochi told me about the incident," Faustino said, shaking his head unhappily. "I thank you for your help. Please be assured that I very much regret the inconvenience."

I listened to the ringing in my ears and had a primitive desire to hit the man who had sent me on a dumb *pistolero*'s errand. But hitting Faustino would have been shortsighted and stupid. Shortsighted and stupid people end up going down stairways on their faces.

"No problem," I said, reaching for Fiora.

She let me pull her to her feet without resisting. Then she hesitated. I didn't catch the signal the first time so she tightened her hand on mine before she disengaged and turned to face Don Faustino.

"I've enjoyed our discussion of international currency flows," she said. "Did you say that you own some mineral claims outside the United States?"

Faustino paused before he nodded. "Brazil and Chile."

"Gold? Silver?"

He nodded.

"Have you ever thought about exporting gold to the United States?" Fiora asked.

"There is little market for gold bullion here," Faustino said. "Most of the world's jewelry is cast in Italy and Israel."

"I was less concerned about markets than I was about a

justification for sending large amounts of funds out of the country," she said.

Faustino's expression remained distant, but there was a sudden spark of interest in his eyes. "Continue."

Fiora smiled the feline money-shuffling smile that sometimes makes me wonder about the state of her soul. On the other hand, I'm in no position to be passing judgments on the state of anyone's soul, so I kept quiet and wondered if I was the only one who could hear the ringing in my ears.

"Reducing the matter to its simplest terms," she continued, "you have too much money in the United States. You want to introduce it into the international banking system, then move it to accounts overseas."

He nodded.

"But to do that," Fiora said, "you have to have a reason for where the money came from. I, as your friendly banker, share that problem. If I accept currency from you and suspect that currency is the result of criminal activity, I am as guilty as you are, under present American law."

Faustino nodded again.

"However," she said, "if you were to come to me as an international gold merchant, a merchant with extensive U.S. sales—say, perhaps a million dollars a week—I could in all conscience accept your currency deposits, then wire-transfer them to Panama, Chile, Colombia, Luxembourg, wherever you wish. Once I had established a pattern for your business, I could even grant you an exemption from the currency-reporting requirement."

"You could do that?"

I went very still, sensing Faustino sniffing the bait Fiora was presenting with such casual grace.

"I have studied the Treasury regulations quite carefully," she said. "Banks can grant exemptions to all kinds of businesses that do a lot of business in currency—supermarkets, parking garages, even your local McDonald's."

"And gold?"

"I'm just a poor little country banker," Fiora murmured.

"If you tell me gold mining is an arcane international business conducted mostly in cash, I could choose to believe you. Then we would both be protected."

Faustino seemed to draw inward, as though he were examining the idea carefully behind his dark, hooded eyelids. "Tell me, would I really have to import gold to convince you I am a legitimate businessman?"

"Technically, no, but it would better if you could show me the rudiments of a business enterprise—perhaps an industrial office with a filing cabinet full of international bills of lading, paperwork of some sort that would be generated by the importation and transportation of gold. That way I could look the Treasury Department right in the eye and say I had seen proof of your bona fides."

Fiora stopped, then smiled her predatory smile once more. "Actually, I'm so naïve that you could show me a shipment of gold-plated lead bars and tell me they were worth a million dollars. On the basis of such evidence I could feasibly grant you a currency exemption and start moving funds for you immediately."

"Tomorrow?" Faustino said sharply.

"Next week," Fiora countered.

I gave her an uneasy, sideways look. I had always known she was a dangerous woman, but until that moment I hadn't known how dangerous. Even worse, I couldn't tell from looking at her whether she was serious or merely blowing fragrant smoke.

Faustino knuckled his upper lip thoughtfully for another moment, then looked at Fiora with an expression that was probably as close to real respect as he could muster for a female.

"That is a very interesting idea, Señorita Fleming. It would need some refinement but—"

"That's it," Fiora broke in, her voice triumphant. "A refinery! If you could show me a refinery somewhere, I'm sure I could start moving your funds immediately. No more of this dangerous charade of changing small bills into hundreds and shipping them out of the country for deposit. We could legitimately accept your currency deposits in small bills, no intermediate steps, if they came as the result of a international gold refining and brokerage business. Think about it."

"I will, señorita," Faustino said. "I certainly will. It has been a fascinating evening."

He offered his hand and Fiora extended hers. With neither hesitation nor the slightest trace of self-consciousness, Faustino bowed at the waist and kissed her knuckles. She accepted the gesture with a grave smile, then retrieved her hand and hooked it through my arm.

"If you will excuse us," she said to Faustino, "I have a lot of work to do."

"But of course."

Denny, the limo driver, was napping behind the wheel, his cap pulled down over his eyes. He came to quickly when I whistled across the parking lot at him. Fiora sat very close to me on the drive home. The privacy glass was in place, but she still spoke softly.

"Who was it?"

"A man with an Uzi."

A ripple of tension went visibly through Fiora. She pressed close, as though needing the reassurance of hearing my heart beat.

"Fiddler?"

"With luck, he was one of the most notorious drive-by shooters in south-central LA. Otherwise he's a dumb shit gunsel face down in a crack house."

"Is he alive?"

"I doubt it."

Her breath came out in a long sigh and she smoothed her hand over my cheek for just a moment.

"Pity it wasn't Faustino," she whispered. "There isn't enough Armagnac in France to take the taste out of my mouth. I almost threw up on his bald spot when he kissed my hand."

"Is this where I say I told you so?"

Fiora lifted my left arm and slipped under it. I could feel her warmth against me as she began to slide down from the adrenaline high she had been riding. She caught my left hand and drew my fingers down until they rested on the smooth, resilient skin just above the décolletage. With her other hand she tried to burrow inside my sport coat, seeking and sharing warmth in the same motion, trying to drive away the cold she sensed in me. Her living heat sank into me.

"That was quite a performance," I said, after a few minutes. "You had me half believing you could put that kind of a deal together."

"I can." She sighed and snuggled closer. "Any moderately capable investment banker understands how to structure a deal like that. It's just that some of us choose not to do it."

"Out of curiosity, how much would you charge him?"

"Five points."

She yawned and I watched her pink tongue curl like a cat's.

"That's a bulk rate," she added, speaking slowly, letting herself relax. "He said something about having a hundred million bucks to move in the next six months."

"Five points on a hundred million bucks," I said, slowly stroking the soft skin above her breasts. "Doesn't five million tempt you?"

Fiora said something, but it was too low and husky for me to understand. I guess she wasn't all that impressed with five million bucks because she was halfway to sleep, her guard down as she snuggled against me. Home safe. With lazy, sleepy fingers, she picked open a button in the middle of my shirt and slid her fingers inside until they threaded through hair to the warm skin beneath. She made a contented little noise and relaxed completely. Within moments she would be asleep.

"You realize we'll be home in fifteen minutes and you'll just have to wake up again," I said softly.

"Carry me. I need all the sleep I can get."

"For once you might try sleeping in."

"Can't."

"Why not? I thought you were giving up the high-pressure life."

"Meeting . . . nine o'clock . . . Jill Swann."

The words came slowly as Fiora slid down the long slope toward oblivion. She fought another yawn, lost, and sent a rush of warm air over my shirt. Her body took on the boneless quality of deep sleep.

The limousine turned, threatening to dislodge Fiora. I lifted her across my lap and sat without moving, watching her peaceful face in the flickering light of street lamps and listening to the ringing in my ears.

19

BENNY WAS LOADING electronic gear in the back of his van when I pulled up behind his garage the next morning. He's the kind of friend who doesn't ask questions. I had just told him I wanted to find out more about Fiora's breakfast date, and he took it from there. He had everything we would need to follow Jill Swann from here to kingdom come.

By the time we got to the restaurant, Benny knew as much about what was going on as I did. Swann had cornered Fiora in the powder room sometime during Faustino's dinner party. The conversation was cordial and inconclusive, but the redhead had hinted that she had some inside dope about Bank of the Southland that Fiora needed to know. Fiora doubted it, but she wasn't about to turn down the chance to pick Swann's brain about Faustino.

I wasn't happy. Tax lawyers aren't usually dangerous, but Swann was too close to the Don. I had agreed to let Fiora talk to Swann as long as I was close enough to do any heavy lifting that might be required. After the breakfast bash I intended to follow the redhead for a while, to see if she was meeting anyone in motels besides Brad.

I pulled into the shopping block adjacent to the restaurant

and parked in the sunlight outside a Builder's Emporium where we could keep an eye on the front door. Then I climbed in the back of the van, pulled the privacy curtain, and settled in as Benny tinkered with his Bearcat scanner.

Everybody keeps awake differently on a stakeout. I read newspapers. It's a great way to waste time. Southern California has become a kind of heaven for news junkies. There's the *Los Angeles Times*, a full-time undertaking in itself, and a flock of local papers, from the *Orange County Register* to the *Huntington Park Signal*. The rest of the world is on hand, as well—*The New York Times* is home-delivered seven days a week in Crystal Cove, and *The Wall Street Journal*, *Barron's*, *Investor's Daily*, and several other specialty papers come by mail. I kill and recycle a tree a day, easy.

Benny doesn't share my tastes. He thinks newspapers are good fish wrappers and little else. He's held this view since the 1968 Tet Offensive in Saigon. The papers all regarded it as a stunning defeat for the United States. Benny knows different. He attended that particular New Year's celebration and saw the enemy all but destroy itself in one stupid public relations stunt. But the stunt worked, and Benny vowed never again to take the media's word on anything.

He has mellowed over the years on some subjects, but he still refuses to subscribe to a newspaper and he can't watch the news without getting into an argument with Dan Rather. To keep up with what's going on around him, he keeps a modified Bearcat radio scanner in the van. The scanner lets him tap in on the news while it's being made, not after it's been homogenized, sensationalized, and editorialized by some news organization that has one eye on advertisers and the other on ratings.

I think Benny's idea has some merit; the news is a lot more flavorful before it's filtered by the media. Benny gets to listen to morning traffic reporters on their air-to-air frequencies, the ones that never get broadcast. He checks in regularly with the radio links between field reporters and the assignment desks of a dozen television stations, often picking up the story behind the story. And he eavesdrops in real time, as things are happening, by keeping track of local and regional law enforcement and fire frequencies.

It keeps him awake on stakeouts, too.

I shook out *The New York Times*; Benny sat in his wheelchair with a pair of headphones clamped over his ears and tapped frequencies into the memory bank of the scanner, looking for something interesting. I hoped he was having better luck than I was; a front-page the-sky-is-falling account of the latest budget crisis in New York was turning my eyelids to lead.

After a few minutes I put the paper down, blinked several times, and looked out at the parking lot through a small gap in the privacy curtains. While I watched, three carpenters piled out of a pickup truck and headed toward the Country Kitchen. Billows of greasy smoke rose from the overworked grill exhausts on the restaurant's roof. A broadside in the window advertised sausage and eggs plus hash browns and toast with real butter for $2.69.

"Hell of a place for an up-and-coming tax lawyer," I muttered.

Benny ignored me.

"It looks like every Country Kitchen I've ever seen from here to Kalispell, Montana," I said. "Pan-fried, deep-fried, chicken-fried, and all awash in double-thick gravy."

Benny switched channels.

Jill Swann arrived ten minutes early for the nine o'clock appointment. She parked her blue Firebird in plain sight fifty yards from us, slung her bag over her shoulder, and strode across the asphalt parking lot with a lithe dancer's step. She was wearing full makeup, a snappy business suit, hose, and heels. She exuded an aura of feminine energy, as though she had just come from a morning aerobics workout or her lover's bed.

"Could you arrange an introduction after this is over?" Benny asked.

"She's a crook."

"So?"

"She's nuts about Brad Simms."

"Forget I asked," he said. "I can overlook many flaws in a woman, but loving a banker isn't one of them."

A faded orange van not unlike Benny's pulled into the parking lot a minute behind Swann. The van circled the lot once, then parked. Nobody got out.

The hairs on the back of my neck prickled.

Two minutes later a cross-country rig with a tall box pulled into the lot and parked between the orange van and the restaurant. The trucker and his relief driver got out and went in for breakfast. A moment later the orange van started up and moved five slots over, relocating to a spot that gave an unobstructed view of the restaurant.

Again, nobody got out.

I watched while the van's driver eased into the closed cargo area and drew privacy curtains so no one could see that the van was occupied. His actions mirrored mine of a few minutes before.

"We've got problems," I said. "Ibañez isn't the only one under police surveillance."

Benny looked up from the scanner. I pointed to the van. He took the binoculars from me and studied the vehicle carefully for a time.

"Clever wankers," he said, handing the glasses back to me. "They have a little periscope built into the roof ventilator. I caught a flash off the mirror when the bloke did a full circle."

I raised the glasses. Benny was right. There was a slanted mirror hidden behind the bug-screen housing in the roof ventilator on top of the van. It was a very professional package, the kind that cutting-edge cops use to shoot surveillance photos and videotapes of cutting-edge crooks. I wondered how deeply Don Faustino's organization had been penetrated and whether Fiora was already too late to save Bank of the Southland. In any case, Fiora didn't need to be linked in police files to a slime like Faustino.

I was reaching for the cellular phone to warn Fiora away when Benny touched my arm.

"Fiora's here."

I was too damned late. Fiora had parked on the other side of the restaurant. She was already out of her silver 750 and locking it. She would walk into that meeting and walk out with her face in some federal, state, or local narcotics squad's mug book.

"Damn!"

"No help for it now, mate," Benny said. "Let it ride." He adjusted the headphones. Pages rustled as he consulted a directory of frequency assignments and punched them into his Bearcat. "Bloody hell," he muttered. "There's a pack of them circling like sharks. Transmission bleeding over half the frequencies on the band."

He switched on a small speaker so I could listen and then went back to fine-tuning reception.

"Can you tell who they are?" I asked.

"They're on the federal bands. DEA or FBI, maybe. I can't get a clean fix."

"*. . . looks like our lady,*" said a male voice on the speaker box. "*Blond, five feet two, built. Somebody get her tag.*"

A few seconds later another male voice read Fiora's license plate number over the radio. The first voice came on again. The voice was authoritative, accustomed to being in command.

"*Run a Ten twenty-eight, wants and warrants, DMV, the works.*"

"*Look at that ass,*" a third voice said. "*Expensive stuff but worth every dime.*"

I must have made some sound, because Benny's head snapped up and he gave me an odd look. I looked out around the block-square parking lot, trying to find the man with the big mouth. There was a plain vanilla sedan backed into a parking slot in front of a shoe store almost a block away. The passenger was watching Fiora through binoculars and talking on a radio microphone.

Part of me was ready to shut the whole thing down, grab Fiora, and leave. But the rational part of me had another view: better the cops than the South Americans. Cops would put Fiora's name in a surveillance report, but they wouldn't hurt her physically.

I stayed in the van.

For the next half hour Benny and I sat and watched through the front window while Fiora ate her English muffin and marmalade, drank her tea, and listened to whatever Swann had to say. It was an easy conversation to script, even if you couldn't overhear. Swann knew she had been outflanked. She was probably proposing some kind of "old-girl alliance," a perfumed partnership in crime.

It was a hell of a commentary on the postfeminist era. Yes indeed, you've come a long way, baby. Now females could be full-fledged outlaws together. I wondered whether women would commit as many crimes for the favors of men in this newly liberated era as men have committed for the favors of women throughout history.

"*Uncle Leader, subjects are moving,*" a male voice said on the scanner.

It sounded like the spotter in the van. He had a better view of the restaurant than the sedan did.

So far I hadn't seen any women cops or heard any female voices. That surprised me. When you're covering two women, it helps to have a cop on the scene who can go through the powder room without setting off a riot.

The authoritative voice came on the air: Uncle Leader, no doubt.

"*The blonde's car is registered to a corporation in Beverly Hills. It's probably a shell. Somebody get on Orange North, have the local PD lend us a motor cop. I want him to make a traffic stop on the blonde when she leaves here and force her to cough up decent identification.*"

"Screw you, Uncle Leader," I muttered, but muttering was all I could do.

Swann and Fiora came out the front door of the restaurant.

I could tell by Fiora's expression that she was amused. Swann looked frustrated. Her mouth was a hard line that made her a lot less attractive. The two women separated without saying good-bye.

I grabbed Benny's cellular phone, punched in the number of Fiora's car phone, and heard it ring. At the same time I watched Swann, who was headed for her own car. Fiora unlocked the door, slid into her seat, and picked up the phone.

"Hello, Fiddler."

"How was breakfast?"

"Wretched."

"The conversation or the food?"

"Both. She must have thought I was an idiot. She kept trying to get me to commit to clearly illegal fiscal actions. I kept pointing out that fact. She became very irritated. End of breakfast. Where are you?"

"About a hundred yards away, over by the hardware store. But don't look around. I've got some bad news."

Swann had reached her own car. She unlocked the trunk and dropped her shoulder bag in.

"I'm sitting down," Fiora said dryly.

"Swann has a tail on her, Feds of some sort. They're dying to know who you are, so they've arranged to have you stopped by a motorcycle cop once you get back out on the street."

"Are motorcycle cops like firemen? Do they have to pass a cute test before they're hired?"

"Damn it, Fiora, this isn't a joke."

"Sure it is. My license, insurance, and registration are up to date."

"Yeah, and you're about to have a brand new file started in your honor, one that says something about money laundries."

"A new entry, maybe, but not a new file. The Feds have watched me like a hawk since Danny and Volker tried to ship a microchip factory to Russia."

Fiora was right. Her twin brother's sole venture into high-tech smuggling had killed him and brought both of us into close quarters with the Feds. But that didn't make me feel any better about this.

A motion at the corner of my field of vision caught my attention. Swann was doing something with her bag while she watched Fiora out of the corner of her eye. It was as though she was waiting for Fiora to leave.

The hair on my neck started prickling again.

"Get it over with," I told Fiora. "Call me afterward on Benny's number."

I kept the glasses on Swann while Fiora started her car and drove off for her rendezvous with a motor cop. The surveillance team came on the speaker instantly.

"Blonde is moving. Tell the motor unit she'll be pulling out into traffic on Chapman Avenue in ten seconds."

"This is the motor. I copy. I'll have her in a few . . ."

It was a new voice, more muddied by the background noise of the street. The sound of a Kawasaki four-cycle revving impatiently came over the speaker. I got the mental image of a motorcycle traffic officer hiding behind a billboard somewhere nearby, waiting.

"I have the silver BMW. I'll make the stop after she goes northbound."

I shifted the glasses to Swann. She had slammed the lid of her trunk and moved to the front door of the car. As Fiora left the parking lot, Swann peeled off the jacket of her business suit, laid it across the passenger seat, got in, and closed the door. Glancing around to make sure no one was nearby, she started unbuttoning her blouse.

I zoomed the glasses to full power. She had a great body, but that wasn't what interested me. As she fussed over her bra, I expected to hear some crude remarks from the cop contingent watching her. Not a peep, even when she arched her back to reach around and pull something out of her waistband.

Suddenly I remembered something and got a sick feeling. The surveillance team had called Fiora "the blonde." There was a familiarity about that, as though they had been expecting her. I started to say something to Benny but couldn't find savage enough words.

After a moment, Swann began to rebutton her blouse. She was slowed down by the fact that she was holding something in her hand—a small, flat plastic box the size of a paperback book. Eighteen inches of thin wire trailed from it.

"Swear for me, Benny. You're better at it than I am."

"What flavor you want, mate? Aussie, Brit, Urdu?"

Before I could decide, Swann reached across to the passenger side of her car to unlock the glove box. There was a two-way radio microphone inside. She picked it up and punched the transmitter button. Suddenly her voice filled the speaker in our van, coming over the Feds' wavelength.

"I told you she was too damned smart to talk out of turn. And next time, friends and neighbors, I will personally castrate the clown who puts the transmitter in the ice chest before I strap it on."

20

"THE TOWN BIKE," Benny muttered.

I lowered the glasses and looked at him.

"Everybody's favorite ride." He shrugged. "Brad, Faustino, and now the cops."

I didn't argue. I was still trying to sort out the ramifications. Uncle Leader came back on the police radio.

"We copied the bug all right, Jill, but it wasn't worth the tape. It sounded like you were talking to Mother Theresa."

Swann picked up her microphone again. *"She's a player, all right. D'Aubisson told me all about her this morning. She has a laundering scheme that is nothing short of brilliant. Simms is nothing but a gofer. We should wash him out of the investigation and concentrate on her. She's the brains behind Bank of the Southland."*

"Can't tell the players without a scorecard," I said. "Shit Marie. This is turning into a game I'd just as soon read about in tomorrow's box scores."

I remembered Swann's face when she met Brad Simms at the motel. Fiora had said it wasn't commerce. Was it art? Was Swann that good an actress?

"You aren't going soft on Bradford, are you, Jilly? His ass is already bought and paid for."

"Haven't you ever heard of trading up? Brad would roll over on that blonde in a minute."

"Who wouldn't? She'd be one hot—"

"Knock it off," snarled a third voice.

Silence. Uncle Leader had spoken.

"We're going over to watch the motor make that traffic stop on the blonde. See you back at the shop."

The vanilla sedan started to move.

One of the men broke in again. *"Jilly from the van. You need backup for anything else? We're supposed to be in court in Santa Ana at ten on that Rodriguez case."*

"Negative. I'll be off the air for a few minutes, stowing this body bug. Then I've got to make a phone call and head back to the office."

The headlights on the surveillance van blinked once, over and out. The vehicle started up and moved away.

No doubt about it. Jill Swann was a cop.

"Clarify something for me, mate," Benny said. "This *is* the girl Bradford Simms says he's in love with, the one he meets for nooners in cheap motels?"

"Yeah."

"Since when do they let cops sleep with suspects?"

"Since never."

"Then she's either ambitious or in love," Benny said.

"Or stupid."

"She's stupid either way."

I slid out from behind the curtains and opened the door.

"Where you going?" Benny asked.

Jill Swann—if that was really her name—looked a little rumpled as she rummaged through the leather bag that was in the trunk of her car. In removing the body-bug battery unit, she had pulled the tails of her blouse out. The pinpoint microphone that had been attached to her bra strap dangled by the long thin wire lead. Her mind seem disheveled as well. I was twenty feet away and closing fast before she saw me. But she recovered quickly, pulling the Smith & Wesson Model 38 out of the bag and pointing it at me in one easy motion.

"Freeze!"

She aimed at the spot between my eyes and thumbed back the shrouded hammer to show she meant business. Her blue eyes were clear, but I could hear the gears in her mind spinning as she tried to figure out whether to play this as a cop or a crook.

That kind of hesitation is a bad sign for an undercover operator. Swann had been playing too many roles in too many games.

"Even if I hadn't heard you a minute ago on the radio, I'd know you were a cop. You don't handle that gun like a tax lawyer. It's the Jeff Cooper combat crouch that gives you away. First time I've seen anyone try it in a tight skirt."

I showed Swann my empty hands. Slowly she straightened out of the crouch.

"Me? A cop?" she said, laughing. "I'm not, but the dude who taught me how to shoot was before they caught him with enough coke to send him away."

"Is he the one who taught you to record every business conversation with a Fargo unit?"

"What?"

I looked at the body bug lying where it had been dropped on the asphalt. "Is that damned thing still transmitting?"

Swann's brain was back in gear. She couldn't explain away the body bug and she knew it.

"What do you want?" she asked tightly.

The pistol didn't waver.

"Is it on or not? I'm about to ask you a question that could embarrass you in front of your brother officers."

She thought a few more seconds. The pistol came down an inch. "It's off."

"Does the Royal Hawaiian Motel ring any bells?"

The fight went out of Swann very slowly. She thumbed the hammer of the pistol back to half cocked. Then, moving

as though she were underwater, she lowered the weapon and
pointed it toward the ground. For a second I thought she was
going to drop the gun completely. When she looked at me,
her eyes were the color of a failed robin's egg.

"It won't work," she said flatly.

"What won't?"

"Blackmail. Tell Faustino I'll put my career in the toilet
and flush before I throw this case. You tell him that."

"Tell him yourself, if you want. As for your career, you've
screwed that up pretty well without my help."

"Who the hell are you?"

"Fiora's partner, among other things."

"And Faustino? What are you doing for him?"

"I'm trying to sell him a ticket to hell."

A flicker of hope enlivened Swann's eyes.

"Look," I said. "Don't you think it would be better if we
found a less public place to talk?"

"Where's your car?"

"Fiora's driving it."

Swann didn't hesitate. "Get in mine."

The Feds don't stint on any aspect of their agents' training.
Swann drove with her hands at ten and two on the wheel,
arms extended, fingers firm yet flexible. She took me to a
quiet old park along the sandy bed of a river that had gone
south for the dry season. The sycamores were green and the
shrubs fully leafed out. We were in the heart of an urban
area, but we were well hidden. I rolled down the window
and let the breeze bring in the sound of a mockingbird running through its repertoire.

"Nice," I said. "You come here often?"

"I used to be a patrol cop in this city. We'd hide out here
when we wanted to sleep on the early watch."

"You're not a local cop now."

Smiling slightly, Swann shook her head. "U.S. Customs
came to town two years ago, recruiting women with law-
enforcement experience. It sounded a lot more exciting than
chasing curfew violators and wrestling with drunk drivers."

"What about the FBI?"

"The Feebies wouldn't take me. I've got all the degrees, all the credentials." She shrugged. "I guess redheads are a little too flashy for them."

"You'll be happier in Customs."

She gave me a bleak little smile. "After this I'll be lucky to get a traffic assignment in Polebridge, Montana."

"Don't blame me. I'm not going to tell Uncle Leader about Brad."

"I think Uncle Leader already knows," she said, gripping the steering wheel and staring narrow-eyed out through the glass at the old fieldstone wall. "But he's not my boss. At the moment I'm not really working for Customs. I'm on loan to a task force—federal and local agencies all under one commander, a lieutenant named Hudson from the Sheriff's Office."

"Uncle Leader?"

"Yeah. He's a prick, but he's shrewd. He scents a rat somewhere. He just can't prove it yet."

"But he's letting you continue to operate undercover in the meantime?"

She nodded.

"Why?"

"Pure, undiluted capital-G greed."

"For what? A big bust? How much coke does it take to make captain, a hundred kilos?"

Swann's laugh was as hard as her eyes. "Where you been, Fiddler, Afghanistan? Cops don't want to seize dope anymore. They want to get their hands on money. 'How much cash did you grab?' That's the new national standard all enforcement actions are judged by."

"Money."

"You don't say it with the proper reverence," she said bitterly. "The bureaucratic name of the game is 'asset forfeiture.' It's turned narcotics enforcement into bounty hunting. Hudson borrows men from every narcotics unit in the county and runs around chasing the money, not the dope.

The only way he can keep his task force alive is to keep
seizing currency or assets from the traffickers. The federal
government takes ten percent of the money, then kicks the
rest back to the local agencies that seized it." Blue eyes
glanced in my direction. "You get the picture."

It wasn't a question, but I answered anyway. "Fifteen million, plus Cochi's Mercedes, and maybe Faustino's ritzy little
condo down the coast, just for good measure. Not a bad
return for a few months."

"Hudson's got even bigger plans," Swann said. "He figures
to seize the whole Bank of the Southland if he can prove a
pattern of racketeering."

The last piece of the puzzle dropped into place so nicely
that I had to smile: A perfect box with Brad, the bank, Fiora,
and me caught inside like rats.

"That's why he's so interested in you and your blonde,"
Swann said. "Is her name really Fiora? That doesn't even
sound like a name to me."

"They misread her mother's handwriting at the hospital.
Fiona became Fiora. You get used to it."

"Maybe, but not today. Today has been a real bitch."

I looked at Swann blankly.

She was digging in her purse. She hauled out a package of
cigarettes. She started to fish out a cigarette, then swore
under her breath and dropped the pack back into her purse.

"I'm trying to quit," she said, through her teeth.

"Why? Because Brad doesn't like it?"

Nails with tips like red daggers gripped the purse. Swann
didn't reply.

"He sucks up a little coke into his sinuses, but he doesn't
like anything socially irresponsible or lower class like tobacco, is that it?"

Swann grimaced and still said nothing.

"Does he know you're a cop?"

After a long count, she shook her head. "I quit treating
him like a suspect a long time ago, but I haven't been able

to tell him the truth. I kept hoping that if I hung in long enough, I'd figure out a way save him."

"Tell him."

"No way. He's a terrible actor. Faustino would smell it on him in a second. Then Uncle Leader's ambitions would be the least of our problems."

Swann glanced at her bag again, still fighting the impulse to have a cigarette. Finally she chucked the bag in the back seat, out of sight.

"Okay, Fiddler, you're the man with the cards. Deal."

I shook my head.

"Are you going to drop the hammer on my career, my love affair, or both?" Swann asked. "I'm kind of interested. I've been asking myself the same question for the last four weeks."

"Is that when the affair started? Four weeks ago?"

"It started the first time I met Brad," she said, leaning back against the seat. Her posture was relaxed, but the body beneath the skin wasn't. "That's what made the investigation so damned easy."

"Love at first sight?" I asked, but my voice lacked the proper sarcasm.

"Laugh all you want. I used to. Then it happened."

"I'm not laughing."

Swann looked at me, really looked at me, for the first time.

"The blonde?"

"The blonde," I agreed.

"Hell of a world we live in." Swann sighed and turned so that she was half facing me. "Brad just kind of happened along one night at the West Coast Club. We had an informant, one of Faustino's money partners. He introduced me into the entire organization at a dinner. Brad was one of the guests."

I waited. Swann's voice was uninflected, but there was pain in the tightness around her eyes and mouth.

"It was all very legit, no laundering talk or anything. I saw right off that Faustino was trying to compromise Brad, giving him free dope, stuff like that. But he interested me. I had a business background, and we just started talking. I knew I should back off." Her breath hissed out around a curse. "The electricity was so thick between us it was like being plugged into a wall socket. Brad felt it too, I could see that. Hell, I could *feel* it."

Swann closed her eyes, then opened them again. They were focused on me.

"Does it ever go away?"

"The electricity?"

She nodded.

"No," I said. "Not even when you want it to."

"I can't imagine wanting it to."

I felt a hundred years old. "Give it time. The day will come."

There was silence, followed by a long sigh. She started speaking again, preferring facts to the turmoil of her own thoughts.

"When Hudson found out Brad was a local banker, the bank suddenly became as much of a target as Faustino's organization. Hudson had sensed the electricity. He wanted me to get close to Brad in order to get information out of him."

"The oldest bait in the world. And still the best."

The flush on Swann's fair skin came from anger, not shame. "It was my job and I did it. Women use sexual attraction all the time. So do men. But I kept everything under control. I never did anything I couldn't testify about in court. I never dated Brad, even though he asked me all the time. I never even talked to him without a surveillance unit in the background somewhere. That's the only way you can run a case."

I waited, knowing that what had begun as a proper, arm's-length relationship had ended up as close as a man and a woman can get.

"After four weeks of that, Brad followed me home one night. I guess I was sloppy."

"Or maybe you wanted him to follow you home."

Swann smiled sadly and didn't disagree.

"It was very innocent at first. We sat and talked in the dark in the garage behind my apartment. I was scared to death."

"Of Brad?"

"Of getting caught. I knew if I let him touch me it was all over. I'd be his woman and that would be that. I've never felt like that. It was like being in someone else's body. So I lied. I told him I couldn't date him because I'd been having an affair with Cochi and that Cochi was very jealous even though I had broken it off."

"Smart lady. Cochi is just the thing to take the lead out of a man's pencil."

"Yeah, I thought so too."

"What happened?"

"It didn't work." Swann made a soft sound, half despair and half remembered passion. She put her head in her hands. "Jesus, what a mess." After a moment she pulled herself together and looked at me. "So what's it going to be, Fiddler? What's it going to cost me, now that I've fallen in love with the wrong man in the wrong place at the worst possible time in my life?"

21

"POOR SWANN," Fiora said. Her sympathy seemed genuine. Leave it to a woman to justify all sorts of trouble for the sake of love. "What did you tell her?"

"The truth."

"Which is?"

We were back in the parking lot in front of the restaurant. For a few seconds I watched greasy smoke rise from the Country Kitchen's vent. The side mirror showed Benny's van. He was back in the driver's seat.

"What the hell could I tell her? I won't go out of my way to burn down her cover, but I didn't buy into this game to protect her ass, either."

"I feel sorry for her. And for Brad."

"They're grown-ups," I said. "I'll save my sympathy for the unwilling players."

I looked at the dashboard clock. Luz would be waiting for us. With Jaime. I hoped the boy had undergone a change of heart. I needed to know some things from him.

Fiora must have read my mind. "Jaime?" she asked.

The question was rhetorical. We both knew there was no other course and damned little time. Things were coming unraveled around us. Fiora started the big car and drove out of the lot. Benny followed.

"The motor cop give you any trouble?" I asked, not wanting to think about Jaime. If he didn't cooperate, I would have to do the kinds of things that leave a bad taste in your life.

"He passed the cute test, except that he had this little love-handle problem. Can't men tell when their shirts need to be let out?"

"Motor cops think they'll be young forever. It's the only thing that lets them climb on half a ton of hot steel every morning."

"That explains it."

"What?"

"He wanted my phone number."

I gave Fiora a sideways look. "What did you say?"

She gave me a very feminine Cheshire-cat grin. "I told him I'd give him mine if he'd give me his. He wouldn't."

"No guts, no glory, pal."

"Mmm." She hesitated, then said quietly, "We should discuss how we're going to deal with Jaime. If you come at him the wrong way, he'll fight you. He has to. He's pretty young, but he's got a lot of male pride already."

"I know. I just hope I can leave him with some of it."

Fiora started to speak, thought better of it, and said nothing. By the time we got to Luz Pico's nineteenth-century adobe home, I must have been looking pretty grim.

"Smile, love," Fiora said tightly. "Unless you're planning on scaring the truth out of him?"

"That's my second option. The first is good old-fashioned treachery."

"I don't want to know if there's a third option."

"You're right. You don't want to know."

Luz opened the front door before we could knock. She's an unusual combination of Latina matriarch and middle-class housewife. She was wearing a set of stylish white sweats and a dark blue sweatband that kept her gleaming black-and-silver hair out of her eyes. She was wiping *masa* dough from her hands with a towel. The smell of fresh tortillas made me hungry.

"How's Jaime?" I asked.

Luz gave me a worried look from her beautiful dark eyes. "He's tried to use the phone several times, but he wouldn't let me dial so I didn't let him make the call."

"Good."

"Is it? What if his mother is living nearby and she's worried and—"

"I stiffed a call in to the Santa Ana cops," I said, interrupting. "I pretended I was a reporter asking about a Mexican kid that went missing yesterday. The cops didn't know what I was talking about. Nobody has reported Jaime missing."

Luz shook her head sadly. "Maybe his mother is here illegally and is afraid to call the police."

"Maybe. And maybe some really unpleasant folks have caught up with her and pulled out all the phones." I squeezed Luz's shoulder. "Thanks. I'll take it from here."

Jaime was sitting on the floor in front of the television set, watching a Lucy rerun. He scrambled to his feet expectantly when I walked into the living room.

"Now will you take me to Santa Ana?" he asked eagerly.

"Sure. Just give me the address."

Jaime's eagerness vanished.

Before I could say anything else, Luz's two sons came thundering into the living room and attacked me with their usual fervor. Ruben and Mateo were nine and seven, growing like the weeds in their father's citrus groves and in constant need of testing their strength. They went to work on my knees and nearly brought me down. I finally got an arm around each of their middles and turned them upside down. They shrieked and flailed and laughed until their faces were red.

For a few moments Jaime watched with an expression of

anger and hopelessness, as though he couldn't believe I would play with other kids but not help him. Then he turned back to watch Lucy.

While I tried to hold my ground against the two Pico boys, Fiora went over and crouched down to Jaime's level. He turned toward her, listened, and shook his head. She smiled sadly and ruffled his dark hair with one hand. He closed his eyes as though savoring a woman's touch, but he would have preferred his mother's hand and everyone knew it.

Mateo bucked hard and whanged his forehead on the pager in my pocket.

"Ow! Is that your gun?"

"Nope. You okay?"

Mateo nodded and rubbed his forehead while I set the two brothers back on their feet.

"Sure felt like a gun," he muttered. "Lemme see."

I pulled the pager out of my pocket and showed it to Mateo. He grabbed it and peered into the blank liquid-crystal display window. Immediately Ruben crowded in and made a pass, trying to snatch the pager away to look at it himself. Mateo turned away, keeping his body between his big brother and the new object of interest.

"I had it first!"

I restrained the bigger brother until Mateo had had his chance. From the corner of my eye I saw that Jaime was watching, curious almost in spite of himself. Boys and their toys, the endless fascination. I understood it well, having a wide streak of it myself. I wondered if Jaime's curiosity was great enough to cloud his caution.

"Ruben's turn," I said.

Mateo surrendered the pager unwillingly.

"How's it work?" Ruben demanded. "What is it?"

The pager went off in Ruben's hand, its yelp so surprising that the boy almost let go. I looked around. Benny had followed us into the house. He was sitting in his wheelchair in the doorway from the kitchen, his portable cellular phone in his hand and an indulgent smile on his face.

"Space magic, boys," Benny said.

Ruben and Mateo forgot all about me and went for Benny instantly. They have all been good pals since the boys were old enough to begin appreciating toys more complicated than wooden blocks. Benny would have made a great father, particularly for boys. He understands what makes them tick because it's what makes him tick, too. Toys—the more, and the more intricate, the better.

"How'd you do that, Benny? Huh? How?"

"Computers and satellites."

Mateo's eyes got big and round. "Really, like with the shuttle?"

Benny smiled approvingly. Mateo is going to be a shuttle commander one day if Benny has anything to say about it.

"Just like the shuttle," Benny agreed. "From my cellular phone, here"—waving the instrument—"to the satellite relay and right back down to Fiddler's pager. A worldwide telephone and not a wire in sight."

Benny's genius is that he sees technology so clearly he can make it intelligible to toddlers. I watched Jaime as Benny told the Pico boys about PacBell's cellular system and how it interfaces with the SkyPager network. Jaime lost all interest in the television, and even in Fiora. Now he was just another kid fascinated with a clever new toy.

Jaime went and peered between the Pico boys for a better look. The other boys moved aside a bit. While Jaime was interested in the technical discussion, the cellular phone kept drawing his eyes.

The idea that had been germinating in my mind grew like jimson weed in spring, and, like jimson, it was addictive. I waited with false patience while Benny finished his lecture. Then I scooped up his cellular phone and tapped Jaime.

"C'mon, *hijo*. I'm going to let you make that call."

Jaime followed me out onto the cool veranda. I sat down on the end of a chaise lounge, which brought me almost to eye level with him.

"I won't turn you loose in Santa Ana to fend for yourself,"

I said carefully, "but if there is somebody out there who is worried about you, I'll let you make a call."

Jaime studied me for a long moment, looking for the trap he sensed was there. His instincts were good. There was a trap, but I hoped to hell he wouldn't see it.

"What comes after five-four?" I asked, punching in the numbers of the common prefix for Santa Ana phones.

"Six—" His mouth snapped shut and he shook his head. "No. I can't tell you. I promised."

"Okay. Dial it yourself." I held out the telephone. "Just punch in the whole number and hold it to your ear."

Jaime looked at the phone hungrily. I hit the disconnect switch, listened to make sure he had a dial tone, then handed him the unit. I hoped to hell he didn't know what symbols on the non-numerical pads meant. The redial button was the important one.

He turned his back to me and keyed in the number.

I waited five seconds. "Is it ringing?"

He nodded.

I reached around his shoulder. He sensed my movement and ducked away, trying to hold the phone out of my reach. I circled his chest with one arm and pulled him close while I grabbed for the phone with my free hand. I punched the disconnect button and pried the phone from his clutching fingers. Then I punched "redial." Jaime's number showed in the readout window.

"Mama!"

Jaime's body arched as though he had been shocked. He tried to twist out of my grasp. I held him close for a moment, surprised at how thin he was, and at his wiry strength. He fought me for fifteen seconds. I let him, knowing he deserved whatever he could get back from me. His struggles reminded me of a small calf on a rope, frightening for the fierceness, agonizing for the weakness. A kick in the stomach would have left me feeling better.

Finally Jaime's body went still.

"I'm sorry," I said. "I know you don't believe it, but I am."

I wanted to hug Jaime, to comfort him, but that would have cost him what little pride he had left.

"Listen to me, *hijo*," I said. "You have a choice. You can walk beside me into the house like the man you will some-day become, or I can carry you like the child you no longer are."

22

THE CAR WAS QUIET as a crypt as we drove toward Santa Ana. Fiora tried to draw Jaime out in conversation, but he answered with single words or not at all, until finally she gave up. I fished a Julian Bream CD out of the file and put it on. Rodrigo's dolorous *Concierto de Aranjuez* soon filled the car, slow notes building toward a hidden climax. I drove carefully, making sure I didn't lose Benny.

When I turned off Standard Avenue at Minnie Street, looking for the address that Benny's telephone company contact had supplied, Jaime's breath hissed through his teeth. I glanced at him in the rearview mirror. He looked like what he was—a frightened child who had been forced to play an adult game and had lost.

I looked away. Jaime's single cry when I grabbed the phone had told me it was indeed his mother he was trying to call. I hoped to hell the address we were heading for would contain nothing more dangerous than a worried mother and her burn-scarred child. I particularly hoped that Faustino hadn't somehow discovered it. The thought of what that cold-eyed Creole would do with hostages kept eating away at me, so I concentrated on the city around us.

Ibañez had picked a good place to hide his family. Minnie Street is a way station for California's newest immigrants, legal and illegal, Asian and Latin American. That means it's also the most congested housing tract in southern California—block after stucco block of 1950s four-plexes that are owned by Beverly Hills dentists and San Marino investors, managed by a professional rental agency in South Santa Ana, and occupied by three times as many occupants as they were originally intended to house.

On the other hand, I've seen the places third-world immigrants leave behind. By comparison, Minnie Street is heaven. That doesn't mean Minnie Street is a tranquil little melting pot. There's a very distinct boundary line between the Latinos and the Asians. The border is a storm gutter that runs down the center of one of the alleys.

South of that gutter lies Latin America, with large families of brown-eyed, dark-haired children. The apartments are crowded with colors and noise and decorated with brightly painted plaster Catholic icons. The lords of these manors are stolid, beer-drinking papas. Broad-beamed mamas watch Mexican soap operas and pound *masa* into tortillas to be cooked on nonstick electric griddles.

North of that gutter lies the highlands of Laos, peopled by equally large families with brown-eyed, dark-haired children. The extended Lao Hmong families live in neat, austere little apartments decorated with well-tended pots of lemon grass and Asian peppers and dominated by huge 45-inch Mitsubishi TV sets tuned to English-speaking stations.

But there are some customs of their new land that the Hmong males simply don't understand. The ritualized warfare of machismo, for instance. Hmongs never mastered the trick of turning combat into a game or a ceremony. When they fight, they fight to kill.

It didn't take long for Santa Ana's Latinos to learn that the gutter in the alley between Minnie Street and Standard Avenue was the New World version of the Berlin Wall. And thank God for it. Minnie Street has become the kind of place where everyone studiously minds his own business and expects the other guy to do the same.

As we got closer to the address, I watched Jaime from time to time in the rearview mirror. He did a decent job of concealing his emotions, sitting in the back seat and watching the world go by as though it were a television show with the sound turned off. He said nothing until I parked behind a produce peddler's faded green step van.

"Why—why are we stopping?" he asked.

In the rearview mirror his eyes were large and haunted with the fear that he had somehow betrayed his father's trust and his family's safety.

"It's all right, *hijo*," I said. "I'm not going to hurt anybody."

Jaime snatched at the door handle. I hit the master lock switch on the console. He made a small trapped sound and hammered on the door. His eyes were pinched shut, as though he was afraid even to look at the little ground-floor apartment for fear of revealing his last secret.

"It's too late," I said, as gently as I could. "Running won't change anything. Your mama and your little sister are in the apartment on the corner, the one with the freshly ironed curtains in the front window."

Jaime's shoulders slumped, telling me that I had guessed right. When I reached over the seat to comfort him, he flinched away. I tried again but Fiora intercepted me with a light touch and a slight shake of her head. I wanted to argue. Instead I called Benny on the cellular. He had parked a block behind me. He answered instantly, a departure from his usual telephone manners.

"I'm going to reconnoiter," I said. "You circle. If there's any trouble, cover Fiora, then get the hell out of here."

"Yo."

Fiora raised her honey-colored eyebrows in silent question.

"I'd hate to run into Cochi Loco," I said.

I looked at her little leather purse and then back at her, wondering if the Beretta was inside.

She nodded.

"Don't be afraid to use it," I said bluntly.

The door to the 750 shut behind me, leaving me alone in a different world.

It was coming on to noon. Ice-cream trucks were prowling the parking lots and streets around the four-plexes like streetwalkers on Harbor Boulevard. The scratchy loud-speaker music of the slowly cruising trucks was as familiar a part of the scene as the broken Budweiser bottles on the street, the roving produce peddlers with their plastic bags of oranges, and the *venderias* who hawked tortillas, eggs, and red licorice from vans parked permanently at the curb.

Everything looked normal. Day laborers who hadn't caught a job that morning sat in the sunlight drinking beer. A pair of low-riders worked on boom-box speakers in the bed of a Chevy pickup. Across Minnie Street, on the other side of the border, an old Hmong warrior sat hunched forward in a plastic chair, his chin resting on a silver-headed cane, his eyes closed. I wondered if he was remembering the triple-canopy jungle and death.

Jaime's apartment was on the ground floor facing the street. The front door was closed. I went through the broken gate, catfooted up the walk, and stood very close to the tattered, rusty screen, listening for sounds from inside.

At first I heard nothing. Then came the faint nattering of familiar voices. It took me a moment to place them—Ernie and Bert from Sesame Street. After a moment, a child laughed with pleasure.

I retreated across the bare dirt, through the broken gate, and back into the car. Jaime ignored me. I punched in Benny's number. He lifted the receiver after half a ring.

"Everything's cool," I said. "We're going in. Keep circling. Page me in case of trouble."

Fiora got out and took Jaime by the hand. He was sullen. I didn't blame him; betrayal does that to you. When we got to the front door, Big Bird was crooning something about friendship and love. The instant I knocked, someone turned down the TV.

No one came to the door. I watched the homemade drapes. The cloth didn't move.

"Señora Ibañez," I called out.

No answer, no sound, no movement.

I knocked again.

Nothing.

"Jaime, tell your mother it's safe."

He gave me a fierce look and kept his mouth clamped shut. I hunkered down on my heels next to him, bringing my eyes level with his. He didn't want to look at me but my hand under his chin didn't give him much choice.

"Listen to me, *hijo*. If I have to kick in this door, your sister will be frightened, your mama will be frightened, and the neighbors will call the cops. Then your mama will have a roomful of money to explain. She won't be able to do it."

Jaime watched me as though he didn't understand English.

"Your mama will be taken to jail," I continued relentlessly. "Your sister will be put in juvenile hall. You will be put in juvenile hall. Is this what you want for your family?"

Tears blurred the defiance in Jaime's dark eyes.

"The choice hasn't changed, Jaime. Me, Faustino, or the cops."

"Mama!" Jaime called jerkily. "It's me!"

The door burst open. A slender, dark-eyed woman swooped out and grabbed Jaime, hugging him almost as hard as he hugged her in return. She crooned to him in soft torrents of Spanish while a dark-eyed little girl came to the open doorway and looked out. The scars on her face were more livid than they had appeared in the family portrait. Her hands, wrists, and arms were also marked by fire.

"*Buenos dias, Josefina,*" I said, smiling as gently as I could.

Her eyes were dark and her long black hair was drawn back in a ponytail. She was dressed in little blue jeans and a pink shirt that made the skin between her scars shine like satin. Her face lit up in a sweet, unexpected smile. Her face might be marked, but her soul had not yet been. If she got lucky, it never would be.

"Hi," Josefina said.

"Hi, honey," I said. I stood up and turned to Fiora. "I'm in love."

Fiora smiled. "You do better with girls. Underneath all that bone and fur and muscle beats the heart of a teddy bear."

For a few more moments mother and son held each other tightly enough to leave marks. Finally Señora Ibañez turned toward us, Jaime still in her arms.

"Where is Ysidro? Why you have Jaime?"

Her English was more accented than her husband's, but quite functional.

"We're Jaime's friends," I said, "even though he isn't very happy with us at the moment. May we come in? It would be much better if we didn't attract any more attention."

Panic registered in the woman's dark eyes. "No. Is impossible. Sorry."

This was one female who didn't sense the steady beating of a teddy bear's heart inside me.

"Señora Ibañez," Fiora said calmly, "if we wanted to hurt you, we wouldn't have brought Jaime home—we would have taken him to Don Faustino."

Frozen by fear, the woman stared at Fiora and then at me.

"You have nothing to lose by trusting us," I said simply. "We don't work for Don Faustino."

She let out a long, shaking breath and set Jaime back on his feet. Without a word she took her son by the hand, walked back into the apartment, and silently stood aside from the open door. Fiora and I went in and closed the door behind us.

The apartment looked more like fifteen dollars than like fifteen million. There was a crooked couch upholstered in lime-green plastic, two mismatched and rump-sprung armchairs, a kitchen table, and three folding chairs. The only illumination in the room came from the television, a motel-room Philco with a color shift that made Big Bird's feathers the color of split pea soup.

Señora Ibañez went to the couch and sat with a child under each arm, looking both defenseless and fiercely protective. She was wearing clean pressed jeans and a cotton shirt. Her round, stoic face had no makeup. Her hair was neatly cut in a short American style. Jaime's mother was no traditional, heavy-waisted country woman but a competent, intelligent immigrant frightened for her children, her husband, and herself. She didn't know what to do or whom to trust.

Jaime had no doubts. He held on to his mother's hand and leaned heavily against her, eyes closed, all but stunned by the relief of being home again. Josefina sat erect and alert, watching Fiora as though she were Tinkerbell or a shimmering blond angel.

"Don't blame Jaime for giving away his address," I said quietly to Señora Ibañez. "I tricked him. There was nothing he could have done about it. Do you understand?"

"*Sí*," she said promptly. Then, slowly, "Yes. He is good boy."

"I know."

Jaime looked at me for a second, blankly, no forgiveness in his shadowed eyes. Then he looked away. He didn't want to see me.

"Stay with your children, señora," I said. "I'll be right back."

The kitchen was empty except for some clean dishes in the sink. The back door, which was locked and draped with a pillowcase, opened out onto a small cement sidewalk that led to the carports. Two bedrooms and a single bathroom opened off a short, dark hallway. The first bedroom contained two suitcases and a pair of bare twin mattresses. The door to the second bedroom was closed.

I opened it and let my eyes adjust to the darkness. The room was empty except for fifteen cardboard boxes stacked neatly in one corner. The boxes were the kind anyone can buy from a U-Haul rental outlet, capacity 1.5 cubic feet, designed for moving and storing books or LP records. Each box had been carefully sealed with wide bands of clear plastic tape.

I jerked the flaps of the top box. Inside were ten bricks wrapped in plastic sheeting and sealed with gray duct tape. I grabbed a brick at random, slit the sheeting with my pocketknife, and looked inside.

That unmistakable shade of green looked back at me. Ten bundles of a hundred bills each to a brick, ten bricks to a box. Ten times a hundred times a hundred.

The brick thumped softly back into the box. I closed the box without bothering to slit the other bricks. I already had enough distractions in my life. I didn't need fifteen million more.

I didn't need them, but I had them just the same. Now I had to get rid of them.

"Get Benny," I called to Fiora. "Tell him to park behind your car."

Señora Ibañez and her children watched passively when I walked through the living room and out the door with three U-Haul boxes stacked in my arms. By the time I got to the front yard, Benny was waiting. The old Hmong warrior watched indifferently from his lawn chair while I loaded the boxes into the back of Benny's van. I made five more trips before all the cartons were stowed away. By the time I was finished, Benny had struck up a conversation in pidgin Lao and Chinese with the old Hmong.

"That's it," I called to Benny as I slammed the cargo door.

He jabbered a few more incomprehensible syllables in the old man's direction and waved as I walked up to the driver's window.

"The old man and I both knew Joe Bashore," Benny said. "He was a bloke from Montana, just like you, only he ended up a loadmaster for the CIA. He'd drop supplies to this man's group in the Highlands, then fly back to Saigon and get drunk with me."

"Small damn world."

"Especially for warriors." Benny's dark eyes focused on me. "Bloody few of us left." He gestured toward the back of the van. "That it?"

"Fifteen million, give or take. You want me to ride shotgun?"

Benny shifted on the seat until I could see the butt of the Browning Hi-Power he had hidden beneath his left haunch. "No worries, mate. Where do you want me to stow the gelt?"

"Use your imagination. Just make sure I can get my hands on the boxes fast."

He started to drive out, then stopped and gave me an odd off-center smile. "No receipt, no instructions, no sweat. You're a trusting bloke, Fiddler."

"You're too pragmatic to be consumed by greed, *compadre*. You know exactly what money will buy. The money is as safe with you as it would be with Chase Manhattan."

"Safer, mate. Banks are piss-poor places to leave money."

23

I DIDN'T REALIZE how much adrenaline was in my system until we pulled out of the orange grove behind Luz Pico's house and back onto Imperial Highway, after dropping off the Ibañez family. Josefina's shy, trusting smile goaded me as much as Jaime's anger and pain had.

Fiora touched my knee with her hand. "Relax. They're safe now. Even if Don Faustino somehow gets to Ibañez, there's no way he could find out about Luz."

I consciously slowed down. "I hope you're right. Those kids know enough about pain."

I punched the number from Jill Swann's business card into the cellular, waited until someone answered, and then asked for Lieutenant Hudson.

"Hudson," a voice said.

Cold, flat, faintly distracted. I'd heard that voice on the radio this morning.

"Simms," I said without introducing myself. I waited two beats. "D'Aubisson." Two more beats. "Ibañez."

I could hear Hudson breathing, thinking.

"There's a point to this?" he asked finally.

"Stay at your desk and you'll know in ten minutes."

Fiora gave me a sideways look as I dumped the phone, pulled the shifter down into second, and cut across two lanes of Newport Freeway traffic to get around a slow Shell tanker.

"Too much of a good thing is still too much," Fiora said.

"What?"

"Adrenaline."

Fiora does that sometimes. She sits beside me, quiet and calm, thinking. Then she sticks a cannon in my ear and blows my head off. I tolerate it because she doesn't really mean to blow my head off. She's just telling me what's on her mind at that moment.

I also tolerate it because there are times when she's right.

"You're treating my car like you treat the Cobra," she explained.

"Like I *used* to treat the Cobra," I muttered, keeping the speedometer needle at eighty. "There wasn't enough of it left to drive after you shoved me off that dirt road and into a boulder."

Fiora wouldn't be distracted by a rehash of that unhappy incident.

"You're on an adrenaline ride," she said. "You've got the bit in your teeth and you're going to run with it no matter who gets in the way. That tactic may get the job done with testosterone freaks like Cochi Loco, but it doesn't play well in the halls of bureaucracy."

"So?"

"We're going to see a government official, a law enforcement bureaucrat," Fiora said patiently, "not some underworld gorilla."

She was wrong about that, but she was also a bit right. I slid the shifter back into drive and backed off a half inch on the accelerator.

"Narcs aren't ordinary cops," I said. "They're game players, maximum hardcases. That's what their job is about."

"Maybe. Maybe not. We won't know until we meet this one. But by the time you've run head on into somebody, it's too late to try being nice."

"Do I tell you how to shuffle money?"

"No, but—"

I cut across Fiora's words. "Just no, period. No buts. Lieutenant Hudson isn't some middle-level pencil pusher from the Environmental Protection Agency. Hudson is a dope cop. The only difference between him and Cochi Loco is that Hudson has a badge. They are both guys who make their living with guns."

"Correct me if I'm wrong, but we aren't doing this for our own ass-kicking gratification, are we? We're trying to resolve a nasty situation in behalf of Jaime and his family and in behalf of our client, Marianne Simms. Aren't we?"

"Get to the point."

"That *is* the point," Fiora retorted.

"No, the point is that we're into the heavy-lifting phase of this operation, and I'm the heavy-lifting expert."

"And I'm supposed to shut up, is that it?"

"Hell of an idea."

But even as I snarled, I was backing off the accelerator another notch.

Fiora let out a silent breath.

One thing the years and the pain have taught us is to read each other's actions, because words are only a part of the truth, and often the least important part. My words said I was pissed. My actions said I was listening.

"I'm not saying you're wrong about Hudson," Fiora said quietly. "But I'd like to try the rational, low-key approach first. The Simmses have been respected members of the community for a long time. They've strayed into the netherworld, granted, but that's no reason to leave them forever bogged down in violence and stupidity."

"What about Jaime's family?"

"The Ibañez family is highly portable. They can pick up and move. They can start all over again in a place where money and drugs aren't synonymous."

"Lots of luck on finding a place like that," I said beneath my breath.

"The Simms family is a different problem," Fiora continued, refusing to be distracted. "Marianne can't throw the Bank of the Southland into two suitcases and fifteen cardboard boxes, head out for a new place, and start all over. That's the problem with joining a community. You surrender some freedom. In exchange you get a feeling of rootedness, of being part of something bigger than yourself. I'd like to see whether we can clear this mess up without uprooting the Simms family tree. I'm not sure Marianne would survive it."

The big silver car was doing only seventy now, just keeping up with the rest of the traffic on the freeway.

"All right," I said. "We'll try the velvet glove first. But I'll tell you right now, I don't think velvet will get the job done. There are too many players involved, too many conflicting interests, and too damn much free-floating cash."

Fiora started to say something, then fell silent.

"As long as we're going to make nice," I continued, "we might get Hudson's attention faster if I wore the velvet and you wore the iron fist."

"You in velvet would get anyone's attention." She smiled. "Unexpected, to say the least."

"That's the whole point. Hudson will look at us and assume that I'm the heavy lifter."

"You are."

"Fiora . . ."

"I'm listening."

And she was. That was the hell of it. She can tease me, run columns of figures in her head, and hold up her end of a conversation with no trouble at all.

"The game is called good-cop bad-cop," I said. "You've heard me talk about it before."

There was a moment's silence. Then Fiora laughed out loud.

Hudson's task force was headquartered in a Santa Ana Civic Center office building that had the mass-produced anonymity of the twenty-first century about it. The interior was every bit as characterless as the smoked-glass exterior. The deserted lobby was dressed with plastic rubber-tree plants and guarded by a closed-circuit television camera on a gimbel. From the front sidewalk to the fifth-floor hallway, we saw only one human being, a blind woman in black glasses behind the cash register in the closet-sized snack bar. The efficient elevators, austere fifth-floor hallway with plain brown-gray institutional carpeting, and off-gray walls were odorless, tasteless, functional, and sterile.

The fifth-floor office doors were a litany of modern anomie. ACME Megabits Inc., Maxi-service Mini-wares, Business Services Inc., FuturTronics. Each card contained only as much information as the tenant wanted the outside world to know. Suite 518 could have housed a telemarketing boiler room, a medical testing lab, or a title insurance company. The sign on the locked door said NTF INCORPORATED. Narcotics Task Force fit, but the average passerby never would have guessed.

Undercover cops have a weird sense of humor. They like to work close to the edge, then laugh at how stupid the rest of the world is for not seeing through their cover. I've known the impulse myself, but I usually control it in public.

NTF's door was locked. I punched the buzzer and heard it go off inside. Footsteps approached. The glass button in the middle of the door darkened while somebody eyeballed us. After a few moments a man opened the door.

"Yeah?"

He was one of the cops who had pulled Ysidro Ibañez out of the car yesterday. He had a flowing mustache, longish hair, and a look of total indifference on his face. The look changed as he studied me with shrewd, dark eyes, trying to place me, knowing he had seen me but not able to remember where.

"Lieutenant Hudson," Fiora said. "He's expecting us."

Without a word the cop turned away. He wore a Walther

in a loop on the back of his belt. The blue steel of the magazine catch had been polished shiny by daily buffing from a jacket.

"Visitors!" he called out.

He stalked back into the office, leaving us to follow if we wanted to.

The announcement was for the bullpen as much as for the lieutenant. There were a half dozen men and two women working at desks in the big room. All were plainclothes investigators. Several people—undercover operators worried about concealing their true identities—ducked reflexively when we civilians walked in.

Jill Swann looked up at us blankly, her expression perfectly controlled, noting Fiora with measured interest and pretending she'd never seen me before in her life. I looked at Swann the way a man looks at a pretty woman, frankly but without personal recognition. Our eyes met for a second; then she went back to the report on the desk in front of her.

I was beginning to like Swann in spite of myself. She had been walking on a very thin high wire—fooling her boss, fooling her lover, fooling the crooks. Now the wire was coming unraveled at both ends and Swann was fighting for balance as the metal strands slid out from beneath her feet one by one. Despite that, she looked as cool as a Margarita.

Hudson was a burly, big-chested man with dark hair and a handlebar mustache long enough to support waxed tips. He looked more like a bartender than a bureaucrat. He didn't get up from his chair. He didn't smile. He just stared at us.

Among football players, there's a name for the expression Hudson wore; it's called your "game face." Cops would probably have a name for it too, if they only wore it once a week.

The nameplate on the rented desk said Hudson's first name was Thomas. There were two other personal touches in the office: a .45-caliber 1911 Colt lay in a holster in the IN basket, and a series of *Los Angeles Times* and *Orange County Register* front pages hung in cheap frames on the walls. I could guess without looking that each front page contained a headline about a narcotics seizure or arrest. Like everyone else, the lieutenant enjoyed keeping score.

Hudson wasn't expecting Fiora, and he certainly wasn't expecting her to take the lead. She stood in the doorway of his office waiting for an invitation to enter, an acknowledgment of our presence, any kind of reaction at all. He stared at us for about fifteen seconds before she let a cool smile show on her beautiful lips. The smile said she wasn't intimidated. It also said she would stand there as long as he wanted to be a horse's ass.

Hudson made a curt gesture toward two chairs opposite him. We sat. Hudson waited for us to talk. Fiora waited for him to take the bait.

"Do I know you?" Hudson asked, but his tone said he didn't care.

"That depends," Fiora said.

Silence, then, "On what?"

"On whether you read the report that motorcycle cop filed this morning."

Hudson's eyes flicked reflexively to the single sheet of paper in front of him on the desk. Then he turned toward me.

"You're the guy on the phone a few minutes ago, right?"

I nodded.

"What do you want?"

"Lieutenant, you're going to make things real tough if you ignore Fiora. This is her meeting, not mine. She gets tired of macho types who assume that the man is always the boss. FYI, I'm the limited partner here."

The handlebars were good cover. They all but concealed the tiny twitch of Hudson's mouth.

"What do you want, Ms. Flynn," Hudson said, glancing once more at the report on the desk and leaning on the Ms. until it sounded like it should be spelled with a long line of Zs.

"We represent the Bank of the Southland. We can help

you recover fifteen million dollars from a money launderer named Faustino D'Aubisson."

For a minute I thought Hudson wasn't going to take the bait. Then he stood up, walked across the room, and closed the door. The office was suddenly quiet.

"Where is it?" he asked, sitting down again behind his desk.

"We don't know," she said. "If we knew, we would be required to tell the police, wouldn't we."

Hudson's pale eyes narrowed. "If you don't know where the money is, why are you wasting my time?"

"I'm trying to determine whether it would be worthwhile for us to locate the money," Fiora said patiently.

He picked up a flat steel letter opener and toyed with it, trying its tip and edge against the desk. The mannerism was unconscious. He did it often, judging from the marks on the desk.

"You work for the bank?" Hudson asked finally.

"We have been retained as consultants," Fiora said.

Her voice was even, uninflected. It suggested an adult's patience in a world full of children. It's her business voice. It drives me nuts.

"What kind of consultants?" Hudson asked.

"The bank's management was concerned about some unusual transactions. We were hired to investigate."

"You're attorneys." Hudson barely managed to keep his lip from curling.

Fiora looked at me in my boots, jeans, and Guatemalan cotton shirt and said dryly, "An attorney? Hardly."

"Private investigator?"

I shook my head.

For the first time, Hudson smiled. I liked him better the other way.

"Then you have no confidentiality privilege at all," he said with satisfaction. "I can haul you in front of a grand jury and drag every bit of testimony I want out of you."

So much for making nice.

I smiled back at Hudson. He took one look and came to attention. This was what he had expected of me all along—the heavy lifting.

"You ever hear of the Universal Life Church?" I asked. "We're both ordained priests. You ever heard of the confidentiality of the confessional?"

"Listen, asshole," Hudson snarled, "if you think you can get away with—"

"Sweet Christ, spare me the male shouldering," Fiora interrupted crisply. "Don't men know anything about structuring a business deal?"

24

FIORA AND HER CANNON. Gets 'em every time. I got
a kick out of watching, because for once I wasn't the target.

Hudson was still back in the early stages of postfeminism.
He thought broad-mindedness meant not calling women
broads. He hadn't run up against many women, even women
cops, who could get their mud in a ball, hold it together in
their little hands, and shove it up his ass.

He was game, though. Stupid but game.

"This isn't a business deal, Ms. Flynn," Hudson said angrily. "This is the criminal justice system. The profit motive
doesn't cut any ice with me. Justice is all that matters."

Fiora's smile was all perfect white teeth and not one bit
of warmth. "Then by all means let's talk about justice. We
can start with the entrapment of an innocent businessman.
You do remember the concept of entrapment, don't you,
lieutenant? That was the defense a businessman named John
DeLorean used so successfully."

Hudson's look said he remembered and didn't like it.

"If you don't like that subject," she continued, "we can
discuss cops who will do anything to keep a task force investigation alive, cops who will go so far as to help inter-

national crooks launder fifteen million dollars of dirty
money."

"That's not wh—"

Fiora kept talking. "Or we can talk about redheaded undercover operators who use the lure of sex to implicate an
innocent citizen in criminal undertakings."

"Now just a minute!" Hudson exploded. "Jill Swann acted
entirely properly! I saw to that personally and I can prove
it. Every conversation between her and Brad Simms is on
tape in there." He jabbed a finger toward a four-drawer file
in the corner of the room, "Read 'em and weep, Ms. Flynn.
We may not know much about profit, but we aren't the fools
you're trying to make us appear."

"That's precisely my point, lieutenant. You don't have to
be a fool to look like one in front of a jury."

Check.

I almost felt sorry for Hudson. Almost.

His game face slipped a little. For a second he looked nearly
human. He knew what Fiora meant. He had done his time
in witness chairs, sweating out some thousand-dollar-a-day
defense attorney's line-by-line examination of undercover
transcripts. The difference between the street and the courtroom is the difference between reality and the ivory tower,
and it's the cop who has to adjust, not the judge.

But Hudson didn't like being threatened.

"I stand behind my people. We are within departmental
guidelines in all our actions. The only deals that went down
were necessary to protect the integrity of the investigation
as a whole."

"Integrity? Did he really say integrity?" Fiora asked, looking at me.

I nodded on cue.

"I wouldn't call it integrity," she said. "I'd call it some
cop maximizing his professional reputation by entangling a
solid, respectable bank in a shoddy little sting operation."

"I doubt that the lieutenant—" I began.

"You go ahead and doubt it. I don't." Fiora turned back to Hudson. "You've been trying to implicate Mr. Bradford Simms in the laundering of illicit funds because that would give you and your squad a chance to seize the assets of the entire Bank of the Southland under the RICO statutes."

Hudson's game face was back in place. He didn't flinch.

"I can see the headline now: CORRUPT BANK SEIZED," Fiora continued scathingly. "Even if you lose the case somewhere down the line, the headline would look very nice up there on the wall next to your other trophies. Unfortunately for your ambitions, the Bank of the Southland is not now and has never been a racketeering operation. The bank directors will spend whatever is required to clear the name of the institution. They can afford to."

Hudson shrugged. "It's their right to try. That's what the courts are for."

"Wrong," Fiora said coolly. "The courts are for those defendants who refuse to make life easier for the cops by plea-bargaining. If you file charges against my client's bank, you and the district attorney's office should be prepared to fight those charges through every pertinent court. And then you should be prepared to defend a civil suit for false and malicious prosecution, as well. The headlines on that might not make the front page of the *Times*, but they would figure prominently in your personnel file."

Hudson came out of his chair, braced his fists on the desk, and leaned toward Fiora, trying out his command presence on her.

"Are you threatening me?" he asked.

"I'm describing the facts of life. If you're threatened by what you hear, that's your problem."

Fiora's cool voice raised Hudson's temperature by about ten degrees.

"Fiora," I said, "let's not lose sight of our mutual objective. Justice. Right, lieutenant? It's justice you're after, not headlines, isn't it?"

Gradually Hudson's jaw unknotted. He carefully traced the sweep of his mustache with his left index finger as he gave me a long look.

"What kind of justice did you have in mind?" he asked.

"The kind of justice you can buy for fifteen million dollars."

Hudson smiled sardonically. "I want more than that."

"We'll throw in Don Faustino."

"He'd have to handle the money himself. Hand to hand, in a controlled situation, something we could videotape."

"Hand to hand," I agreed, "but no videotape and no body bugs. They're looking for them. And I'll do the deal, not her," I added, glancing at Fiora. "From now on she's not going any closer to that asshole than a telephone."

Fiora gave me a quick look of disapproval but didn't say anything. She was too smart to interrupt the process of earnest bargaining, once it had actually begun.

"I don't care who hands the money over, so long as D'Aubisson is the one picking it up," Hudson said.

"Agreed. In return, Simms and Ibañez walk."

"No dice. I don't give a shit about the Colombian. He's just a mope. But Simms is going to have to stand up in front of a judge and plead to something."

"Why?"

"I've got my people to think about. We've spent too much time chasing his sick young ass around the county, watching him suck up nose candy and play the big-shot banker. He's not going to skate. He's going to have to plead guilty to something, if only for the morale of my squad."

"Are you more worried about your squad or your own career?" Fiora asked, glancing at the clippings with cool disdain.

Hudson glared at her, then turned back to me as though the question didn't deserve an answer.

"Will morale be served by a misdemeanor guilty plea?" I asked.

"Fiddler, that's not wh—" began Fiora.

"Sorry, *partner*," I said over her words. "He's gonna fall. All we can do is try to pad the landing."

Fiora tapped her nail against her purse, shrugged, and went back to examining the clippings on the wall. Hudson looked gratified, which had been the point of the whole sideshow. Give a little, get a lot.

"I'd rather have a felony plea," Hudson said.

"I'd rather be fishing for salmon in British Columbia, but I'm here trying to cut a deal with a cop who believes in fairy godmothers," I said. "You can have a free misdemeanor plea or you can fight like hell against an entrapment defense on a felony. If you go for the misdemeanor plea, it has to be handled quietly, in the judge's chambers. No headlines that would ruin the bank."

"Guilty pleas in criminal cases are public record."

The undertone of satisfaction in Hudson's voice brought Fiora's attention back to him.

"Lots of things exist in the public record but never make the newspapers," I said, hanging onto my nice-guy act. "All I'm asking is your promise that neither you nor any of your people will tip the press and turn Brad's guilty plea into a public circus."

"I don't control the press. What if they find out on their own?"

"Then you'll tell them wonder boy was just in the wrong place at the wrong time, that he's really a pretty good kid, and that shit happens even in the best families." I gestured toward the walls. "There are a thousand ways to blow a situation all out of proportion, and there are another thousand ways to deflate it. Do we have a deal?"

Hudson looked at me a long time with his clear, pale eyes before he said, "You two make quite a pair. You do this for a living?"

"She does. I protect my amateur standing against all comers."

He shook a cigarette out of a battered pack, pulled a lighter out of the desk's belly drawer, and lit up. He examined the cigarette and my offer from all angles, then shrugged.

"Okay. The mope gets a walk and Brad gets a slap on the wrist, in camera. We get D'Aubisson and fifteen million."

"More or less," I said.

"What's this 'more or less' shit?"

"You'll get the contents of fifteen U-Haul boxes, wherever they might be. I haven't counted the bundles, so I don't know exactly how much there is. If you're short a few thousand, don't come crying to me."

There was another long silence.

"Don't screw with me, cowboy."

Fiora looked at the ceiling but held her tongue.

Hudson glared at her, then shook his head in defeat. "I'll have to clear it up the chain of command," he said. "But I think they'll okay it."

"Fine," Fiora said. "We'll do the same with our clients. You going to be here at five o'clock? I'll call you then."

Hudson grunted. "What if your clients don't agree?"

"No worries," I said. "We'll get out of the way and let you, God, and the South Americans sort it out."

"What about the money?"

"What money?" Fiora said.

George Bradford's ninety-year-old redwood Victorian two-story had stood up to time very well. Painted white with green trim, the house stood in the midst of a well-groomed lawn enlivened by beds of rosebushes as old as the house. It was a graceful showpiece from the last century, a dowager aunt with a cameo broach at the collar of her high-necked wool dress and sensible, expensive shoes from Buffums on her tired feet.

I began to feel sorry for Brad. When the confinement of community and family began to stifle me, I had packed a violin case and a knapsack and gotten in the wind. Brad didn't have that luxury. His family roots nailed him to the town that shared his name. He was lugging a century of family tradition on his shoulders. History can be a hell of a burden, even the relatively brief history of a southern California family like the Bradfords.

"This time you get to be the good cop," I said.

"Do we tell Brad the truth about Jill?"

"No way. He's having enough trouble keeping his mud in a ball as it is."

Mrs. Simms was hovering behind the pale, graceful day curtains of the old mansion. She opened the door before we could knock. She was dressed in a matched sweater and slacks, rather than her work clothes, and she looked tired, almost haggard. I wondered whether she and Brad had been talking or just staring at one another in the dim, cool twilight of the old Victorian sitting room.

"We need to talk to Brad," I told her bluntly. "We don't have a lot of time. It would be quicker if you'd take a turn around the garden with Fiora while I outline his options for him."

"No."

Direct and to the point. Quick, too. The wrong damn answer, but you can't have everything.

She turned and walked toward the drawing room without a backward glance, and we had no choice but to follow. I liked the woman's style. She was tough and decent and willing to fight for what she believed in. Unfortunately, none of that would help her son and too much of it would hurt him.

Brad was sprawled in a leather recliner, wearing a Ralph Lauren rugby shirt and jeans. He looked up but didn't say a word.

"You take it," I muttered to Fiora. "The urge to spank him is becoming irresistible."

Fiora sat down and calmly outlined the task force investigation, making it seem that we had discovered the cops by backtracking Ysidro Ibañez instead of by running Jill Swann

to ground. Then Fiora sketched the details of the negotia-
tions with Hudson. As soon as the guilty plea was mentioned, Mrs. Simms shook her head fiercely.

"Absolutely not."

Her face was ashen and grim. She didn't look at her son,
only at Fiora.

"The facts can't be changed or finessed," Fiora said without heat. "Brad broke the law. If he pleads guilty to a misdemeanor, the matter will be handled quietly. Bank of the
Southland will survive."

"I won't permit my son to be labeled a criminal."

Mrs. Simms's face was a death mask. Only her eyes
showed life. They burned with an energy that wasn't quite
sane, the fierce intensity of a lioness protecting her cub.

The cub in question was still sprawled comfortably in his
expensive clothes. I locked my jaw to keep from saying
anything.

"Marianne," Fiora said carefully, "if Lieutenant Hudson
wants to push, Brad will face a long, very public trial, followed by conviction on money-laundering and racketeering
charges, followed by prison."

Mrs. Simms neither said nor did anything. She sat as
though frozen.

"The press would report every allegation, every word of
testimony, day after day," Fiora continued unemotionally.
"Even if Brad were acquitted—which is *not* likely—the
bank's reputation would be ruined."

"The bank's reputation is attached to the Simms name."

The tense, uneven quality of Mrs. Simms's voice made
me an unwilling participant in her pain. Looking at Brad was
also painful, but it was a pain that could be cured. At this
point we had nothing to lose. Mrs. Simms wasn't going to
budge.

"Hey, wonder boy," I said. "Did Mommy cut off your
tongue, too?"

Brad flushed. He moved his leg and sat up straighter. He

opened his mouth to speak, but Mrs. Simms was quicker. Furious, she turned on me.

"Stop it!" she commanded.

"No."

My flat refusal surprised her.

"That's the risk you take when you don't hire a gentleman," I said. "Now you can sit back and shut up or you can stand up and walk out. Alone. All that's on the line for Brad is a slice of family pride, but there's another kid out there in the real world. His whole family is on the line. They could be killed by the folks whose dirty money your son so happily laundered."

Mrs. Simms opened her mouth. No words came out. She looked at Brad as though pleading with him to say my words were lies.

"I'll write out my resignation now, if you want, or you can fire me, whatever is better for the bank," Brad said, breaking his silence. "I'll sign over the voting power of my stock to you, so you can have a free hand in reorganizing operations." He glanced at Fiora. "Unless you have a better way to minimize the agony for everybody involved."

Three of us knew who else Brad meant. His mother didn't. I wondered how he was going to react to the news that his "everybody" had been living an extended lie.

Mrs. Simms would have preferred her son to be silent. She wore the miserable, rigid expression of someone who is learning the unhappy truth about the connection between the road to hell and good intentions. She held her hand out to Brad even though he was sitting well beyond her reach.

"This isn't what I wanted when I hired them. I had hoped—" Mrs. Simms cleared her throat. "I do love you, Brad. No matter what, that won't change. But I don't—" She cleared her throat again. "I don't expect you to believe me."

Brad started to say something, but it was lost in the sound of the doorbell.

"You expecting anyone?" I asked.

Brad shook his head. So did Mrs. Simms.

The doorbell rang again. I reached for the Detonics, which had been digging into the small of my back. Mrs. Simms looked horrified when she saw the gun in my hand.

Fast and quiet, I went to the hallway and stood to one side of the solid wood door, relic of a time when peepholes weren't necessary. The bell rang again.

"Who is it?" I said.

"Jill Swann."

I reached for the doorknob, wondering what the hell else could go wrong.

It didn't take me long to find out.

25

I STEPPED onto the porch and pulled the heavy front door closed behind me. Swann's skin was the color of bleached flour. She looked like she was hanging on to control by a fine steel thread.

"What's wrong?" I said flatly.

"Faustino has Ysidro Ibañez."

"Shit. What happened?"

"Somehow Faustino found out this morning that Ibañez was in jail. Faustino called in his lawyer, and thirty minutes later a judge had set bail and Ibañez was gone. Cochi Loco met him at the jailhouse door. If I had to guess," she added tightly, "I'd say they're beating the crap out of Ibañez right now, trying to find out where the money is."

"Ibañez is going to have a tough time telling them. He doesn't know anymore."

"I figured that out from what Hudson told us. We've got to do something, Fiddler. They'll kill him."

"Not until they find the money. Cochi doesn't kill for pleasure." I shoved the gun back into my belt. "Okay, Special Agent Swann, you've delivered your message. Now go tell

Hudson our deal is off. That fifteen million is going to buy a daddy back."

"You tell him. I have to talk to Brad."

"That's a really dumb idea, lady. He doesn't need that kind of distraction right now."

"I'm not too crazy about it myself, but if he finds out from someone else, I'll never see him again."

"He won't find out from me."

That wasn't good enough for her. She stepped around me, pushed the door open. If I'd thought I could get away with it, I'd have grabbed her and carried her out to her car. As it was, all I could do was follow her in and hope to pick up some useful pieces after she exploded her bomb.

Brad scrambled to his feet when he saw her. "Jill? What the hell . . . ?"

She tried to smile.

"What's wrong?"

Brad had a few masculine instincts. He moved to his woman and caught her up in a hug she returned with a kind of desperation, as though she was storing up memories.

"What's wrong?" Brad repeated.

For a long moment, Swann didn't answer. She just clung to him. Then she broke away and stepped back.

"Brad—"

Swann's voice got away from her. When she spoke again, it was fast and hard, as though she wanted to get it over with before she lost control.

"I'm a cop, a Customs agent. I'm part of a task force investigating Faustino. And you."

The words didn't register for a moment. When they did, Brad's expression changed, showing a fury that was unexpected in a true gentleman. Swann's own mask slipped, showing the agony underneath.

Brad didn't see her pain. He stared at her, his expression distant, as though he had never seen her before. And in many ways he hadn't. Special Agent Swann was a hell of a lot different from his very own passionate Jill, the love of his life.

I cursed silently and waited for Brad to blow up in front of us. I needed him intact. He didn't know it yet, but he was Jaime's shining hope. And mine.

"I'm sorry," Swann said, her voice almost hoarse. "I've made a mess of everything—your life, my life, the investigation, everything. I never expected to fall in love. I just wasn't prepared. I'm sorry."

Brad continued to stare for another minute before he said calmly, "Are you here to arrest me?"

His voice was different. Nothing tentative. Nothing ingratiating. And nothing fragile. I began to see a faint hope of having some useful pieces left.

"No," Swann said carefully, fighting for her voice. "I don't think I'm going to be arresting anybody anymore, not after Hudson finds out about us."

"Are you saying that screwing me wasn't part of your assignment?"

Swann flinched. She blinked rapidly, trying to deny the tears. It didn't work. They flowed like large hot drops of rain. But nothing in Swann's eyes changed, nothing in her stance, nothing in her determination to see it through. As I watched her, I sensed that Brad was about to learn what Fiora had long since taught me: tears don't prevent a woman from clear thinking . . . or from pulling the trigger on a recalcitrant male.

"You bastard!" she said savagely. "I fell in love with you!"

"Yeah. Sure. That's why you made a fool of me too, right? Or was that just sort of a—"

"Sit on it," I said, talking across whatever else Brad intended to say. "There are bigger problems in the world than your love life. Faustino has Ibañez."

Brad blinked, trying to switch gears. Fiora had no such problem. She was on her feet, ready to move, her mind racing as she looked for a way to control the damage.

"I thought Ibañez was in jail on a no-bail immigration bond," Fiora said.

"He was," Swann said, managing to switch gears like the good undercover operator she was, despite the shine of tears on her face.

"What happened?"

"An attorney walked into the jail with a signed court order voiding the immigration hold and setting bail on Ibañez at twenty-five thousand. Cochi Loco posted the appearance bond in cash. Everything went down in half an hour. We didn't even know until afterward."

"How can that happen? What judge would sit up and bark for Faustino?"

Fiora beat me to that question, but probably because I already knew the answer.

"Her Honor Elaine Shartel, judge of the Superior Court," I said before Swann could speak.

"How did you know that?" Swann stared at me with the cold eyes of a cop.

"Uncle Jake told me. But don't worry. He won't be telling anyone else. He's dead."

I could see George Geraghty and Elaine Shartel collide in Fiora's memory. Her expression changed from disbelief to frank distaste.

"And to think I once considered a career in law," she muttered.

"I don't understand," Mrs. Simms said crisply.

"You're fortunate," Fiora said. "Tell her, Fiddler. I'm too angry to do a good job."

"In tracking down Ibañez yesterday, I called in a favor from a defense attorney named George Geraghty," I explained. "I didn't know George was tied to Faustino, although I should have considered that possibility."

"But how does that relate to Elaine Shartel?" Mrs. Simms objected. "She sits on the Golondrinas board with me. She's a fine woman. She doesn't take orders from criminals."

"No, but she does listen to George. She was his law partner

after they both left the Public Defender's Office. Now she's a sitting judge. When George needs a favor, he goes to her like a bee to a private honey pot. I can just hear George now. 'The no-bond hold is a miscarriage of justice, Elaine. My client is a family man with deep roots in the community. He has citizenship equity. He has good friends who are willing to vouch for him. He is entitled to bail, whether he believes himself worthy of it or not.' "

Mrs. Simms winced at my tone, but she listened.

"Naturally Judge Shartel leaped to aid the poor, downtrodden illegal alien." I made a disgusted sound. "God save us from good intentions, my own included."

"Don't blame yourself," Fiora said. "You had no way of knowing George would double-cross you."

"I knew he was capable of it. I'm just surprised he bothered. The rent on a corner suite is a lot higher than a lawyer's morals."

"If he's that corrupt," Mrs. Simms said, "why did you go to him in the first place?"

"George isn't corrupt, not in his own mind. Corruption is a meaningless moral construct to him," I said. "Justice is a big game between his clients and the cops, and he's along to make as much money as he can, selling tickets, hawking peanuts, and rolling drunks behind the bleachers."

"It's worse than that," Swann said. "We have information that Geraghty crossed over. He *belongs* to Faustino."

"What kind of information?"

"I'm not free to—" she began.

"It's too late for that bullshit," I said angrily. "If you start playing by the nice bureaucratic rules, Ibañez is dead meat."

Swann swallowed, then nodded. "The task force has made some very big money-laundering cases in the past few months. Every time we take a defendant down, anywhere in southern California, Geraghty shows up and monitors the case, whether he represents the defendant or not. We picked up the pattern, but we couldn't figure out what he was doing. Then, last week, another agency turned up an informant who says Faustino offered Geraghty a million-dollar cash retainer. The money is payable when Geraghty figures out who has been supplying the task force with all their information."

I looked at Swann with a new respect. "How does it feel to have a million-dollar bounty on your head?"

Brad's cold expression thawed a little as he began to realize how much was at stake.

Swann shrugged. "It comes with the territory."

"Is Geraghty close to earning that million?" I asked.

"Not so far. He still thinks it's somebody inside the group. I'm just a hanger-on." Swann's smile was swift and cold. "Of course we've gone to a lot of trouble to make him think that."

"Do you enjoy being a spy?" Brad asked.

Swann drew a ragged breath and faced him. "I was wrong not to tell you. You have every right to be mad. But I won't apologize for anything I've done to Faustino and his people, and I sure as hell won't apologize for being a cop. That's my job, a job I'm proud of, a job I do well." Her mouth twisted. "At least I used to do it well. I haven't covered myself in glory since I met you."

Brad looked like he wanted to argue but couldn't exactly figure out where to begin. Without a word he walked past Swann, headed out the back door. I caught his arm and stopped him.

"Do you know the difference between good and perfect?" I asked.

"That's easy," Brad snarled. "Nothing's perfect."

"But some things are very good. Think about it before you throw away something good, just because it wasn't perfect."

Brad shook off my hand and vanished down the hallway. A few moments later a door slammed at the back of the house. It was very quiet in the room. Mrs. Simms walked up to Jill Swann and looked her over curiously.

"We haven't met," Mrs. Simms said, "so forgive me if I'm too personal. Do you still want him?"

"Yes." Swann's answer was clear, unequivocal.

"The door to the back yard is down the hall and through the kitchen."

Swann hesitated.

"Marianne's right," Fiora said. "If you're going to be emancipated, you have to teach your man how to deal with it."

Swann looked at me. "Is that how it works?"

"When it works, yes."

"And when it doesn't?"

"That's when you wish you had a way to turn off all that electricity."

This time Swann understood what I was saying.

"I'll take my chances," she said, heading for the back door and her angry lover. "I don't really have a choice."

"But you have a choice in what you tell Hudson," I said.

Swann stopped and looked at me, unsure of my meaning.

"I've got an idea," I said, "but to make it work, I'll have to know what Hudson is doing at all times. You're the only one who can give me that."

She thought about it for a minute. "I won't betray my badge."

"I'm not asking you to. I just don't want any nasty surprises. In return, I'll give Hudson something he wants more than a headline."

"What?"

"George Geraghty's ass."

26

BENNY ANSWERED on the first ring. The hollowness of the connection told me the call had been forwarded to his portable cellular phone.

"Where you at, home boy?" I asked.

"Little Saigon, the Bolsa mini-mall. Best bouillabaisse this side of the Cordon Bleu School. Makes you proud of imperialism."

"I'll take your word for it. You still have our cargo?"

"Of course not," he said cheerfully. "I used it to pay for lunch."

"Funny, Benny. Speaking of the bad old days, you remember how Victor Charlie used to make scrap metal?"

"Too bloody well, mate."

"Fix our cargo the same way."

"Are we talking about the same Victor Charlie?"

"Think of it as a money-back guarantee," I said. "If we have to give the money back, we want to guarantee nobody will ever spend it."

Sometimes Benny has a really evil laugh. It's one of the things I like best about him.

"No worries, mate. One money-back guarantee coming up."

"Just make sure there's a long trip wire on it, okay?"

"No worries. But can we use something besides my van to make the delivery? Hand controls are bloody hell to rig. I just got the bugs out of these."

"I'll pick up a Ryder and see you back in Newport in an hour."

I dropped the cellular back in its cradle between the front seats. Fiora gave me a slanting, hazel-green look. She doesn't like it when Benny and I talk in code around her.

"What was all that about?" she asked.

"All what?"

"Fiddler—"

"We were just being careful. Cellular lines are open-air, you know."

"You're not on the phone anymore. Stop being careful."

"I don't want to burden your mind with unnecessary details," I said.

"Now wait a damn minute. I promised I wouldn't do anything in this partnership that I didn't tell you about first."

"Uh-huh."

"Well?"

"I never made a similar promise."

Anger burned along Fiora's cheekbones, but she never stopped thinking. After a few moments she let out a long breath.

"That bad, huh?" she asked.

"I doubt it, but when it comes to screwing around with the likes of Cochi Loco, I'm a careful man."

She seemed to accept that. At any rate, she was silent as we drove to George Geraghty's Newport Center office building and parked the car.

"This won't take me long," I said.

Fiora reached for her door handle.

"Wait here." I heard the tone of my own voice and reconsidered. "Please wait here."

"Are you planning on murdering him?"

"No. Just cutting a deal."

"That's my forte, remember?"

"Not this kind of deal. This is the deal that gets cut with the devil."

"Then I'll listen and learn."

"Fiora . . ."

She got out, shut the door, and looked at me across the roof of her silver car.

"I won't say one word unless you explicitly ask me to," she said.

It was the best I was going to get. The only other alternative involved using my superior strength and inferior wit to tie her to the goddamn car.

"Right. Not one word."

Geraghty had the early warning defenses and diversions deployed. When I asked to see the boss, the salon-tanned secretary sighed with profound unhappiness, showing me four inches of cleavage.

"I'm so sorry, Mr. Geraghty isn't in," she murmured. "He didn't say when he would be back. He's such a busy man. In the future, to save being disappointed, it would be wise to make an appointment in advance."

Just to make sure my trip hadn't been completely in vain, she heaved another cleavage-shaking sigh. The whole performance would have been more impressive if I hadn't been more interested in the lights on the AT&T Wizard telephone console at her desk. One of Geraghty's lines was in use, and this bimbette was the only employee in the shop.

I sniffed. Fresh cigar smoke in the air.

"Don't worry," I promised her. "I'll tell him you tried."

I headed for the corner office, Fiora silent behind me. Before the receptionist could buzz Geraghty, I threw the heavy oak door open. It made a nice sound when it met the rubber door stop embedded in the wall.

Geraghty was sitting behind his desk, cigar in one hand

and telephone in the other. He studied me for a moment, then hung up without saying good-bye.

"Rude, George, really rude. I thought law school was supposed to teach you manners."

"You could use a few yourself. What do you want?"

"Some advice. Only this time I'll pay for it. Seems like the stuff I got for free may end up costing me fifteen million bucks."

Geraghty blinked at that. Then he cocked his head to one side and studied Fiora.

"Hello, Fiora. You're more beautiful than ever. I kept hoping you'd call me some day. I thought you were smarter than to stay with Uncle Jake's idiot nephew."

"One sentence," I said to her, holding up my index finger so there would be no mistake.

"Go to hell," she said.

I couldn't tell whether she meant me or Geraghty. Neither could he. He simply put the cigar in the big crystal ashtray, got up, and closed the office door. Then he went to an oak file cabinet, opened a drawer, and pulled out a flat box with a short antenna. Cochi Loco kept one like it in his trunk.

"Say it ain't so, George."

Geraghty didn't say a thing. He frisked both of us electronically. Fiora watched him like the snake he was. So did I. He kept his hands on the black box when he went over Fiora, giving me no excuse to do what I so badly wanted to do to him.

No needle jumped. No alarm sounded. Geraghty ran it over me again, grunted, and put the box back in the file.

"Sorry about that," he said. "Win a few cases, and suddenly you're a target for every cop in the country."

"No problem. We both know how far we can trust each other."

He sighed and lied again. "I'm sorry about Ibañez. I didn't realize until some time later—this morning, actually—that your friend worked for Don Faustino."

"You didn't call Faustino until a few hours ago because it took you that long to figure out where your biggest payoff would come—him or me."

"Not a payoff. A fee for legal services rendered."

"Legal services? Setting up some poor mope for execution?"

"I have absolutely no knowledge of that." Geraghty said it offhandedly.

"Nice legal phrase. It ranks right up there with 'not to the best of my recollection.' "

"You do what you have to do, Fiddler. I do what I have to."

"My God. You still have enough humanity to feel defensive. You're a bloody marvel, George."

Geraghty flushed angrily. "Get to the point or get out."

"Simple. I want to prevent a murder, assuming it's not too late already."

"I told you I know nothing of—"

"Save the bullshit for Elaine Shartel. We can't negotiate a deal if you keep trying to act like you don't know what's on the table."

Geraghty sucked on the black cigar, discovered it had gone out, and opened the belly drawer of his desk. "I'm listening."

"I have the fifteen million and Faustino has Ibañez."

"Does he?"

"Ask Cochi Loco."

Geraghty rummaged in the drawer. "Go on."

"I'll swap half the money for Ibañez."

"All of it."

"No way, pal. A promise isn't worth that much."

For the first time, Geraghty began to relax. "I wondered what was in this for you. Same old dumb Fiddler—tilting at windmills nobody else gives a tinker's damn about. Who did you promise?"

"Nobody you know."

Geraghty looked at the cheap lighter he had found in the drawer. He chewed on the cigar and turned the lighter end over end in his quick, clever fingers. After a minute he looked at Fiora. So did I. Her face was without expression, a death mask, and her eyes were the cold bottomless green of a river pool.

"Don Faustino wants all his money," Geraghty said.

"Tough shit. Cochi can connect Ibañez's pecker to a field telephone and crank all day long but nobody's going to answer. Ibañez doesn't know where the money is. I do."

Geraghty rolled the cigar in his mouth. "There's the matter of internal discipline. Don Faustino intends to make an object lesson of Ibañez, sort of a message to the troops."

"That's where you come in." I lifted my left boot and planted the sole on the polished rim of the desk. "You're going to talk Faustino out of this tough-love approach to management."

"I am?"

"Yeah. And I'm going to be so grateful that I give you the snitch who's been operating inside D'Aubisson's ring. Think of what that would do for internal discipline."

Even defense lawyers have autonomic nervous systems. Geraghty's pupils got real big and he drew a deep involuntary breath. He wasn't thinking about internal discipline. He was thinking about earning his seven-figure bounty.

"How do I know you can do it?"

I smiled. "Trust me."

"I'm serious, Fiddler."

"So am I."

The lighter's wheel rasped and a three-inch flame shot up. Geraghty sucked hard, took the cigar out of his mouth to examine the hot spot, then shoved it back in the fire. The end of the cigar that had been in his mouth looked like Kwame's frayed rawhide chewbone. Geraghty chewed and sucked and chewed and sucked until he was happy with the stink. He took out the cigar and examined both ends with satisfaction.

"You'll have to be able to prove it," Geraghty said. "A name out of the hat won't get it done."

"I may look stupid, but I'm not. Think about it."

"I have been. That's why I'm still talking to you. Have you seen Cochi Loco?"

"Yes."

"Think you could take him?"

"I don't think it matters," I said. "Fiora has a theory that violence is the result of bad organization. Since we've become partners, I'm organized as all hell."

Geraghty sucked and chewed some more before he said, "All right. It's a deal. But if you're not as organized as you think, my money is on Cochi Loco."

I was betting on the big bodyguard too, but not in the way Geraghty was.

Fiora kept her silence until we got to the car. Before she could say anything, I tossed her the keys, hoping to distract her by making her drive.

It didn't work.

"Communicate," Fiora said, snapping the shifter down into reverse and backing out of the parking space.

"You're running out of gas. I noticed that on the way over, meant to mention it. Also, the engine is a little ragged at fifty-seven hundred rpms. Time for a tune-up."

She gave me a look.

"You don't want that kind of communication?" I asked. "Okay. If you want specific communication, you have to ask for it."

"Don't go mulish on me now," she said, snapping the shifter into drive. The big car shot forward. "What are you planning?"

"You heard me in there. You know as much as I do."

"Frightening thought," she muttered.

"But true."

"That's crap. You aren't planning to keep half the money."

"Geraghty thinks so."

"Geraghty has the brains of a turd. You aren't going to turn Jill Swann over to Faustino, either."

"You have more faith in me than Geraghty does."

"That wouldn't be hard."

I smiled slightly and ran my fingertip from Fiora's right shoulder to the hand curled around the steering wheel.

"You're right, love," I said. "I'm not going to trade Swann. But I am going to use her."

"How?"

"By using Brad. I'm going to keep wonder boy at my side every step of the way. Any nasty surprises that happen to me, happen to him."

"Don't you trust her?"

"Against Faustino, yes. But if the choice was between what I want and what the cops want . . ." I shrugged. "Swann's a cop. I don't want to put her in a position where she's going to have to choose. That's my best chance of organizing this charade so no one gets killed."

Silence came while Fiora ran the situation forward, backward, sideways, inside out, and upside down through the ultra high-speed Cray supercomputer hidden beneath her sleek blond hair.

There were lots of flaws in my plan, but it was irritating as hell that she found the worst one on her first try.

"Brad is coming off a serious addiction problem," she said. "Can he handle this?"

"We'll find out."

What I didn't say was that I was betting my life he could.

Fiora didn't say it either. Some things are just better left unsaid.

27

THE OCEAN whipped by, little shocks of blue flashing between the buildings along Coast Highway. I ran variations of the kidnap/ransom game through my mind one last time. Nothing new. Nothing improved. It was what it had always been, a crap shoot with the devil, and the dice were being passed to me.

I picked up the phone and punched in a number. Lieutenant Hudson picked it up on the first ring.

"Hudson."

"Our clients gave us the green light. How about you?"

"I've talked to the prosecutor. Your boy can get off with a wrist slap, so long as it's in the interests of justice."

Hudson lied like a psychopath or an undercover cop, without qualm, without hesitation. It shouldn't have made me angry, but it did. Maybe I was just tired of being treated as though I had the IQ of a room full of hair.

But at least Jill hadn't lost her nerve and confessed to her boss.

"What about Ibañez?" I asked.

"Like I told you. He's a mope. Who the hell cares about one mope more or less?"

The mope's family, that's who, but pointing it out would only distract Hudson.

"Okay," I said. "On those terms it's a done deal."

"It's a done deal when we get our hands on the fifteen million."

Ah, sweet justice.

"How about your suspect?" I asked. "Don't you want him?"

"Everybody's a suspect in this game."

"I was thinking about a certain South American businessman."

"He's just another mope in an expensive suit," Hudson said. "Yeah, sure, we want him. What the hell do you think is the point of this whole exercise?"

"Dirty money and headlines to match."

"Listen, asshole, I don't have to take this from you."

"Really? You have someone else you can take fifteen million dollars from?"

Hudson breathed hard and said nothing.

"You get the money and the man tonight," I said. "I'll call you later and let you know when and where."

"Hold it, cowboy! You're way ahead of yourself. We don't run our roundups like that. We call the shots, not you. We set up the delivery and the transfer. We control the situation from beginning to end."

"Not this time. I'm not your employee. I'm not even your snitch. I owe you nothing, least of all control of the transfer. Have your men ready. I'll call and tell you when and where. Are you in or out?"

The line was silent.

"Okay," I said. "I'm sure Newport PD has someone they can spare to gather up fifteen million and the biggest money launderer in California."

"We're in." Hudson's voice was strained through clenched

teeth. "Just don't push me too far, cowboy. You could end up in jail for obstructing justice."

"Obstructing your career isn't the same as obstructing justice."

I hung up before he could respond.

"Where to?" Fiora asked after a moment.

"There's a Ryder rental office on Seventeenth Street."

She glanced at the clock and started pushing stoplights. Even so, the girl at the Ryder office had the CLOSED— CERRADO sign in her hand when Fiora dropped me off out front. I could have gone to U-Haul, but I really wanted the visibility of a bright yellow Ryder van. So I used my unfair biological advantage and opened the door before the girl could lock it.

She wore a plastic tag that said her name was JANI. Jani tried to act businesslike, but with a name like that and working for $4.50 an hour, it's tough. To make things worse, her boyfriend sat out front in a Volkswagen bug, playing Def Leppard at maximum decibels and making obscene tongue gestures at her through the windshield.

"I need a van for two days," I said.

"You have to have a commercial license."

"Not for a van." I smiled to show how harmless I was. "I've done this before. Go ahead, check your rules. I'll wait."

I might have waited, but the bozo outside was randy and ready to fly. Jani looked outside, then shoved a rental form across the counter at me. I filled out the top with a phony name and address. Jani took over for the rest of the form. She asked for my California driver's license. I flashed it at her, then read her the numbers off the license, scrambling three of them in the process.

"Major credit card, please."

"How about two days' rental, cash in advance."

"The card isn't for the rental. We take an imprint for the deposit. Then if you don't bring the truck back, we charge everything to your credit card."

"What's a van worth?"

She shrugged. "I don't know."

"More than five hundred dollars?"

She gave me a look. "Sure."

"Then my credit card won't do you much good. There's a five-hundred-dollar limit on it."

Jani got the joke but she didn't laugh. She was distracted again. Bozo in the VW was bouncing up and down in the seat, demonstrating his mattress technique.

"How about a thousand bucks, cash, as a deposit?" I asked. She shook her head.

"It's perfectly legal. Check the service contract. Trust me. I've done this before."

She glanced sideways at me, then at her boyfriend out front. She sighed and turned over the service contract form and came face to face with enough fine print to hold us both until midnight. Bozo hammered on the horn in time to the music, a beat that was about as subtle as the last thirty bars of *Bolero*.

I fanned a dozen hundreds on the counter and discovered Jani could count.

"That's more than a thousand dollars," she said.

"Not if you subtract two bills. I figure that's the least I can do for coming at closing time and causing your date to get restless."

Nobody had ever offered Jani a bribe before. She wanted the money but wasn't quite sure what to do. I turned my back, wandered over, and stared out the glass front door. Bozo was playing drummer on the steering wheel. When his solo ended, I went back to the counter. There were ten hundreds lying there. I don't know where she put the two bills, because she wasn't wearing a bra and there were no pockets in her miniskirt.

Bozo was probably in for the surprise of his randy young life.

Jani finished filling out the rental agreement, time-stamped it, and pulled my copy. "There you are, Mr. . . ."— she checked the form—"Johnson. I gave you the van with the plush carpet. It's really rad." She winked at me. "Have a nice night."

Benny was working in the garage when I pulled up. He stared at the interior of the bright yellow van with distaste.

"Looks like a bloody whore's Christmas," Benny said.

"The girl said it was rad."

"The young are easily impressed."

When Benny wheeled around and opened the back of his own van, I was the one who was impressed. Benny has genius. No matter how simple or complex a technical problem might be, he will discover a solution to it that is both elegant and direct. The direct part was C-4 moldable plastic explosive; Benny always has the stuff around because he uses it to start his barbecue. But the elegance of the device came from Benny's understanding of human psychology. He had put all fifteen cardboard boxes on a wooden pallet, strapped them in place with plastic binders, and strung bright red wires from a power source to each of the boxes.

"Most of the wiring is phony," Benny said matter-of-factly. "All the boom is in the center box, the one with the receiver. But this way looks more impressive to the civilians." He peeled back the flap of one of the cardboard cartons. "I put a liter of gasoline in each box as an accelerant."

"Are you trying to kill somebody with this bomb?" Fiora asked. "Is that the part of the plan Fiddler left out?"

There was a certain careful lack of emotion in the questions that bothered me. Benny answered before I could.

"I'm not trying to kill anyone," Benny said. "What about you, Fiddler?"

"Nope."

"Besides, it's not a bomb," Benny continued. "It's a standoff destructive device. If you call it that, you'll feel better."

"I doubt it," Fiora muttered.

"Then call it life insurance," I said. "Faustino is a backshooter, the kind of man who would have a sniper with

orders to waste us all once he had his hands on the money."
I looked at Benny. "What are you using as a trigger?"

He tossed me a palm-sized plastic box that was slightly
bigger than a pack of cigarettes. There was a clip on the back.

"Lose that and you owe me a new remote-control Genie
garage-door opener, catalog price $39.68," Benny said.

I looked at the pushbutton in the center of the box.
"Range?"

"Two blocks. That's why I suggested you do this little
dance out in the country somewhere. Genie only uses a
dozen different frequencies for these remotes. I'd hate to have
some civilian come home from the movies and open his
garage door while you were trying to consummate your deal
two blocks away. There's a one in twelve chance he'd blow
you into the next century."

Fiora didn't say a thing. She didn't have to. The idea of
one more variable, and an explosive one at that, wasn't something she wanted to hear.

"I'll transfer it to the Ryder," I said.

Fiora looked at Benny, as uneasy about the bomb as I am
about sticking bare wire into live electrical sockets.

"Harmless as a baby," Benny assured Fiora. "It's not armed
yet. You don't think I'd let your man drive around city streets
with a live bomb in back, do you? I'll wire the power supply
into the circuit when we get to the exchange point."

She wasn't entirely reassured, but she moved to the other
side of the pallet. There she eyed the roughly sawed lumber
and cardboard boxes as though they were a hundred pounds
of sleeping snakes.

"Let's get it over with," she said.

"Don't snag your silk," I said.

She gave me a disgusted look, then bent over and grabbed
hold of the bomb.

Considering its value, the pallet wasn't heavy. But it was
damned awkward to handle. Together we slid it through the
side door of the Ryder van. Fiora gave the bomb one last

look and slammed the door shut, as though to prove the device didn't scare her. Unhappy but determined, she turned to me.

"Now what?" she asked.

"Now I jack up Jill."

I used Benny's cellular to call the task force office. A strange voice answered.

"Is Jill Swann hanging around?" I asked, trying to sound like a dinner date.

Swann picked up.

"Can you talk?" I asked.

Swann recognized my voice. "Hello, Tom. Sorry I didn't get back to you sooner about dinner. Things have been kind of tight. You know how it is."

"Yeah. Your boss is playing games with me. He thinks I don't know Cochi bailed Ibañez out."

"Sorry about that, but it's out of my hands."

"Is it? Time to choose sides, Jill."

There was a long pause. "I already have. You know it as well as I do."

"Then you won't mind if Brad is my Siamese twin tonight, will you?"

"You bastard!" she breathed.

"I try. Are you in or out?"

She was silent for what seemed like an hour before she said, "In."

"I don't need anything fancy. Just give me a warning if Hudson moves. You have Fiora's cellular number on file, right?"

"Sure," she said in a normal tone. "Sounds like fun. But it might be too late for dinner before I get out of here. The boss is being tight-assed again. He's keeping us hanging around but he won't tell us what's going down. I'll try to call you when I know. Really."

"Good. The more I know, the less chance someone gets killed. Keep it in mind."

I hung up.

One down. Four to go.

I punched in Brad's number at the ancestral home. He answered in three seconds flat.

"How would you like to run a little ringer on your old customer Faustino?" I asked.

"I'd love it."

He still sounded angry and eager to vent that anger on somebody. That was fine with me. I had somebody in mind.

"Stay by the phone," I said. "I'll call you."

"Wait! What about Jill?"

"She's safer than you'll be."

"But wh—"

"Pretend she doesn't exist until this is over," I interrupted. "If you're thinking about her when you should be thinking about your own ass, you'll lose both."

I hung up.

Two down.

Fiora was sitting on Benny's couch, watching me. Her expression told me she was wondering if I ever took my own advice. Before she could ask me, the phone rang. I picked it up.

Cochi Loco was on the other end.

28

¿*QUE PASO, VATO?*" I asked. "I thought you'd leave the negotiating to your tame lawyer. Or are George's hourly rates too steep?"

"I do not use lawyers." Cochi's voice was rich with contempt.

"Yeah, I know what you mean. Is the banker with you?"

"Yes."

"Does he still have all his arms and legs?"

"Yes."

"Congratulations. You're as smart as I thought you were. Let me talk to him."

There was silence.

"You're wasting time," I said. "I'm not going to purchase merchandise that's too damaged to talk."

An instant later Ibañez was on the line. His voice was hoarse and shaky as he gave the standard Spanish phone salutation.

"*Bueno.*"

I talked fast, knowing Cochi would get restless. "Your family is safe, all three of them. You can be, too."

"They will not let me live."

"They won't like it, but they'll do it. Just follow orders when I give them. ¿*Comprendez?*"

Cochi took the phone back before Ibañez could reply.

"What is your plan?" Cochi asked.

"Nothing down, no interest, and no balloon payment at the other end. You and your Creole friend bring the banker. Meet me in Santa Ana Canyon. There's a hamburger stand named Knowlwood, just west of the intersection of Imperial Highway and Orangethorpe, a mile north of the Ninety-one Freeway."

Cochi grunted. "I understand."

"There's a phone booth in the parking lot, underneath a streetlight. Be there at eleven P.M. Let the banker get out of the car and wander around in the light so I can see him. I'll give you a call on the pay phone, and we'll take it from there."

"My employer will not be with me. He does not bother himself with such matters."

"He will this time. I'm not going to turn those cartons over to anybody else."

"Are you very sure?"

"Sorry, hombre. I'm sure. Be patient a little while longer. And remember—neither one of us is as stupid as he looks."

Cochi was crazy like a fox, not a pig. There was a two-beat pause, and then he went on talking as though nothing had happened.

"I think you will have us drive around while you make sure we are alone."

"You know how it is," I said. "I hate party crashers, especially when they're carrying assault rifles."

"I told my employer to expect such caution from you. But he has travel plans. Could you limit the foolish driving to one hour?"

"That depends on who's smarter, you or your boss. I'm betting on you, Cochi."

Cochi chuckled deeply, reminding me again of that old China boar. He was still laughing when I disconnected.

250   A. E. MAXWELL

Three down.
One to go.
I punched in the number for George Geraghty's office.
Some stoned surf bunny at an answering service tried to
convince me to call back in the morning. When I suggested
Geraghty would fire the service if he didn't get this call, the
girl finally agreed to try tracking him down. I left the portable
cellular as the call-back number.

The key to what I had planned was the cellular phone, the
greatest communications breakthrough since the ballpoint
pen. Cellular phones have completely revolutionized the
daily lives of thousands of people. No more waiting around
by a phone that never rings. Now you can take the phone
with you and conduct your life while you wait.

To a cop, cellulars are an absolute nightmare. Cops have
been able to trace phone calls since Alexander Graham Bell
built his third instrument, but now, with phones that can
roam all over the world, the old game of call-tracing has
become impossible. A smart cop like Hudson could lock on
an incoming call and trace it back to its origin in a matter
of minutes, but as long as the call came from a cellular, all
he'd have was a number, not a fixed location.

Of course there is a drawback to cellular phones. They use
open-air channels, the equivalent of party lines. Hudson was
no fool. He knew a number of players in this game, including
both Fiora and Cochi, had cellulars. By now he had probably
set up some kind of monitor on the open-air channels in the
cells we were likely to use, whether or not he had a wire-
tap authorization to do so.

On the other hand, there are a lot of calls going out in the
clear from southern California. All I could do was keep moving, avoid mentioning any more names, and pray that the
party would be over before Hudson sorted out the invitations
from the background noise.

Which meant it was time for all of us to get on the road
again.

I sent Benny out to roam the late-evening traffic in his

own van and Fiora over to pick up Brad. I threw a tarp over the standoff destructive device and took the Ryder van on my own errand. Two fast stops, one at an electronics store in Orange and one at a music store on Tustin Avenue, and I headed back to Luz Pico's place. If it all went from sugar to shit, I wanted to leave Jaime with something more than anger and guilt and shattered pride.

The night air in the citrus grove was damp, cool, sweet. The waning moon was little more than an amorphous glow through the thickening marine haze. I parked beside the adobe house and shut off the engine. The night was infused with the sound of water running through irrigation furrows. I stood for an instant with the two presents in my hands and listened as though I had never heard the sound of water before and never would again.

Luz opened the door before I knocked. Mrs. Ibañez was right behind her. The smell of *carnitas* and chiles clung to them like an earthy perfume. I looked at Mrs. Ibañez.

"I talked to your husband. He's as well as can be expected. I told him that the three of you are safe."

"*A Dios gracias,*" she said, crossing herself.

I looked at my watch. "Is Jaime still awake?"

"*Sí.*"

I followed her to the back of the house. Josefina had already fallen asleep on a couch in the television room. Roger Rabbit was playing on the VCR. The three boys were transfixed. Jaime saw me, stopped smiling, and went back to watching. He looked ten years older than the Pico boys.

I put one of the wrapped packages beside Josefina on the couch, took the afghan from the back of the couch, and covered her against the slight chill in the room. In the low light her face looked almost unmarked, as serene as a madonna. I turned away.

"Jaime, I need to talk to you. Alone."

Without a word he stood up and followed me out onto the veranda. The yellow bug light in the outdoor fixture gave a peculiar cast to the night. I offered Jaime the remaining package. He looked at me warily, but without real anger. I wondered what his mother had said to him that had eased his pain at being tricked.

"No strings," I said. "Take it."

The sound of paper tearing overshadowed the crickets for a moment. Then Jaime's head snapped up and he stared at me.

"A Walkman," he said, pulling out the player and earphones.

"I took a chance and got one for your sister too. Do you already have one?"

He shook his head, then said slowly, "Thanks, I guess."

I pulled a cassette tape out of my pocket and handed it to Jaime. "Ever heard of him?"

Jaime read the back of the tape box and shook his head.

"Beethoven is a very great composer." I smiled slightly and added, "Even greater than Bruce Springsteen."

Jaime looked skeptical.

"The tape is of the Violin Concerto in C Major. It's the music that taught me the difference between being a boy and a man. You probably won't like the concerto the first time you hear it. That's okay. Hang on to the tape. Some day when the world seems like a prison, put on the tape and listen, really listen. Then you'll know that freedom, like manhood, is in your mind. No one can take either one away from you, Jaime. Not me. Not Cochi Loco. Not Don Faustino. No one."

Jaime looked at me for a long moment. There was more understanding in his eyes than I had expected and less than I had hoped for.

"Cochi Loco and Don Faustino are holding your father hostage. I'm trying to get him back. If everything works out, you'll be eating breakfast with your daddy. If not, I wanted you to know who was responsible." I searched for more words and didn't find any. "Play the tape once for me, *hijo*."

I left Jaime in the strange yellow light with the crickets singing in the darkness beyond.

By the time Fiora and Benny were set up in the parking lot of a convenience market on the other side of the river, it was ten-thirty. I cruised the Knowlwood parking lot once. There were a dozen light pickups and old-style muscle cars in various states of disrepair and restoration. The Coors Brigade was finishing its ritual dinner of grease-burgers and six-packs. One of the pickups had a bumper sticker that said it all: BEER IS GOD'S WAY OF MAKING SURE CONSTRUCTION WORKERS DON'T TAKE OVER THE WORLD.

I tried the phone booth in the parking lot. Dial tone, complete number pad, no chewing gum in the coin drop, clear connection. Satisfied, I drove back to the other side of the nearly dry river. I was at a traffic light on Imperial when the cellular buzzed on the dashboard. I pulled over and picked up the receiver. George Geraghty was the only player with my number, so I didn't even bother saying hello.

"The slick Creole is trying to stiff you out of a million-dollar fee," I said.

"Is that supposed to mean something?"

Geraghty's voice was a trifle slow, a shade thick, a bit hoarse, as though he had been sucking up $50-a-bottle chardonnay at Antoine's or bourbon with water back at the Plank House. I guessed the Plank House, judging by the "live" music in the background; some luckless semitalented son of a bitch was trying to make himself and his out-of-tune piano heard over a room packed with drunks.

"Save your dummy routine for juries," I said. "I'm not recording this call."

"I can't hear you."

"This is a cellular number, George. Anybody who wants to can listen in. Why should I waste money on tape?"

"It's a free country. Say whatever you want."

"I'm going to buy a mope an hour from now. Afterward,

the Creole is headed south. And I mean *south*. No return ticket and no forwarding address for outstanding debts."

"That slimy little cocksucker!"

"Yeah, yeah, and his mother wears combat boots. Get real. You knew he would try to stiff you. Only a fool would pay a million bucks when he could have the same information for free. The Creole's no fool. But he can be had."

I could practically feel Geraghty come to attention. Like most defense lawyers and all stuntmen, he had this thing about the size of his balls. They had to be the biggest on the block.

"Yeah? How?"

"Meet me in thirty minutes in the parking lot of Yen Ching, on Glassell, just north of the Twenty-two."

He was silent, trying to think fast when he had eaten too well and drunk too much. The crystal sound of ice cubes bumping against glass came over the phone, combined with a frank slurping sound. Bourbon on the rocks, the manly American libation. Two an hour keeps the blood-alcohol level somewhere in double digits.

Attaboy, Geraghty, suck hard on that icy tit. Make my job easier.

"Why are you doing this?" he asked. "What's in it for you?"

"I owe the Creole one. A big one."

Geraghty hesitated. "Yen Ching, huh? Okay. And—uh, no hard feelings about the mope, right? It was just business."

"No problem here."

"Jake wouldn't have understood."

"Jake's dead."

Geraghty sighed. "Yeah. Damn. You know, I'd trade it all to be nineteen again."

"I wouldn't trade any of it. Half an hour. Don't be late."

I hung up.

Four down, none to go. Targets coming up on the scope.

I parked the van in the shadows behind the market, next

to the empty 750. Fiora and Brad were with Benny in his van. The boy wonder was dressed in blue jeans and a dark green cotton bivouac sweater. His eyes were too bright and too wide open, reminding me of a kid on his first overnight. He jumped when I opened the van door and got in.

"Relax," I said, punching him in the shoulder, trying to knock some of the bullshit and hot air out of his system.

Brad laughed nervously but began to let down a little. The four of us sat in Benny's van, eating a bag of Cheetos Fiora had bought in the market. While we crunched, we listened to the Bearcat prowl the radio waves. Every few minutes Benny entered a new round of frequencies with the keypad, looking for radio traffic, picking up bits and snatches of law enforcement calls.

"Domestic disturbance, second call from the neighbors. Somebody's going to have to respond. . . ."

"Four-five-nine silent at . . ."

"Cancel two-eleven in progress at Seven-Eleven. Back-fires, not shots."

". . . wants and warrants on vanity plate J-A-R H-E-D. Send backup. Car is full of drunk marines."

Benny laughed as the scanner moved on.

"Send Vietnamese translator to thirteen twenty East . . ."

". . . in pursuit of stolen car at ninety miles an hour, eastbound on the Ninety-one approaching the Fifty-five. He's staying with the Ninety-one, pushing a hundred on the clock."

Benny held the scanner on the spot.

"Hundred and five. Ten. Fifteen. Twenty. He's gonna TC! Vehicle hit center divider, flipped, skidded across the one, two, and three lanes, now upside down in fourth lane, no sign of . . ."

Benny set the scanner off and running again.

"This goes on all the time?" Brad asked, half fascinated, half appalled.

"Believe it," Fiora said. "Turning one of those scanners

on is like turning over rocks at the beach. The top is smooth and sun-warmed and clean. But the underneath—" She shook her head.

"Your world can stay clean and warm," I pointed out. "All you have to do is walk away when the rocks start rolling over."

"Don't start in on that again."

"Listen, woman. If we didn't need an extra set of wheels you would be back in Crystal Cove right now, and you know it as well as I do."

"Does Cochi drive a white Mercedes?" Brad asked.

I turned and looked. Cochi's white Mercedes was gliding down the ramp, signaling for a left turn onto Imperial Highway. Inside the vehicle, backlit against the traffic light, three figures were clearly visible.

"Go," I said.

Benny started the van and slid unobtrusively into the sparse traffic on Imperial. Three hundred yards ahead was a broad band of Mercedes taillights. Cochi signaled and made the left at Orangethorpe. Moments later he was in the parking lot. The white Mercedes stuck out among the Coors Brigade vehicles like a diamond in a bowl of dirt.

Cochi was making it easy for me. The dome light was on even before the man in the back seat opened the door and stepped into the garish circle of purple mercury-vapor light. I lifted the binoculars. As we slid by on Orangethorpe, I could see Ibañez clearly. His face looked puffy and bruised but he was walking on his own.

I picked up Benny's cellular and tapped out the number of the pay phone in the parking lot. Cochi answered on the second ring at 11:01 and thirty seconds.

"You're late," he said.

"Shit happens. Is the banker out in the light where we can see him?"

"Of course."

Cochi sounded impatient, as though he had expected a better organized operation.

"Give me five minutes to verify the ID. If you haven't heard from me in that time, get back on the freeway and head toward Newport Beach. When you reach the junction between two freeways, choose the right-hand one. Then turn on your dome light. Leave it on for exactly four miles, driving the speed limit. Any questions?"

"No."

I hung up.

"Misdirect, mislead, and generally muddy the waters," Benny said approvingly. "You missed your calling. You would have made a fair illusionist."

"Did I miss some nuance?" Fiora asked.

Benny smiled. "Your former husband just made certain that Cochi is going to be examining every vehicle that passes Knowlwood for the next five minutes, trying to figure out which one we are in."

"It's like baseball, football, or seduction," I said. "You just keep putting the ball in play. Sooner or later, something will sneak through."

Benny made a pair of lefts that brought us back to Imperial, then a right turn back to the market. I gave him directions to the little park beside the dry riverbed where Jill had taken me, put Brad into the Ryder van with the bomb, and walked Fiora to the 750.

"You've got the number on the portable?" I asked.

She nodded.

"In about two minutes, Cochi is going to come back down Imperial and get on the freeway toward Newport," I said. "Follow him at a discreet distance. When he turns on the interior lights, cruise by and see who's inside. He'll be looking for a man, not a woman, but don't hang around too long. Just make sure the other men in the car are Faustino and Ibañez."

"But you said you had seen them in the car already."

"That was in the parking lot. I want to make sure Cochi doesn't substitute two ringers carrying Uzis."

Fiora became very still. "And if he does?"

"Then we'll back out quietly and try another approach."

She gave me a searching look. "You aren't usually that generous when somebody tries to stiff you."

I passed up the bait. "After you call me, go to the coffee shop at Chapman and State College. At eleven-fifteen, call Swann. Have her meet you there with Hudson and his men at precisely eleven-thirty."

"What do I do with them?"

"Wait until I call."

"Hudson will want to know more," Fiora said.

"You can't tell him what you don't know, which is why I'm not telling you anything."

I glanced at my watch, then looked across the freeway toward the Knowlwood parking lot. A set of bright double-beam headlights came on. A Mercedes. Ten seconds later the big car made a turn back onto Imperial.

"I'll be right behind you," I said and turned away.

"Fiddler?"

I stopped, looked back at Fiora. She was just within arm's reach. The instrument lights threw a rosy chatoyance over her face and hair. She was alert, alive, so beautiful to me that I could barely breathe. In that instant I wanted her more than anything else in the world.

She knew it.

"I heard what you told Brad about dividing his attention," Fiora said, her voice low and husky. "I don't want you to be looking over your shoulder for me when you should be watching Cochi Loco."

"Then stick to the program. That way I won't have to look. I'll know where you are all the time."

I kissed her fast and hard, because we both knew there were too many variables to put much faith in any program.

"Go."

The 750 vanished like a sleek silver ghost, leaving me behind.

29

BRAD WAS PERCHED on the passenger seat like a crow with a stiff neck, peering out at the world through his stylish glasses. He twitched when I slammed my door getting in. The van's engine didn't start until the second time. That made him twitch too. I maneuvered the van into place a hundred yards behind Fiora.

"Relax," I said. "This sort of thing is like making love— a lot of fun as long as you stay loose in the knees and tight in the hips."

His laugh was like his posture. Too tight. He was going to fly apart if a car backfired. If bad jokes couldn't distract him, maybe something tangible would.

"Can you handle a gun?" I asked.

"My—" Brad's voice cracked. He cleared his throat and tried again. "My high school was a military academy. Most of it didn't take, but I was a good shot."

"Rifle or pistol?"

"Both."

Once in a while you get lucky. "There's a revolver in the glove box. Try it out."

He opened the glove box and removed the two-inch .38

Smith & Wesson Airweight. His mind might have been nervous, but his hands knew what to do. The muzzle of the gun stayed pointed between his feet as he snapped the cylinder out and checked the loads. Brad was no Cochi Loco, but with any luck he wouldn't have to be.

"Five rounds, double-action," I said. "If you have to use it, just aim and pull the trigger."

Brad knocked out the cylinder, checked the load again, and snapped the cylinder back into place.

"I've never shot at anything except paper targets."

"You'll feel right at home. Lawyers are nothing but paperwork and hot air."

Brad put the pistol in his pocket. I kept track of Fiora's lights, letting her set the pace while I looked for strangers who were doing the same.

Fiora stayed in the fast lane at an unobtrusive sixty until the 91–55 split. Then she picked up a few miles an hour, dragging me along. A hundred yards ahead of her, a dome light came on in a car in the number one lane. Fiora picked up her pace, changed lanes, and made her pass.

I let her go, holding behind the Mercedes. She slid by the Mercedes at seventy and kept going into the night. A minute later, the portable cellular went off. I picked up the receiver.

"Is he a man of honor?" I asked.

"I wouldn't go that far, but Ibañez is in the back seat and Faustino is at the wheel."

I hung up and punched in the number of Cochi's car phone. He answered immediately.

"You passed the first inspection," I said. "Now get off the freeway at the next off ramp, make a left, and drive for ten minutes. Then turn around and come back to the off ramp. Be there at precisely eleven-thirty. If I'm not there, wait for me. Got it?"

"We are losing our patience with your game."

"If the Creole doesn't like driving that much, switch places."

I hung up before Cochi could answer.

Ahead, the Mercedes signaled off at Chapman obediently. I drove past the exit and kept going.

"Now what?" Brad asked.

"Do you like Chinese food?"

"Not particularly."

"Good. The restaurant is closed."

I made the transition from the 55 to the 22. The lights of the Glassell off ramp burned brownish yellow in the damp night air. The Yen Ching restaurant hadn't seated a customer for more than an hour, but there were a few cars left toward the front of the lot, close to the miniature golf course. I parked way in the back, in the deepest shadow I could find.

"Here's the program," I said, turning to face Brad. "Listen hard because it might go down at any second. A piece of legal slime called George Geraghty has been trying to earn a million-dollar fee from Faustino."

Brad whistled. "How?"

"By identifying the police informant inside Faustino's organization."

For a minute Brad was blank, then realization sank in. "That's Jill!"

"Yeah, but we're going to say it's you."

"But what if—"

"No," I interrupted. "No arguments. Just follow my lead, answer my questions, and listen real hard to what Geraghty says because someday you may have to testify to it under oath."

"But if he—"

"Shut up and listen. Take the gun out of your pocket and stick it under your belt in the small of your back."

Military schools are good for something. Brad followed direct orders.

"Now lean forward and lock your fingers together behind your back as though you were handcuffed."

He did.

"Can you reach the gun easily now?"

Brad grunted and fumbled.

"That's not good enough. Move the gun until you can get to it."

While I watched, he reversed the handle of the gun and shifted it to the right a few inches. Headlights glared in the van's sideview mirror as a car headed toward the darkness where we were parked.

"There," Brad said. "That feels bet—"

I backhanded him hard enough to break the skin on his lip but not hard enough to stun him. Before he could get his hands up to fend me off, I gave him another rap, this one on the nose, making his eyes water and his nose bleed. He tried to protect himself but I was already done. I pushed his hands down.

"Easy does it," I said. "Turn your head toward the window."

"Go to—"

"*Do it.*" I slammed Brad's head against the window hard enough to shake the safety glass. A car turned out of the parking lot, its headlights illuminating both of us for a moment. I looked at Brad's face critically. He looked a bit shocky. Blood from his nose and the corner of his mouth glistened blackly against pale skin.

He started struggling. I held him hard against the glass.

"I want Geraghty to believe I've just finished beating the shit out of you," I said. "And that's just what I'll do if you don't settle down."

I eased off the pressure. Reflexively, Brad shook his head and wiped his mouth with the back of his right hand, smearing the blood that was trickling from his nose and mouth. Then he blinked and stared at me with eyes that weren't as trusting as they had been a moment ago.

I finally had his attention. All of it.

"As soon as Geraghty has dug his grave with his big mouth, I'll give you the word. Then you'll pull out that gun and screw it in his ear. Got it?"

Brad nodded.

"Questions?"

He shook his head slowly.

"Good."

There was no time for fine details or flourishes. Geraghty's silver XJ-12 Jaguar was pulling in along the far side of the van. He parked in the shadows and shut off the engine.

Moving slowly, letting Geraghty see that my hands were empty, I got out and walked around to the driver's side of the Jag, taking time to read the vanity plate: COPB8TR. Geraghty wasn't so much a defense lawyer as an anarchist manqué.

The electric window on the driver's side slid down. The air in the Jag smelled of bourbon and cigars. Geraghty's eyes looked too sober for my comfort. He glanced at the van.

"Not your usual style, is it?"

"When a vehicle is carrying fifteen million dollars, style doesn't matter."

For a moment Geraghty didn't believe it. Then he did.

"You broke the bank! Jesus Christ, you're crazier than Jake ever thought of being!" Geraghty leaned closer, staring at the figure slumped against the van's window. "Who's that bleeding all over the glass?"

"A coke freak and sometime banker named Brad Simms. He's been bird-dogging Faustino's operation for the task force, buying off a beef for felony possession. Come on, he'll tell you the whole thing."

Politely I opened the door for Geraghty. The dome light came on. It revealed the shiny chrome-steel revolver he had been pointing at me through the car door. Geraghty eased out of the Mercedes.

"All right, Fiddler. Let's take a look at your million-dollar snitch."

The gun made my spine itch, but there was nothing I could do about it at this point. I had expected Geraghty to be armed. I just didn't like it.

"Simms is a little the worse for wear," I said as I walked

back toward the van. "We had to reach an understanding."

"Can he still talk?"

"Hell, yes. What good is a snitch that can't talk?"

As we got to the passenger side of the van, I reached for the little Maglite in my hip pocket. Geraghty was about a half a beat slow in jabbing me with the gun. Booze doesn't disrupt the reptilian part of the brain too much, but it plays hell with the higher functions.

"Just a flashlight," I said. "See?"

The beam hit Geraghty square in his dime-sized pupils. They reacted to the light slowly. He batted at the flashlight with his gun hand. I thought about feeding him the pistol but didn't. Instead, I turned around, opened the van door, and dragged Brad Simms out.

Geraghty blinked and peered, but his eyes were still stunned by the beam of light. He could see that Brad's hands were behind his back, but that was all.

I played the flash across Brad's face, further distracting Geraghty. The cold white beam of the halogen bulb washed the natural color from Brad's skin. The places where he had been struck appeared heavily bruised by contrast. His eyes looked a bit shocky. The blood coming from the corner of his mouth and his nose was fresh.

"You did work him over," Geraghty said, surprised. "You've changed, Fiddler. You never used to like hurting people."

"Snitches aren't people. Isn't that right, Brad?" As I spoke, I grabbed Brad's left elbow, positioning my fingers to mash down on the ulnar nerve. "Speak up. Tell the nice defense lawyer how you've been passing Faustino's secrets to a lieutenant named Hudson."

"I find out things," Brad said sullenly. "I tell Hudson."

"You're the one with the bank in Newport, right?" Geraghty asked.

"Yeah."

Geraghty turned toward me. "Not good enough. The leak

has been going on longer than your snitch has known Faustino."

Shit.

George had been doing his homework. Brad might incriminate himself falsely, but he wasn't going to be happy about telling on his lover. I'd have to make sure that he didn't have time to think about it.

"Tell him the rest of it, wonder boy," I said, tightening my grip on his arm. "Tell him about your girlfriend's other job."

Brad glared at me. "Go to—"

My fingers found his ulnar nerve first before he could finish. He groaned and twitched like a moth on insecticide.

"Tell him."

Face pale and sweaty, eyes clenched shut, Brad fought for control. Even though I had lifted the pressure almost immediately, he gave a good impression of a man in continuing pain. Maybe Jill had underestimated her lover's ability as an actor. Just in case she hadn't, I brushed the nerve again. His breath came in raggedly.

It was Geraghty who provided the final touch. He shoved the gun into Brad's groin.

"Talk or die, kid."

Brad might have wondered about my ultimate morality, but he had no doubt whatsoever about Geraghty's.

"I've been working with a woman," Brad said jerkily. "She's a federal agent."

I squeezed very gently, cutting him off from further speech.

"A Fed?" Geraghty yelped. "I thought it was just a local task force! What's her name?"

Brad looked at me.

"Tell him," I said softly, not liking the look in Geraghty's dilated eyes.

"Jill—Jill Swann." Brad groaned, trying to shrink away from the muzzle of the gun. "She's passing herself off as a tax consultant."

"Swann? Holy Christ!" Geraghty's eyes narrowed. "Are you sure?"

"Yes," Brad said, defeated.

"But she's got an office in Century City and another in Newport Center. They exist. I know they do. Faustino had one of my investigators check her out completely before he started doing business with her. We ran her every way I could think of, and she always checked out." Geraghty leaned on the gun, burying it deeper in Brad's groin. "Not that it matters. As soon as I tell Faustino, she's dead meat."

And so was Geraghty, except for one small detail; he still had the muzzle of his gun digging into Brad. I started easing away from the center of the action. I got three steps before Geraghty realized what was happening.

"Where you going?" he said warily, automatically bringing the gun around to cover me. The muzzle was the size of an open manhole.

"Any time, Brad."

My tone was conversational. Geraghty didn't understand what was happening until he felt the cold round bore of the Airweight imprinting itself in his cheek.

"Drop it!" Brad said.

His voice was a little shrill, but Geraghty wasn't in any position to make artistic objections. Neither was I, for that matter.

"Call him off or die, Fiddler."

Geraghty's voice was definitely shrill. The chromed barrel of his gun quivered in the faint moonlight.

I looked at Brad. "If he shoots me, you'll be next. So keep pulling the trigger until he stops twitching."

"Uh-huh," Brad said. His voice was calm and confident.

I looked back at Geraghty. "You're a great trial lawyer, but there's no appealing a through-and-through head wound. Think about it. Then drop your gun."

Geraghty thought about it for the longest ten seconds of my life. Then he blinked. The muzzle of the gun drooped fractionally. Before he could blink again, I had the gun. I

slammed him up against the side of the van, pulled out a
Tyton plastic handcuff, and bound his hands behind his back.
   "Jake would be very disappointed in you," Geraghty said.
   "I keep telling you. Jake's dead."
   "When Faustino finds out, so are you."

30

BENNY WAS PARKED unobtrusively on Glassell a half
block from the entrance to the little park where Jill Swann
and I had talked that morning. He wore a black watch cap
over his dark hair and a wolfish grin.

"You really made a believer out of Cochi Loco," Benny
said, as the hydraulic lift in the tailgate deposited his wheelchair on the asphalt. "Those three gents are sitting on their
bums in a Standard station right beside the freeway, just like
you told them to do."

"How much time do you need?"

"Thirty seconds, unless you've been cocking about with
circuit wires."

Benny propelled himself back to the open cargo door of
the Ryder van and levered himself inside with his massive
forearms. I flashed the Maglite around the interior of the
van, revealing Brad Simms and a very angry George Geraghty. In addition to the indignity of Tyton plastic handcuffs,
I had taken off one of my socks and gagged him with it.

"What have we here?" Benny asked.

"Family barrister. Genus *Defense*. Species *asshole*."

"That's what I thought, a balding *Rattus rattus*."

Geraghty tried to return the compliment but the sock got in his way.

Benny cocked his head as though he were listening closely, then shrugged. "Don't jump salty with me, Barrister, or I'll wire your old feller into this firing circuit. Twelve volts might be more of a shock than your heart could stand."

While Benny rummaged among the U-Haul boxes, Geraghty started to say something else. Then his eyes focused on the red plastic-coated wires, the liter bottles of gasoline, and the receiver. His eyes got very big.

"That's right, you silly bugger," Benny said as he deftly mated wire with wire. "It's a bomb. I've got a very sensitive switch wired into the circuit. Bounce hard or talk loud, and a bad taste will be the only difference between you and strawberry jam."

Geraghty became very still. Benny checked the connectors and looked up.

"Good to go."

I reached for the telephone and punched up Cochi's number. He answered quickly.

"You're three minutes early," Cochi said.

"In three minutes, get back on the freeway, come straight west to the traffic circle, then south on Glassell to Hart Park. Take the road into the park and come straight back until you see me. Do you understand?"

"Yes."

"Listen, Cochi. We're both simple men. This is a simple job. Let's keep it that way."

I hung up before he could answer.

After I turned around, Benny gave the receiver one last check, looked up, and nodded.

"I'll open the line when we're in position," I said. "If you hear any conversation you don't like, hit the button."

"You really sure you want me to put the torch to all this gelt?"

"The longer I'm around this stuff, the more sure I become. Half the world is corrupted already, including the cops, and the other half is dying for the chance."

"In that case, get that can out of the front seat of my van."

Benny levered himself back into his wheelchair while I went forward and found the red five-gallon plastic jerry can on the floor in front of the heater vent. I brought it back.

"Put that bad boy right in the middle of the stack," Benny said.

"What is it?"

"Motor oil and gasoline, the closest I could come to napalm on short notice. Money can be a bitch to get started." He handed me the control unit. "This is your trigger. Don't worry about accidentally setting it off. Just don't sit on it by mistake."

I glanced at the trigger. It looked like what it was—the remote control for a garage door opener.

"So I push and it goes boom, huh?"

Benny gave me a pained look. "Boyo, this is a standoff destructive device, not a bomb. It will take about thirty seconds for the wires on the liter bottles to heat up and melt through. Even then, it won't look like Krakatoa right away, more like Paul Hogan's barby. But sooner or later the message will get through that jerry can, and then things will get real hot real fast."

"Good enough. Do you have the other trigger?"

Benny's thick, deft fingers vanished beneath his loose shirt and came up with the second remote unit.

"You're usually not this nervous," he said.

"I'm usually not this well organized."

"That's the problem with being organized. You get to worrying about all the variables instead of staying loose and ready to jump. Don't forget—when all else fails, you can pull out that bloody great cannon you're wearing and reduce the variables to a few stones' weight of cooling meat."

I gave Benny thumbs up. Where he came from, the gesture

means *bugger you*. He doubled the signal and returned it, then wheeled off to his own van.

When I was certain that Benny was in place, I turned the key in the Ryder. The van started on the second try. I turned down the park road, trading the well-lit street for the dark shadows thrown by sycamores and eucalyptus. I didn't see Benny's van. Apparently he had turned off his lights already. I didn't know where he was now, but I knew he was within two blocks, the effective range of the transmitter.

Brad sat half turned in the passenger seat, watching Geraghty spit into his gag. The young banker still held the short-barreled .38 in his right hand.

"Ready?" I asked.

"I'd just as soon it was over with."

"Amen."

The night moved past me slowly while I let my eyes adjust to the darkness. The marine layer had moved in early, putting an opaque lid over the land. The air was dark and glistening. The low ceiling caught the radiance of city lights and diffused it through the dense air. The resulting illumination was treacherous, rather like a night scope. Shadows were deeper and pools of light glared, playing tricks with depth perception.

I drove with the window open, listening to the moist sound of tires on the pavement, the early summer rasp of crickets, and the furtive rustling of air among the broad leaves of the sycamores.

"My grandfather donated the money for this park," Brad said absently.

I grunted.

Two hundred yards into the park, I found the little pocket where Swann and I had parked a few hours and lifetimes ago. The hideaway was empty and dark. I backed the van into a parking slot and killed the engine. From the medium distance came the sound of traffic on the freeway. From nearby, a horned owl hooted in a palm tree. I punched Fiora's number into the pad.

She answered immediately. "Where the hell have you been?"

It was as close as she would come to saying how worried she was.

"Stringing wires," I said. "Any sign of the headline hunters?"

"Swann should be arriving at any—hold it. This might be her."

There was a ten-beat pause.

"It's her. She's got about ten guys with her. They're pouring in here like the finale of a bad cop movie. What should I tell them?"

"The truth."

"Which part of it?"

"You don't know where I am. I'll call again as soon as I'm ready for them."

I wanted to say more, much more, or maybe just one thing. But the time wasn't right. Besides, she already knew.

Suddenly a pair of powerful headlights flared in the darkness at the entrance of the park. I broke the connection with Fiora and punched in Cochi's number. He answered immediately.

"Kill the headlights," I said. "Come straight ahead."

Before Cochi could speak I hung up and called Benny. He picked up instantly.

"We're on," I said. "You hear shots or anything else you don't like, *open the garage door.* Got it?"

"Ten-roger. And remember, mate, she'll get over a few dead bodies so long as one of them isn't yours."

I set the receiver aside without answering, but I didn't break the connection.

The Mercedes' bright headlights had disappeared. Faustino drove slowly, cautiously. He was still a hundred yards away, entering the park's darkness with reluctance.

"Get in the back of the van," I told Brad. "If Geraghty makes a noise, shoot him through the head."

I didn't care whether Brad would do it. I just wanted Geraghty to think about the possibility.

"They'll hold on to Ibañez until they've seen the money," I continued. "I'll bring Faustino here. When I open the van's back doors, don't say anything. Just point your gun at Faustino. I'll take it from there. Understand?"

"Yes," Brad said. His voice was surprisingly steady. "What about the bomb? How will we know if Benny triggers it?"

"If you smell something burning, bail out and run like hell."

"What about Geraghty?"

"Carry him out or let him fry, but don't waste any time over it either way."

With the phone in one hand and the bomb trigger in the other, I climbed down from the van, took a deep breath, and stepped out from behind the screen of shrubbery. The Mercedes was thirty yards away. When it was thirty feet away, it stopped. I could see Cochi's silhouette in the passenger seat. Ibañez was in the back. The Creole was still driving.

I stood in the middle of the road, my hands in plain sight, letting the Mercedes see what I was carrying.

"Turn it off," I called out.

The smooth Mercedes motor switched off. Simultaneously the passenger door opened and Cochi Loco stepped out. I caught the glint of light off his Magnum. The gun wasn't pointed at me, but it wasn't pointed away from me, either. In the frame of the Mercedes' back window, I saw Faustino put a small handgun to Ibañez's head. Obviously I wasn't the only one worried about the possibility of a sniper in the bushes. Faustino was a very cautious man. He must have wanted the money badly to put himself at such risk.

The thought of Faustino's nervousness was pleasant. If he was that desperate, his position was vulnerable ... and Cochi Loco would know it.

"The money," Cochi Loco said. "Where is it?"

I held up the cellular unit. "This is a telephone. The line is open. A friend of mine is listening very carefully. He's holding one of these."

I held up the bomb trigger.

"Explain," Cochi said.

The tone of his voice made me suspect that he had a good idea of how I had stacked the deck.

"It's a remote-control device. A transmitter. If he hears anything he doesn't like, or if I see anything I don't like, the button gets pushed. After that, fifteen million dollars in cash and fifteen dollars' worth of gasoline will get together and burn like unleashed hell."

There was a glint of white in the dim light, Cochi Loco smiling. He reached back into the car and threw the passenger seat forward. Then he pulled Ysidro Ibañez out with one big hand. The banker's own hands were bound behind him.

"How are you doing, Ibañez?" I called out. "Can you walk?"

"Sí, señor."

I couldn't see his face well, but he sounded as though he were in reasonably good spirits.

"Good. In a few minutes you'll be on your way to a family reunion. Until then, don't do anything to startle anybody."

The driver's door opened slowly and Faustino stepped out. He kept the open door between us.

"No one leaves until Cochi counts the money," Faustino said.

"Not Cochi," I countered. "You. I don't trust anybody around that money but you. You can count it yourself or you can take my word for the amount."

"That is not acceptable."

"Tough. If I'm going down a dark alley, it'll be with you. I'm not betting fifteen million on my ability to handle Cochi Loco. End of negotiation."

The Creole started to object but I held up the flat transmitter and moved my thumb in the direction of the recessed button. Cochi and Faustino studied me, trying to decide whether I'd really punch them out of fifteen million dollars.

Finally Cochi grunted and pointed the barrel of his pistol at Ibañez's head. With his free hand, Cochi lifted the banker to his knees, then sprawled him out face down on the damp pavement. Cochi stood over him. The barrel of the gun pointed at the back of the banker's skull.

Faustino came out from behind the car door. His gun was pointed at me.

"Come here," Faustino said.

Telling myself I was no worse off than I had been a minute ago, I walked toward the Creole with my thumb over the button.

"Give Cochi Loco your pistol," he said. "He wants to examine it while we count money. He has not seen a pistol like it before."

"If I go unarmed, you go unarmed."

After a glance at Cochi, Faustino uncocked his pistol and tossed it through the open window of the Mercedes. I broke the Detonics out of its holster, reversed the gun, and offered it to Cochi butt first. He took it without a word. His hand was as big as mine. The gun looked at home against his palm.

"It's a Detonics Four fifty-one," I said. "Exotic but very accurate. I put a new barrel in it after the last time it was fired."

Cochi's eyes met mine. Both of us remembered the last time it was fired. He nodded slightly.

"Let's get counting," I said to Faustino, "or you'll miss your plane."

I walked toward the van without looking back, feeling Cochi stare at my spine every inch of the way. As Faustino and I approached the Ryder, he caught a whiff of raw gasoline. I threw open the back door, and the fumes became thicker. Faustino didn't seem to notice. He was too busy staring down the muzzle of Brad's gun. Faustino stood very still, his hands raised slightly, more malice than surprise in his expression.

"You are dead," he said in a low voice. "All of you."

"I'm betting Cochi is smarter than that," I said. "If I lose, you'll be the first to know. You can enjoy your victory for about a hundredth of a second. Then you'll be dead too."

I grabbed Faustino and shoved him into the van. His shins banged hard against the bumper. With a little more encouragement, he bent over into the van far enough to get a mouthful of carpet. I grabbed his hands and pulled them behind him.

Brad was a quick study. He laid the cold muzzle of the pistol beside Faustino's ear while I reached in my hip pocket and pulled out another Tyton binder. I had to yank hard to get the job done. Faustino's wrists were tiny and delicate.

"Two down, two to go," I said softly. "Keep these clowns quiet until I tell you it's safe to come out. Cochi has my gun, so if you hear any shots, kill Faustino first."

"Do you want this one?"

"No, thanks. If I'm right, I'll be safer without it."

"But what if you're wrong?"

"Then I'll be shit out of luck and you'll have fifteen million dollars, two hostages, one bomb with a lit fuse, and Cochi Loco to play with. Have fun."

31

"THREE MINUTES," I told Fiora. "Then bring them in."

"Where?"

"Ask Swann. She knows the territory."

I disconnected, reconnected with Benny, and walked back to where Ibáñez lay face down on the pavement beside the open door of the Mercedes. Cochi Loco had better equipment than I did; stainless steel handcuffs glinted on his prisoner's wrists. Cochi stepped out from behind the door when I approached. When he saw I was alone, he pointed his long-barreled revolver at the back of Ibáñez's head.

But Cochi never took his eyes off of me.

"Where is Don Faustino?"

"Counting his money."

Cochi's black eyes went from my face to my hands. He saw nothing but a bomb trigger and the red light on the cellular that indicated an open line. His eyes searched the park's darkness for the sniper he would have stationed, had he been the one staging the exchange.

I held my breath.

The sound of Cochi cocking the hammer on his pistol was

like a dry stick snapping. Ibañez drew a broken breath and began praying in strained, tumbled Spanish.

"Don't do it, Cochi," I said quietly. "Your boss is out of it and the cops are on their way. But you can still walk away, if you do it right now. It won't be any trouble for you to get to the airport. Use Faustino's ticket. He won't be needing it. I hear the Colombian highlands are real pretty this time of year. Rio isn't bad, either."

Cochi narrowed his eyes. "Why are you letting me go?"

"It was either try to kill you or let you fly." I shrugged. "My partner has a thing about violence."

"The blonde."

"Yes."

"You are police?"

"No, but for the moment I'm on their side. You have maybe two minutes before they get here."

"If I run, Don Faustino will think I betrayed him to the police."

"It's that or fifteen years to life in a federal prison."

"I could still kill you." Cochi lifted the cocked Magnum and pointed it at me.

"But you won't. It gains you nothing and causes you a world of grief."

For what seemed like a long time we stared at one another over the three-pound pistol. The big, round eye of the muzzle watched me without wavering or flinching. Finally Cochi thumbed the hammer of the Magnum and lowered it.

"A life for a life," he said, referring to the crack house where I had kept both of us from getting killed. "But do not test me again, Fiddler."

I took a deep breath. "I don't plan on it. Get in the car, make a left at the street, and jump on the freeway. But I'd ditch the Mercedes real fast. Every cop in southern California will be looking for it within half an hour, max. Move it, hombre."

Cochi Loco slid into the front seat like a big shadow.

"You'll never get my Detonics through airport security."

He chuckled, ghostly echo of a long-dead boar. Then he dragged the Detonics out of his belt, flipped the big gun deftly, and caught it by the barrel. He handed it back to me butt first. The instant I took the gun's weight I knew he had removed the magazine.

"It's hard as hell to find replacement parts for a Four fifty-one," I said.

Cochi didn't reply. He backed the car, turned, and drove off quickly, without headlights. When he was a hundred feet away, his hand appeared through the open window. I heard the sound of something metallic hitting the pavement.

I ran forward, holding the phone to my mouth. "Cochi is coming out."

"Want him stopped?" Benny asked.

A mental image came to me: the Ice Cream King sitting in the shadows near the entrance to the park, a short-barreled riot gun across his lap and a long-barreled rifle with a sniper scope propped against the seat.

"Forget it," I said. "He wouldn't do well in captivity."

"That's not how I planned to stop him."

"Don't tempt me, *compadre*. I'm trying to show Fiora what a good boy I am."

"Then you're a bloody stupid bugger, aren't you," Benny said coldly.

"What the hell is your problem?" I asked, surprised by his anger.

Benny's answer was a barrage of antipodal invective. By the time he got to "prick with ears," I'd heard enough. I put him on hold and punched in Fiora's number. She answered almost before the phone had a chance to ring.

"Has Swann figured out where we are yet?" I asked.

While I spoke, I squatted on my heels, looking for the glint of metal in the diffuse light.

"She's still thinking," Fiora said.

Swann was taking no chances of Brad being at risk. I appreciated the thought, but it was no longer necessary.

"Tell her I'm exactly where we were when she and I talked

this morning. Everything is calm, no need to break out the Uzis."

"Does that mean nobody is hurt?" Fiora asked.

"Geraghty's feelings are bruised. So are Faustino's. Brad has a bloody nose and cut lip for Swann to coo over. Now get Hudson down here so we can cut our deal and go home and you can coo over me."

"I don't coo."

"If I can be nonviolent, you can bloody well coo."

I hung up and put Benny back on the line. He was wrapping up an intricate description of my imbecility that might have amused me under other circumstances. I turned the volume down and walked along the road, looking at the dark ground.

The first thing I saw was a small flash of shiny metal—a handcuff key. The Detonics magazine was in a patch of shadow a couple of feet away. The metal was clean, even the flanged end. I slammed it home, bringing the Detonics up to fighting weight. Then I went back and used the key to free Ibañez.

Even with my help he was slow getting to his feet. The light was bad, but it showed me enough. Ibañez had gotten the kind of working over I had only pretended to give Brad.

"Cochi didn't believe you, huh?" I said.

"It was Faustino." Ibañez shrugged, flexing his shoulders and arms, rubbing blood into his hands where the tightly ratcheted cuffs had left marks. "He wanted to slit my throat."

No surprises there. I hustled Ibañez back to the Ryder van and began unloading human cargo. Ibañez took Faustino and Brad took Geraghty. I pointed them to where the Mercedes had been parked, then flashed a light around the inside of the van once more to make sure the wiring was still in place. One of the bricks of neatly bundled currency had come unwrapped. Ben Franklin stared out at me with that prim little shit-eating smile.

Tires wailed through the darkness, the sound of cars being driven by cops with visions of a fifteen-million-dollar bust.

I slammed the van door and headed for the shadows. One after another, vehicles leaped out of the night and squalled to a stop nearby, blinding everyone with lights. Doors slammed and men shouted conflicting orders over drawn pistols.

Between one minute and the next, the park was bursting with officers, mostly plainclothes and undercover types, except for one unhappy patrolman who had latched onto the tail of the high-speed convoy trying to figure out what the hell was happening on his beat.

I stayed in the shadows and watched while the cops gathered around Brad and the prisoners. If Swann hadn't already confessed her sins, Hudson would have known anyway. She held onto Brad the way a worried woman holds on to her man. He had the it-was-nothing grin of a teenager on his artistically bloodied face.

Fiora cut Hudson out of the crowd without a ripple and led him toward the shadows where I was standing. He carried a heavy black five-cell Kelite flashlight in his hand like a nightstick, with the bulb end pointed toward the ground. When I stepped forward, he turned on the light and aimed it my eyes as though he were conducting a field sobriety test.

"I'm going to bust your smart ass," he snarled. "You're under arrest for obstruction of justice, and that's just the start."

I held the garage door control where he could see it and asked, "Do you want to make captain?"

That made him pause.

"Yeah, I thought so," I said. "Take a good look."

He did. Then he looked around warily.

"Right the first time," I said. "It's the trigger to a bomb. It's connected to a mixture of gasoline and motor oil. The whole package is wrapped in nichrome wire, the kind that's used for industrial heater coils, and it's surrounded by five boxes full of hundred-dollar bills. All I have to do is punch out and watch the most expensive bonfire since Dresden."

Hudson's mouth came open and stayed that way for a moment. Then it snapped shut. He spoke through clenched teeth.

"Where is it?"

I jerked a thumb over my shoulder.

He turned the flashlight on the screen of shrubbery. The vivid yellow shape of the Ryder van gleamed through the branches and leaves.

"You might want to tell your men to stay away," I said. "The guy who did the wiring says it's kind of touchy."

Hudson glared at me for only an instant before he turned and called out to his men.

"Throw up a perimeter around that van! Nobody closer than two hundred feet!"

The impression that he was being cooperative lasted only until Hudson turned to face me again. He held his 1911 .45 in his right hand. It was pointed at me.

"You're under arrest. Hand over the transmitter."

"Sure thing, officer." I flipped the transmitter toward him.

Hudson dropped his flashlight and made a grab for the plastic box.

"Jesus Christ, are you crazy?" Hudson demanded, catching the unit just before it hit the ground, then holding onto it gingerly, as though it were a bomb instead of a trigger.

"Yeah, I'm crazy," I agreed. "I just put you in charge of fifteen million bucks. Fiora can corroborate my testimony, if it comes to that. You are now legally responsible for the loot."

Hudson's head came up slowly. He knew he hadn't won yet but he didn't know why. "What the hell does that mean?"

"Simple," I said. "I no longer control the fate of all that combustible cash. You do. If you screw up and hit that button by mistake, don't blame me. If the money is burned to fine white ash, it's your fault, not mine."

I held up the cellular phone, letting Hudson see that the keypad was lit and that the line was open. "Of course, you could always try to convince your superiors that I had somebody on the other end of this line, somebody with a trigger just like the one you have in your hand, somebody who is going to set off the whole mess if I don't call him off in the next thirty seconds."

Hudson opened his mouth. Nothing useful came out.

I glanced at Fiora. "What do you think? Would they believe Hudson if he took the SODDI defense?"

"SODDI?" asked Fiora.

"Some Other Dude Did It," I explained. "Someone that no one else saw, no one else heard, and no one else found any sign of."

Fiora looked at Hudson. "I don't know. How gullible is your boss?"

Hudson didn't answer. He just looked from the trigger in his hand out into the surrounding night. His intent, all-encompassing glance reminded me of Cochi Loco. After a few moments Hudson stared at me as though he could see through my skull to the plans beneath. Ambition, pride, greed, anger, and intelligence struggled behind his own eyes.

While I waited to see which combination would win, I reached out and touched Fiora on the shoulder. She moved closer and then closer still, until she was pressed against me. She felt like warm silk beneath my fingers, and she watched Hudson with eyes as cold as the night.

"Damn you, Fiddler," Hudson snarled. "What kind of deal do you want this time?"

Four down.

None to go.

EPILOGUE

FIORA LOOKED at her watch, but it wasn't necessary. Sunrise is sunrise, no matter what hour the clock says. The first pale light was already gliding over the ocean, dividing water from sky and darkness from dawn. Kwame's dog door made its familiar *whap-slap* sound as he padded in from his sentry go.

"Did Benny say what he wanted?" Fiora asked, stifling a yawn.

I was struggling against my own yawn. "Nope. He just said he wanted to see us as soon as we got home." I gave in and yawned. "Ten more minutes and I'm going to say to hell with it and go to bed."

Fiora sighed and ran her fingers through her hair in a distracted gesture that always strikes me as sexy. I would have reached for her but Benny was bound to show up at the worst possible moment. She yawned again and stretched. The motion made light shimmer and twist over the surface of her white embroidered robe. The edges fell open invitingly. I thought about calling Benny and telling him to make it noon.

"Marianne was pleased," Fiora said, stretching again.

"She should have been. The Bank of the Southland is being

touted as an example of institutional social responsibility. Bradford the boy wonder didn't even get a slap on his aristocratic wrist. He's being painted as a civic hero for his dangerous undercover work helping the police to arrest the biggest money launderer in the history of currency."

"Don't sound so cynical. Brad did do a good job and it was dangerous," Fiora said. "All you had to do was look at his face to see that. How did he get so banged up, anyway?"

Kwame barked once, cutting off what would have soon degenerated into a wrangle over my violent tendencies. The dog's bark was both warning to us and welcome to the visitor who had arrived. Kwame charged through the dog door to greet his pal.

"Benny's here," I said.

I opened the kitchen door when I heard the wheelchair on the redwood deck. Benny came steaming through the door as though he were on rails. He was still wearing his watch cap and dark sweater. His face was tight, as though he had been chewing on something bitter. He didn't bother to look at me or say hello on the way by.

"Next time I won't open the door," I said, closing it behind him. "I'll let you run into it."

He didn't say anything.

"Good morning, Benny," Fiora said around another yawn. "At least I think it's finally morning. Hope you got more sleep than we did." She bent and brushed a kiss over his cheekbone just above his black beard. Then she got a look at his face. "What's wrong?"

Benny turned and looked at Fiora. For once his eyes didn't crinkle at the corners with indulgent pleasure at the sight of her. He was well and truly pissed. I've seen him that way twice: both times when I refused to drop the hammer on a killer from ambush.

Saying nothing to Fiora, Benny swung his black-maned head around and looked at me with bleak eyes. "Are all the finicky little details nailed down?"

"Brad and the bank are clean," I recited. "Hudson is going

to keep his suspicions about Swann and Brad's love life to himself. Faustino is going to spend the rest of his life in federal slam. The Ibañez family is getting a new name, a new citizenship, and a guarantee of whatever medical treatment Josefina needs."

"What about Geraghty?"

"That's the bad news. At worst, George will be disbarred. He'll skate on the rest of the charges in exchange for his testimony." I shrugged. "I'm not worried. Someday I'll open a door and find him alone."

Benny grunted. "Cochi Loco?"

"Neither hide nor hair."

Benny switched the lethal black brilliance of his glance to Fiora. "Are you pleased with this well-organized nonviolent partnership of yours?"

Uh-oh.

"Benny," I said quickly, "that's—"

"Arf off, mate. This is between me and her."

Fiora looked at him with wary green eyes. "I know about Brad, if that's what you mean."

"Bugger Brad. If it had been me doing the stage dressing, the little sod would have been spitting teeth and pissing blood. Did Fiddler tell you about Cochi Loco?"

"Just that he acted reasonably and—"

"Reasonably!" Benny's voice became as savage as his eyes. "Fiddler hands over his only weapon to Faustino's chief enforcer and you call it *reasonable?*"

Fiora looked at me.

I looked for a fast way to shut Benny up. Short of shooting him, there wasn't any.

"Let me tell you what your knight in shining armor did in order to stay in his fair lady's good graces," Benny said. "Faustino made your lover turn over his gun. Then Fiddler went up against Cochi Loco holding a garage door opener in one hand and a bloody cellular phone in the other. And I had to lie on my belly and watch through the sniper scope while Cochi's finger tightened on the trigger!"

Benny gripped the wheelchair until his knuckles were white. All of his frustration was focused in his bleak, savage eyes. "There wasn't three eighths of five eighths of sweet fuck-all I could do to save Fiddler's life, *and I knew it*."

The room was absolutely still for a moment. Then Fiora drew a shaky breath and turned to me.

"Is that true?"

I was too surprised to answer. I didn't know Benny had been out in the bushes waiting for a chance to drop Cochi Loco.

"Don't look at Fiddler," Benny snarled to Fiora. "He can't help you. As long as you have his balls in your purse, he's a dead man walking."

Fiora went pale. "I didn't mean to—"

Benny kept talking. "The next time you start congratulating yourself on how clever little minds overcome violence every time, remember this: you fell in love with a warrior, not a bloody pacifist. There is only one reason Cochi Loco let Fiddler live. Cochi had seen Fiddler move. He had seen Fiddler shoot. He had seen Fiddler *kill*. He didn't believe Fiddler was stupid enough to tamely turn over his only weapon to his executioner. Cochi figured there had to be a backup somewhere in the bushes.

"And your lover was just bright enough and just crazy enough about you to bet his life on Cochi Loco's warrior reasoning."

Benny swung his black glance back to me. "Cochi was right, boyo. The only reason he's alive is that his gun barrel was on you or Ibañez every instant. He was good, Fiddler. Too bleeding good. So help me God, if you ever put me in the position of watching your execution again, *I'll kill you myself*."

Benny's massive arms flexed beneath his black T-shirt. The wheelchair reversed directions.

He left.

Later I tried to tell Fiora that Benny was wrong, but she just shook her head and held on to me. We didn't talk about it again. Maybe we both knew Benny was right. Maybe we just couldn't see a way around that truth.

But Fiora must have been thinking, because a week after Benny's exit, a flatbed auto transporter pulled down the winding little road from Coast Highway into Crystal Cove. Under Kwame's watchful eye the driver knocked on the door of the cottage. When I looked past him to the rig, I saw the outline of an open-body roadster beneath a canvas drape. Where the canvas didn't completely cover, there was the familiar gleam of flared magnesium alloy wheels.

For an instant adrenaline shot through me and I felt like I was flying. Then reality struck and I landed hard. The Cobra was dead. I ought to know. I had been present at the execution.

Fiora came out of the living room. She stood in the doorway next to me, her face carefully expressionless.

"Where you want it?" the driver asked me.

"Who said I wanted it?"

He looked at the invoice on his clipboard. "Trust me. You want it."

"Why don't you take a closer look before you send it back?" Fiora said.

Her expression was still neutral, but there was a shimmering dark-green light in her eyes that I couldn't deny. With Kwame at my heels, I walked unhappily toward the truck. Fiora stayed put.

I looked at the wheels close up. Flared magnesium alloy wheels, all right. Fiora must have talked somebody into making a pass at fixing up my trashed Cobra. But no matter how good the mechanic was, it wouldn't work. I had replayed the accident a hundred times in my mind. The body metal on the left side had been ruined, and the force of the impact must have bent the frame. Fixing the Cobra would have been like wiring up a Thoroughbred's shattered cannon bones and asking it to run straight and clean and fast again.

But apparently someone had made a hell of a try with my

Cobra. The closer I got, the better the rims looked. Jewel-buffed and flawless, showroom fresh.

Too fresh.

Oh, Christ. Somebody has sold Fiora a shiny new replica and I'm going to have to look pleased and make happy noises over a fake Cobra. No matter how good the damn thing might be, it isn't what was bent around a boulder in the desert.

The driver levered himself up on the flatbed and carefully unstrapped the custom-made canvas car cover. With the care of a fan dancer, he began to undrape the car, starting at the front.

I had to admit the nose was nicely done. The chrome-rimmed mouth was clean and perfect. The swoopy front with the round medallion was bright and hard and beautiful. Someone had even gone to the trouble of putting in a phony auxiliary oil cooler underneath the radiator, just like a real Cobra S/C. Hell, even the 427 plaque just forward of the door looked authentic. Whoever had done this knockoff was a real artist.

I glanced at Fiora. She was watching two sea gulls circling just above the lip of the bluff.

The body of the car was rounded and flawless, the deep blue paint clean and glowing, as though it had never felt even the gentle touch of a chamois. I hadn't known that fiberglass could look that pretty.

Staring at that plastic replica was like being nineteen again, just for a second, both bitter and sweet. I walked closer, admiring the car in spite of its bastard origins. Every last detail was correct, right down to the cooling vent that had been cut into the sheet metal of the front wheel well.

Sheet metal?

The hairs on my neck stirred. There's something eerie about a replica that's so close to the original.

"Well, back it down," I told the driver. "We may as well take a good look at it."

Kwame wandered over and lifted his leg against the wheel of the transporter.

"You'd better put the dog away," the driver said.

"Why?"

"He pisses on that car once, and the value drops by a hundred thousand bucks."

I opened my mouth. Nothing came out but a strangled sound.

"Mister, this car has been sealed in a bag full of argon since 1967," the driver said. "There are exactly sixty-seven point three miles on the odometer."

I heard, but I couldn't believe. I couldn't speak, either.

"Kwame," said Fiora. "Come."

Kwame went to her.

"Stay."

He stood as though nailed to the ground.

Fiora came and stood next to me as I watched a beautiful blue piece of art and history slowly slide off the tilted bed of the truck. Dust from the driveway rose and settled onto polished rims. I didn't move.

"Go on," Fiora said softly. "It won't bite."

Afraid to touch all that perfection, I kept my hands in my pockets, leaned into the cockpit, and read the odometer. Sixty-seven miles, three tenths.

Sweet . . . Jesus . . . Christ.

I turned and stared at the woman I loved and wondered if I would ever understand her.

"It's not my birthday," I pointed out.

Her expression was bland, but her color was high. I'd rarely seen her look so vivid. She smiled and said nothing.

"You don't like Cobras," I said finally. "You never have. They're muscle cars. They lack subtlety. They aren't comfortable. All they're good for is to go like blazing blue hell. You've said it a hundred times."

Fiora took a deep breath. "I've been rethinking my position."

I looked back at the Cobra, fresh from decades in some collector's argon-filled bag. Born and bred to prowl. . . . I could practically feel the leashed power of the engine flowing up through the frame to vibrate beneath my hands.

Until that instant I hadn't admitted how much I missed my wicked heirloom.

"This one is too damned perfect," I said huskily. "I'd be afraid to touch it for fear of scuffing it up."

"Well, if that's all that's bothering you . . ."

Fiora walked up to the Cobra and drew back her foot, ready to deliver a roundhouse kick to the passenger door. I yelped and grabbed her, lifting her off her feet.

"Are you out of your mind?" I demanded.

"No. I'm just coming *into* it. Good things shouldn't be packed away, Fiddler," she said, running her fingertips over my mustache and the knife scar it concealed. "Good things were meant to be used, even if it means risking dents and scratches . . . and scars."

Before I could say anything, Fiora kissed me, putting everything she had into it. Gravity doubled. Holding on to her hard, I leaned against the Cobra and kissed the woman who loved me enough to let me run free.

Fiddler and Fiora are the creations of ANN and EVAN MAXWELL, writing as A. E. MAXWELL. Beginning in 1985 with *Just Another Day in Paradise*, the Maxwells have written five other novels involving Fiddler, the low-key yet lethal southern California troubleshooter and Fiora, his shrewd, wordly lover and ex-wife. The Maxwells' careers are less dangerous than their characters'. Ann, the author of more than thirty-five books, has been a full-time novelist for twenty years. Evan is a nationally known reporter who has covered international crime and national security for the *Los Angeles Times*, *Reader's Digest* and other publications. Together, the Maxwells have coauthored eleven novels, including six involving Fiddler and Fiora. Unlike their characters, the Maxwells have been well and truly married for twenty-four years.